NEVER SAW YOU COMING

ALEXA RIVERS

To all the mothers out there.
You've got this.
You're awesome.
You're doing a great job.

PROLOGUE

"That's it. Good girl, mama." Gabby finished cleaning the last of the litter of puppies, settled her with her brothers and sisters, and scratched the exhausted new mother behind the ear. "You did so well."

"Are they all okay?" the owner asked. She'd been a bundle of nerves throughout the delivery, fidgeting with her clothes and obsessively checking each pup after it made its way into the world. As if Gabby, a veterinarian, might have missed something. But Gabby didn't mind. Whatever made her feel better.

"Yes, they're all in good shape." Gabby straightened and glanced around the room. She usually cared for larger animals, but the small animal veterinarian had been out of town when the dog went into labor so she'd been called in. She had to admit, she understood the attraction of small animal care. The birth had been far tidier than it would have been for, say, a cow. "It looks like you have everything they need."

The owner had gone all out with beds, blankets, food, and toys. Gabby felt like she could leave, safe in the knowledge that these puppies would be spoiled like crazy.

"Thanks for coming on such short notice," the owner said. "She wasn't supposed to be due for another two weeks."

Gabby shrugged. "Nature runs on her own schedule. I'm just happy I was around to help."

She ran the woman through instructions for care, washed her hands, and headed home with a smile. Delivering a litter of puppies wasn't a bad way to spend a morning.

When she arrived at the sprawling property she owned on the edge of Huntly, she parked on the concreted area outside and waved to the half-dozen goats grazing in the adjacent paddock. She took a moment to appreciate the view. Green grass stretched as far as the eye could see. Perhaps it wasn't as nice as being near the beach, like her brother Shane's house was in Haven Bay, but it had its own rural charm. Her ginger cat, Thomas, greeted her at the door and butted his head against her legs, purring loudly.

"Hey, buddy." She patted him and went to her bedroom, where Luna—a deaf sweetheart of a kitty—was curled on the bed. She blew Luna a kiss and stripped out of her dirty clothes, then grabbed a towel from the cupboard in the hall and showered. When she got out, Thomas was waiting for her. He was the clingiest of her fur babies, although he tried to mask it by acting as though he was the man of the house.

Gabby dressed in jeans and a t-shirt, put her dirty clothes in the laundry, and checked the time. It was nearly 2 p.m., which meant Marley would be over soon. She and Gabby planned to watch cricket together. Gabby's boyfriend, Henry, was on the New Zealand men's team, who were playing against South Africa, and after the match, he would be free for a whole week. It had been close to a month since Gabby had seen him, so she intended to surprise him with a visit tomorrow.

She was excited to spend time with him. After dedicating most of her twenties to her career, and suffering through one bad date after another during the first couple of years of her thirties, she thought Henry might actually be the one. He was outgoing, fun, and wanted the same things she did: a family, and a place to settle down.

"Hey, hot stuff!" Marley's voice rang through the house. Gabby must have been so distracted she hadn't heard the car pull up. "I have snacks. I have booze. And I've got a hunch you might have a ring on your finger by the end of the week." Marley appeared in the laundry doorway and winked one shimmering eyelid. "You ready?"

"Give me two seconds to let the girls in, and I'll be there."

Marley grinned. "How are my beautiful snookumses today?"

"As cheeky as ever."

Marley followed Gabby to the back door. When she opened it, Thelma and Louise, her two rescue dogs, bounded toward them with the same enthusiasm with which they embraced everything. Louise's movements were a little unbalanced because she was missing a leg, courtesy of a hit and run. Thelma loped beside her, her squashed bull terrier face panting happily.

"Hi, girls." Gabby knelt to cuddle each of them.

"Hey, boo!" Marley exclaimed as Thelma licked her. "Aren't you the sweetest thing?"

Gabby led the way to the living room with the dogs—and Marley—following behind. She flopped onto the sofa and Thelma immediately tried to jump onto her lap. Gabby shifted her to the side. She was too big to be a lap dog. She found the channel the cricket match was on and settled in to watch. Marley claimed the other end of the sofa, opened a bag of caramel popcorn, and passed it to Gabby.

"Do you really think he might propose soon?" Gabby asked as the match began.

"Of course." Marley tugged a hand through her high-lighter-pink hair. "You guys are so cute together it makes me sick. He's going to want to lock you down as soon as he can."

Anticipation tingled in Gabby's gut. "I hope so."

Henry was perfect. He didn't mind how direct she was, and he hadn't run when she spelled out her intentions on their first date—unlike most of the men she'd dated. They tended to find her too intense or say that she came on too strong. At first, she hadn't minded their reactions. She'd thought she was weeding out the ones who were wrong for her. But after a while, it had gotten depressing. Then Henry came along and changed everything.

The match went on for hours, but in the end, New Zealand won. Gabby and Marley cheered and raised their wine glasses to the team. When the interviews began, Gabby was thrilled to see Henry's handsome, square-jawed face fill the screen. The interviewer asked a few questions about the match and then gave a sly smile that Gabby suspected meant the conversation was about to take an interesting turn.

"You're notoriously private about your personal life, but I've heard rumors that a certain special lady has been seen wearing a ring," the interviewer said. "What do you say to that?"

Gabby frowned and looked down at her hands. No ring.

"What the hell?" Marley muttered. "Must have gotten the wrong guy."

"Must have," Gabby agreed, but her stomach soured. She had a bad feeling about this.

On screen, Henry grinned. "It's true. Vanessa and I are engaged."

"*Vanessa*?" Gabby shot to her feet, dislodging Thelma, who grumbled in dissatisfaction. "Who's *Vanessa*?"

The interviewer looked like he was about to wet himself with excitement. "You heard it here first. Not only is Henry Gosling off the market, but we can also officially confirm his involvement with Auckland attorney Vanessa Hallborn."

"What?" Gabby's jaw dropped and her heart squeezed painfully. She couldn't take her gaze from the horror unfolding in front of her even though tears prickled in her eyes and a hollow pit in her stomach told her this wasn't a nightmare. She was awake, and the man she'd planned on building a life with was apparently engaged to someone else.

"What the fuck is going on?" Marley demanded.

"I don't know." Gabby reached blindly for her phone. Maybe a phone call with Henry would clear this up. She found his number and hit 'Call,' but he didn't answer. Of course he didn't. He was still being interviewed. The voice-mail prompt played.

"You're engaged?" Gabby asked incredulously. "Seriously? Is this real? I don't understand what's happening. Please call me back. I need to hear you tell me this is all a big joke." She hung up.

Marley wrapped her arms around Gabby and hugged her tightly. "I don't think this is a joke."

Heat rushed to Gabby's cheeks. She squeezed her eyes shut. If this was really happening, it meant that Henry was a liar and a cheat, not the good, honest man she'd thought he was. He'd played her, and she'd fallen for it. God, what a fool.

She felt sick. What if her parents were watching this from their home in Wellington? Or her brother? She and Henry had agreed to keep their relationship quiet, which he'd claimed was to protect her from public scrutiny, but she now realized must have been so he could keep her and this Vanessa lady in the dark about each other. Despite that, she'd told her family and Marley. They'd be horrified. What would they think of her? Would they believe she'd known about the other woman? Or just that she was blind and stupid?

Henry had disappeared from the TV and another player was being interviewed, so Gabby tried calling him again. When he didn't answer, she sent him a text message instead.

Gabby: *Call me.*

She flopped back onto the couch, breathing heavily. Was she supposed to just lie here and wait for him to respond?

Fuck that.

She was driving to Auckland and she was going to ask him to explain face-to-face. She deserved that much.

"Come on." She grabbed her purse and strode to the door. "We're going to Auckland."

"Are you sure that's what you want to do?" Marley asked.

Gabby shot her a look that said she was one hundred percent certain.

"Okay, then. I'll drive. We can call Blake to feed the animals later if you need." Blake was her twin brother.

"Thanks."

Twenty minutes later, they were hurtling toward Auckland in Marley's pickup truck when Gabby's phone pinged with a text alert. She checked the screen and, seeing there was a message from Henry, hurried to open it.

Henry: *Yes, I'm engaged. I'm sorry you had to find out this way, but it doesn't have to change anything between us.*

What. The. Fuck?

Did he expect her to be his side chick? How the hell could he say that to her when, even in an alternate universe where she might have been okay with helping him cheat on another woman, he knew it was her dream to have the two point five kids and white picket fence? She could hardly have that while their daddy ran between their home and someone else's.

Shit, had she *been* his side chick already? If he was engaged to Vanessa, then Gabby couldn't be considered his main girl. She'd been aiding and abetting a cheater. Nausea rolled through her.

"The nerve of this boy," Marley spat, leaning over to read what he'd said.

A sob burst from Gabby, startlingly loud in the silent vehicle. With tears streaming down her cheeks, she opened the window and threw her phone through it as hard as she could.

"Are you crazy?" Marley demanded. "Now we're going to have to go find that."

"Don't stop," she said. Whatever was on that phone, she didn't want it. No doubt Henry would message again, and so would Mum and Shane. She couldn't deal with it. If she needed to call someone, they could use Marley's phone. "And don't turn back."

"Hell no." Marley reached out and intertwining her fingers with Gabby's. "We're still going to Auckland and we're going to fuck shit up."

1

LOGAN PRIDE POURED A BEER FOR AN AMERICAN TOURIST AND scowled across the bar to where Gabrielle Walker sat opposite a stocky guy in a plaid shirt and holey jeans. She was on another date. Logan didn't recognize the guy, which meant he must have been from out of town. As the owner of The Den, the only pub in Haven Bay, he knew the locals by sight, and in most cases by name too.

Whoever this man was, he wasn't good enough for Gabby, who'd gone out of her way to look nice for the occasion. The least her date could have done was scrub the dirt off his boots.

"Cider, please."

Logan jerked in surprise and forced himself to smile at the pretty brunette who'd been trying to get his attention.

"Sure thing, honey." He poured the drink and took her payment, watching as she rejoined a group of women at the table in the back corner. On another night, he might have tried to flirt with her, but he was off his game. He had been ever since Gabby strolled back into his life after a year-long hiatus and proceeded to go out with every man under forty-five in a fifty-mile radius except for him.

He couldn't lie. When she'd turned up in town a few months ago, he'd hoped they might pick up where they left off before her last relationship—arguing and falling into bed once or twice a year, while never, ever mentioning it to anyone else. Unfortunately, she hadn't had the same idea. Instead, she'd gone into avoid mode. The only times he saw her were either when she was on a date or with her brother, Shane—his close friend. She hadn't replied to any of his text messages and wasn't home the evening he'd gone over to say hi. Or, you know, to persuade her to have another romp for old times' sake.

It wasn't that he wanted to date Gabby, or that he even particularly liked her—although he respected her plenty—but their chemistry was off the charts, and bantering with her made him feel alive in a way that flirting with other women didn't. There was something about her that he found addictive.

"Maybe she's ignoring you because she's looking for The One," he murmured to himself. God knew that wasn't him. After being abandoned by his father and raised by a single mum, the last thing he wanted was to fall into the trap of thinking he could have a happily ever after. He knew what he was. A player and a flirt, just like his dad. He wasn't capable of committing to a woman long-term, and if he tried to, he'd only end up hurting the person he was supposed to love.

He kept an eye on Gabby and the man he'd internally dubbed "the farmer" while they shared a romantic meal of fries and pizza and drank a couple of pints. Gradually, the other patrons left the bar, until they were the only ones remaining. Logan edged closer as he wiped down tables, trying to eavesdrop on their conversation. The farmer was rambling on about a recent hunting trip. Logan cringed, waiting for Gabby to put him in his place. She was a vegetarian and a staunch believer in animal rights. But she didn't say anything. The farmer moved on to making crude remarks that were presumably supposed to be flattering—clearly angling to take her to bed.

He finished with, "What do you say we get out of here and head back to my place?"

"No." Gabby shot him down with no emotion. Logan cheered internally. It was about time. "Thank you for dinner, but I won't be going home with you tonight. I already told you that I want to take things slow, and if you can't respect that, then we won't be having a second date."

The guy stared at her for a moment, as if he couldn't believe what he'd heard, then he chuckled. "I think you're taking what I said out of context, sweetheart. We can wait to get to the good stuff." He waggled his eyebrows, then looked her up and down. "You look like you'll be worth it."

Logan turned away from them and rolled his eyes. Did Gabby not realize she could do better than that? Sure, she was a pain in his ass half the time, but there was no denying she was gorgeous, with thick dark hair, delicate features, and eyes that seemed golden in the dim light. She was an animal doctor too. Pretty, smart, the whole package.

He moved further away. Gabby and her date exchanged a few more words, growing heated, until the man stalked out of the pub and she dropped her face into her hands. Her shoulders sagged. He wished he could give her a hug, but if he tried, she'd probably bite his head off.

She raised her eyes to his and glared. "I suppose you think this is funny, do you?"

"No, I—"

"Is it too much to ask for a guy who wants to know what's going on in my head in addition to wanting to get me naked?" she interrupted, then pressed her lips together.

"You do look great naked," he quipped, instantly regretting the comment when her face fell. "Hey, sorry, what I meant was—"

"I know what you meant, Logan," she snapped. "You're no better than the rest of them. At least they're open to discussing the possibility of a relationship."

"Hey." Her words hurt more than they should have. "Maybe I'm just more honest than them. I tell women what I am and am not capable of before I blow their minds. That's better than playing along until I've got what I want, like some of those assholes you've been dating recently."

Her jaw dropped and her eyes glittered dangerously. "Call it what you want. The outcome is the same."

"A happy woman in my bed?"

She huffed. "Ugh, why are you so frustrating? Sometimes I just want to scream in your face."

"Same goes, Gabs. I'd love to have you screaming under me again." He shouldn't antagonize her, but the anger blazing through her now was better than the defeat he'd caught a glimpse of earlier. Gabby was a firecracker. She should never let the world get her down.

"You." Her hands fisted on the table. "You're insane."

He shrugged one shoulder. "Maybe. Maybe not. But I bet I could be a hell of a distraction."

"Nope." She held her hands up as if warding him off. "No, no, no. Don't even think about it. You're not touching me."

He sighed. At least he'd tried. "All right, then."

He turned to wipe down another table but as he laid the cloth on the surface, a hand gripped his shoulder and spun him around. A couple of seconds later, a pair of soft, warm lips landed on his, and his arms were full of Gabby. He grinned against her mouth. Well, damn. She tasted just as intoxicating as she used to.

WHAT THE HELL WAS SHE DOING?

Gabby had been firm with herself ever since she moved to Haven Bay to be closer to her brother and his family. Under no circumstances was she to hook up with Logan Pride again. Yet here she was, her lips pressed to his, her legs wrapped around his hips. His hands curved around her ass and squeezed gently. His tongue plundered her mouth as skillfully as it had half a dozen times before.

No. Bad Gabby. Get off him.

Logan was her personal kryptonite. Over six feet of tousle-haired, blue-eyed, flirtatious goodness, who could make her come harder than any other man she'd been with. He was also, unfortunately, not in the market for a girlfriend. Never had been, and probably never would be. All he seemed to want was to screw as many people as possible in as many ways as possible, and she was a little ashamed of how many times she'd succumbed to him in the past. Especially when she knew how it ended: with him cooking her breakfast and sending her on her way, and her lying to Shane about where she'd spent the night.

She hooked her arms around his neck as he carried her through the "staff only" door and backed her against a wall, out of sight of prying eyes. Their mouths bumped, teeth clashed, and he pulled away.

"Do you want me to stop?" he asked, his voice dark with passion.

She weighed her options in a millisecond. Say "yes" and protect her moral high ground, or say "no" and wallow in the way he made her feel desirable more than any other man ever had. Even though she knew she couldn't have a future with Logan, he was a master at making her feel like the sexiest woman on the planet. Tonight, after yet another demoralizing date, she needed that.

She took a breath. "Don't stop."

He grinned, his baby blues twinkling. "I'm so glad you said that." He loosened his hold on her and she slid down his body. "Come on. I can't carry you up the stairs. I'm too old for that shit."

She laughed. "Are you trying to get me to stroke your ego?"

"No." He pouted, drawing another laugh from her. Logan may have his faults, but God, he was *fun*.

"You're only thirty-four," she called after him as he went to lock the front door.

"In retired sportsman years, that's ancient," he said, hurrying back to join her as she climbed the stairs to his apartment above the pub.

"So it is." She waited while he unlocked the door, then stripped off her dress, dropped it and her purse, and danced out of reach. "Come and get me, Granddad."

He narrowed his eyes. "Oh, you'll pay for that."

She ran toward the bedroom, hearing his footsteps thudding behind her. Just as she reached the bed, he grabbed her waist and tackled her onto the mattress, landing on top of her and pinning her down. Her breath hitched, and she wriggled her butt, brushing against the hard imprint of his erection behind the fly of his jeans. He rocked into the cleft of her ass, creating delicious friction both where he touched her and where she was flattened against the bedspread, only the thin fabric of her panties between them.

His hands stroked down her sides, stoking the fire inside her hotter. She moaned and arched against him. His fingers feathered along her ribcage, and then, as she tried to twist around to kiss him, he tickled her underarms. She shrieked and pulled her arms against her sides. When that didn't stop him, she tried to buck him off.

"Cut it out, you ass," she hissed, rolling her hips, pivoting from side to side. He finally stopped the torture in favor of gripping her hips so she couldn't dislodge him. She flopped against the mattress, panting, and turned her face enough to glare at him. "Not cool."

He lowered himself along her body, his clothes scraping over her sensitized skin, until his mouth was beside her ear. "I told you you'd pay."

So he had. And honestly, she kind of liked it. Not that she'd ever admit as much. His tickling had gotten her out of her head for a moment, and that was worth everything.

He peeled himself off her back and rolled her over, so they were face to face. She shot him the bird. His eyes darkened, and focused on her mouth. Her lips parted and he groaned. "You are the sexiest thing I've ever seen, even when you're flipping me off."

She wet her lips, watching his pupils dilate. He yanked his t-shirt off over his head, exposing a gloriously tanned and muscled chest. Her gaze zipped to his ripped abdomen, where a golden happy trail delved beneath the waistband of his jeans.

"Take them off," she said. "I need to see you."

Despite all the dates she'd been on after moving to Haven Bay, she hadn't been intimate with a man since Henry. There was something comforting about knowing that this was Logan and that even if he drove her crazy at times, he'd never hold back with her or let her believe she was anything other than a sex goddess.

"Like this?" he asked, one side of his mouth hitching up as he slowly dragged his zipper down.

"More."

His grin widened. He shoved the denim down his hips to

reveal a defined V and a dusting of hair above the part of him she knew could make her feel better than anything else. "Is this enough?"

"You know it's not," she complained. "Get it all off. I haven't had a non-self-induced orgasm for months. Now's not the time to tease."

He paused. "Really?"

She fought the urge to tell him to hurry again. "Yes, really. Now please, take your jeans off. The underwear too."

He winked. "Your wish is my command."

He shucked off the remainder of his clothes and rose above her, naked and toned and gorgeous. Then he lowered himself over her and peppered kisses from the bottom of her ribs down to her sex, settling over her panties and laving his tongue against the softness beneath. Gabby sighed and rolled herself against his mouth, riding his tongue, desperate for more. He pulled her panties down and she gasped as he licked her as if she were his favorite dessert. He pinned her thighs down with his forearms and feasted on her until she was whimpering, wet, and desperate for him.

"Please," she begged, too far gone to be embarrassed by how needy she sounded. "I need you inside me." She wanted him to erase the memories of Henry, even though she knew that wasn't fair. "There's a condom in my purse."

His eyes narrowed. "Who were you planning to use that with?"

"I don't know." Nor did she much care right now. "I just always have one."

That seemed to settle him because he reached for her purse and withdrew the condom. He sheathed himself and notched his body between her thighs.

"Last time to change your mind, firecracker."

Guh. As if she'd change anything when he was pressed so tightly to her heat.

She raised herself onto her elbows and nipped at his throat. "Do it."

"Gladly."

He sank inside her, and she exhaled slowly, forcing her muscles to relax. It had been a while. When he was buried deep, he knocked against her clit and her head fell back, her eyes closed in pleasure.

"You're so fucking gorgeous." The words were rough. He withdrew and thrust into her again, bumping against the bundle of nerves that drove her wild. Gabby circled her legs around him and locked them behind him, meeting each thrust as they drove her higher, wound her tighter, and she spiraled out of control.

Logan clasped her tightly to him and kissed her ferociously, as though trying to taste her very essence.

She needed this. Needed him.

"Harder," she whispered, trusting him to give her what she asked for. Logan wasn't the guy who was overly careful with women. He was the guy who ruined them for all others.

He slammed into her, angling her so she saw stars every time their bodies came together. "Is this what you want, honey?"

"Yes." She clung to him as pleasure built, clutching his strong shoulders, and buried her face in the side of his neck. "More."

He slid into her again, and again. Her head lolled and her eyes closed .

"Look at me," he ordered.

Her eyes fluttered open.

He grunted approvingly. "Need you to know who's making you come."

Oh, wow. That was too much. She gazed into his eyes as her release barreled into her, making her shake and cry his name.

"That's it, baby." Their mouths met in a messy kiss as he pumped his hips once more and buried himself deep inside her. His cock jerked and she tightened her channel around him, smiling with satisfaction as he cursed and shuddered.

When he stilled, he drew out of her and got rid of the condom, then grabbed a cloth and cleaned them both up.

"Get off the covers," he said, and she felt a pang of disappointment. Was he kicking her out already?

He snorted. "Not like that. I just want to get under the blankets. Come on, you know I'm a cuddler."

She smiled. He was, and she loved that. Somehow, one-night stands felt less businesslike when they were followed by cuddles. She scooted under the blankets and waited until he snuggled up behind her, pulling her back against his chest. Then she closed her eyes and let sleep claim her. She'd worry about regretting him in the morning.

2

GABBY WOKE IN THE DARK WITH A SINKING FEELING IN THE PIT of her stomach. She'd done it again. She'd fallen into bed with Logan Pride. Did she have no self-control? After trying too hard to keep her distance from him for weeks, she'd given in the instant they were alone.

Shame tightened her throat. Not shame over being with Logan, but for failing to keep her word to herself and for once again doing something she'd have to hide from Shane. It shouldn't be so difficult to resist Logan when she knew he couldn't—or wouldn't—give her what she wanted. Children. Marriage. A family. But she'd never been able to stay away from him. Even when they fought, it inevitably led to the bedroom. For years, she and Logan had shared furtive nights together. She'd justified not telling Shane because it was more a series of one-night stands than any type of relationship, and when she'd moved here, she'd promised herself it would never happen again.

Yet here she was.

With a sigh, she extricated herself from his embrace, freezing when he murmured in his sleep, but he didn't wake. She placed one foot on the floor and then the other, gradually easing herself away, afraid that if she disturbed him, he'd convince her to go for round two. One slip-up she could live with, but two would be stupid.

She left the bedroom and searched the darkened living room for her dress and purse, then pulled the dress over her head as silently as possible. She abandoned her underwear —she'd wake him if she went back for them—and kept her feet bare, the better to make her escape. Fortunately, February mornings were mild, so she didn't have to worry about her toes freezing. She let herself out of the apartment, gently closed the door, and tiptoed down the stairs. At the bottom, she left via the fire exit, which automatically locked behind her, and beelined for her car. She pressed a button on her key fob to unlock it and climbed into the driver's seat.

"Why?" she asked herself in frustration as soon as the door shut behind her. "Why do you sabotage yourself? No matter how hot or fun Logan is, he's never going to be the father of your children." He'd made that obvious the first time they met. He'd given her the talk she suspected he gave all of his hookups.

All I want is fun. No strings. I'm never going to settle down. I'll be a bachelor until the day I die.

Yada yada yada.

Honestly, it had been a little insulting that he'd thought she needed it spelled out. She'd told him so and started to walk away, but he'd made a smart-ass remark that immediately lured her back. They'd bickered, and before she knew it, they were in his bed. That seemed to be how it went with him. He overrode her good sense. Being with him, even for one night, messed with her head. She needed to focus on her goal of finding the right guy to make a family with. She was in her thirties, after all. She couldn't afford to waste valuable time or mental real estate on Logan or to fall into that old pattern with him.

She started the car and drove to her new home, a few minutes outside of Haven Bay on the inland side of town. Fortunately, she'd fed the cats and dogs before she went on her date, otherwise she'd have had a whole other layer of guilt to contend with. She parked near the door and let herself in. Thomas greeted her, meowing loudly, his eyes shining green in the light from her phone. Behind him, two other furry outlines with glowing eyes waited. Probably Mouse and Karen. Luna would be asleep. She was more independent than the others.

"Hi, babies," she said, feeling like a teenager who'd been caught sneaking out of her room. "Sorry I'm late."

Thomas bumped his head against her leg and meowed again. She scooped him up and buried her face in his furry body. He purred as loudly as an engine. She carried him through the house and held him with one arm while she used the other to open the back door. Thelma and Louise were waiting outside. They had crates with blankets on the back doorstep but much preferred sleeping in the house when they got the chance. Louise shivered in a way that was no doubt designed to make Gabby feel guilty.

"It's not that cold," she muttered, although the breeze was a bit chilly. "Never mind. Come to bed."

She brushed her teeth and slipped beneath the blankets, finding a warm ball of fur already waiting for her. Luna. The other animals surrounded her and she smiled. She loved being close to them and sharing in their unconditional love.

"No more Logan Pride," she promised them. "That was the last time."

Karen made a judgmental sound, as if she doubted Gabby's word. She wasn't the only one.

Logan's arms were empty. As was his bed. He blinked his eyes open and looked around. There was no sign of Gabby. Groaning, he sat up and stretched, then scanned the floor. Her underwear were still there, but when he stopped to listen, the apartment was dead silent. Disappointment flashed through him at the thought that she'd probably left. He'd have liked to see her this morning. He could have cooked her breakfast and chatted about what she'd been up to since she moved to town—aside from dating everyone other than him. He'd heard from Shane that she'd joined the staff of the rural veterinary clinic, but he wasn't sure what that entailed. Working with the local farms, perhaps. There weren't too many stock farms in the area, but there were a handful, and the next nearest clinic was quite a drive away so their clinic probably covered the entire district.

Now, he wouldn't get the chance to ask her about it. He flopped back against the pillows and stared at the ceiling. Perhaps it was better that way. Gabby intrigued him, and the more time he spent with her, the more he wanted to know her better. That would lead nowhere good. He'd only end up hurting her, and that would be a shitty thing to do, especially when she was fresh out of a relationship and probably nursing wounds because of it. He didn't know much about her ex, but from what he'd heard, it hadn't been an amicable breakup.

"Leave her alone," he muttered to himself. "She's been through enough. She doesn't need you messing with her any more than you already have."

If he tried to get close to her, there was no doubt he'd hurt her somehow. All his life, Logan had been told how similar he was to his no-good father. He had the same hair, the same carefree attitude, and the same reputation as a womanizer. Not to mention they shared a love of surfing and wide open spaces. Summed up, this equaled one truth.

Logan would be a crappy boyfriend or husband, just like his dad had been.

Stop wallowing in self-pity.

He forced himself to get up, confirm that she was gone, shower off the smell of sex, and don a clean outfit. When he was presentable, he went downstairs to finish last night's cleanup. It only took a half hour to have The Den smelling of disinfectant rather than spilled beer. Then he wandered out the front door and across the town square, smiling at the people clustered around the fountain in the center of the square, until he reached Cafe Oasis. The tables inside were nearly full, thanks to the tourists who flocked to the bay on the weekends.

He walked inside and joined the short line, checking the cabinet before deciding on a cream cheese and salmon bagel. He ordered from Lana, the middle-aged woman who owned the cafe, and took one of the few remaining empty seats in the corner. He enjoyed a latte and ate his breakfast while listening to Irene and Nell from the Bridge Club—a group of retirees who spent more time gossiping than playing cards—discuss their romance sweepstakes.

They'd been running the sweepstakes for a couple of years, betting on which people would form couples and when. The pool of singles was dwindling though, and it sounded as if poor Gabby was now their biggest subject of speculation. At least they were leaving him alone. Earlier on in the sweepstakes, they'd tried to include him, but now they seemed to take him at his word when he said he wouldn't settle down.

He left the cafe with a friendly wave for the two ladies and headed for the beach. Since it was before eight on a Sunday, hardly anyone was around. He spotted a runner in the distance. Perhaps Sterling from the bed and breakfast, or Michael, the school principal. He went to the trailer he rented for the surfing school he ran, and grabbed his wet suit from inside. Then he glanced around to make sure no one was watching, changed into the wet suit, and tucked one of the surfboards under his arm.

He drew in a lungful of sea air as he made his way to the water, and smiled. God, he loved that smell. The ocean was his favorite place. As a teen, he'd spent hours riding the waves, which had stood him in good stead for his years as a professional competitive surfer, and now for running his own surfing school. He waded into the shallows. It was cold at this time of day. When he'd gone far enough that the waves lapped at his waist, he climbed onto the board and started paddling. He loved the burn in his arms. He could surf all day, if not for his bung knee. Most of the time, it didn't slow him down too much, but he'd never have the same effortless grace he used to, and if he overdid things, he'd regret it later.

He positioned himself in the water, waiting for the right wave to roll under him. He tuned in to his surroundings, allowing everything else to drop away. Out here, all was peaceful. Or at least, it usually was. Today, for some reason, he couldn't shake the guilt of betraying Shane's trust again. He'd just have to stay away from Gabby from now on. Otherwise, he'd be forced to have a very awkward conversation with his friend.

3

By some miracle, Gabby had managed to keep her distance from Logan after the night they shared together. For the last six weeks, she'd stayed away from The Den, and he must have been doing his part to avoid her too because they never ran into each other in the minimart or at The Shack—the local ice cream parlor and cupcake shop. A couple of times, she saw him leading a surfing class from a distance, but she knew better than to approach.

Despite her success on that front, she hadn't gone on any more dates. She was being more cautious in vetting people because she knew she needed to prevent a repeat of the circumstances that had led her to Logan's bed in the past, which meant no more self-pitying episodes after terrible dates. Ergo, there could be no more terrible dates.

Fortunately, she didn't need to worry about men tonight. Well, except for little ones. It was Friday, which meant that Shane's friends were meeting for poker. She was catching up with Faith, Shane's partner, and Charity, Faith's sister, while they looked after Shane's sons, Dylan and Hunter.

"Come on," she called to Thelma and Louise, who were coming with her. The boys adored them, even if their cat,

Tinkerbell, was less of a fan. The dogs jumped into the back seat of her car and stuck their noses out the partially open windows while she made the drive to the old villa where Shane lived with his family. His car was parked out front, so she pulled to the side of the road and let the girls out. They bolted toward the front door. Gabby jogged up the path behind them and knocked.

"It's open!" Faith called from within.

Gabby turned the handle and held the door wide enough for Thelma and Louise to enter, then closed it behind herself.

"Doggies!" Hunter cried, rushing out of one of the bedrooms and engulfing Louise in a hug. Shane's youngest was six, and while he could be shy at times, he was crazy about her pets. Honestly, he was just a pint-sized joy to be around. Dylan, the older boy, was thirteen and beginning to think he was too cool for the adults around him, but he was still a good kid.

"Hey, Gabby." Shane emerged from the room he shared with Faith, tugging on a t-shirt. His glasses sat askew on his nose and his brown hair stuck up at interesting angles.

"Hi, big brother." She hugged him, wondering once again how someone as sweet but clueless as him had won over sassy, curvaceous Faith.

"How are you doing?" he asked as they separated. He scanned her face, and his forehead creased with concern. "You haven't seemed like your usual self lately. Is everything okay?"

Gabby rolled her eyes. "You're always trying to take care of everyone. It's nice, but not necessary in this case. I'm fine." She hesitated, wondering whether to share some of the thoughts that had been on her mind. His earnest expression encouraged her to take the plunge. "I've just been tired lately. Or maybe I've got the blues because of being single when everyone around me is in blissful relationships." Having someone of her own like that was her dream, and it had factored into her decision to move here. While the main driver had been a need for change and a desire to be close to Shane, it had crossed her mind that many new happy couples seemed to pop up in Haven Bay. She'd thought... why not her? She wanted to share in their ooey gooey happiness, and to be the center of someone's world—something she obviously hadn't been for Henry—but so far, she'd defied the bay's matchmaking magic.

"I'm sorry, Gabby." He touched her shoulder. "It'll happen."

"I hope so." She forced herself to brighten. The last thing he needed was her dragging him down when he finally had everything he wanted and deserved.

He glanced at his watch. "I'd better go. I'll just say bye to Faith and the boys."

While he went to say his farewells, Gabby joined Charity in the living room.

Charity flashed her a smile that was gone as quickly as it appeared. "Dylan is playing video games," she said. "He's invited Hunter to join him, so it should be a quiet night."

"Great." A peaceful one, hopefully, too. With the age gap between Dylan and Hunter, they didn't always want to do the same thing, so there was a chance Hunter might tire of games or that Dylan would want to play at a higher level than Hunter was capable of, but they should occupy each other for a while at least.

Thelma trotted into the room and launched herself onto the sofa beside Charity, who patted the top of her head but didn't look thrilled when the dog tried to climb onto her lap.

"Down," Gabby ordered. Thelma looked at her mournfully, and she sighed. "Fine. Come over here." She sat on an armchair and made as much space as possible for

Thelma to join her, wincing as the dog's elbows dug into her thighs.

A few minutes later, Faith joined them, carrying a tray of mini cupcakes.

"You have to try these," she said. "Megan is testing new flavors for The Shack. The limoncello cupcake is divine."

Megan was Faith's business partner. She was a classically trained pastry chef who'd left the city lights behind to bake cupcakes in Haven Bay after falling for the cook who worked at Sanctuary, the local bed and breakfast.

"Ooh, nice." Gabby plucked one up. "Does it actually have alcohol in it? I don't want to be over the limit when I drive home later."

Faith shook her head. "No, she used other ingredients to mimic the flavor. She said she wanted everyone to be able to eat them."

Gabby bit into the tiny cupcake and a burst of lemony flavor filled her mouth. She moaned. "That is so good. Oh my God." A little sweet, a little tart. Delicious. "Tell her she's onto a winner."

Faith dropped onto the seat beside Charity. "Louise is with the boys. Hunter wouldn't let her out of his sight."

"Cute." Gabby's heart sighed. She wished she had a gorgeous little boy of her own.

"So, what's new?" Faith asked.

"Kyle and I are moving house," Charity said. "We signed the sale and purchase agreement today."

"Congratulations!" Gabby raised a cupcake toward her as if she were toasting them. "Is that the place a couple of blocks away from here?"

"It is." She smiled, and it softened her hard edges. Charity could be prickly, but when it came to the man she loved, she was a marshmallow.

"We'll help you pack," Faith said. "Just tell us when."

"I will, thanks."

They talked about the new house for a few minutes before lapsing into temporary quiet.

Faith turned to Gabby. "Are you okay? You seem a bit off."

Gabby pulled a face. "Are you all trying to tell me I look haggard or something? Because Shane already mentioned it."

Faith shrugged. "We're worried, that's all."

"I know." She appreciated it. Having people who cared meant a lot to her. "Like I told him, I think I'm just melancholy because I haven't got my own happily ever after yet." She pinched off part of a cupcake and popped it into her mouth. "I mean, even Corinne has found love."

Corinne was Logan and Kyle's mother.

"She and Lawrence are so sweet together," Faith said. "I'm so glad they went away to Switzerland and were stuck with just that one bed." She waggled her eyebrows.

Gabby sighed. "Exactly. They have that, and I'm just sitting over here like a pumpkin. The worst part is..." She trailed off, deciding she shouldn't go down that path.

"What?" Faith asked.

"Nothing."

Charity's eyes narrowed. "Nuh-uh. Whatever is going on in your head right now, it's not nothing. I can tell it's stressing you out."

Gabby sighed. Sometimes it was inconvenient to have perceptive friends. "I just don't seem to be interested in anyone lately, other than a guy I've had an on-and-off thing with for a while, but nothing long-term is ever going to happen with him. That message doesn't seem to be getting through to my brain."

"A guy?" Faith sounded excited. "What guy? Is he from your old hometown?"

Gabby took a moment to pull her thoughts together. She didn't want to give them enough information to figure it out. "We've known each other for ages. Half the time, I don't think we even like each other, but there's this magnetic pull between us."

"A magnetic pull is a good sign," Faith said. "Have you thought about giving a real relationship with him a try?"

Gabby snorted. "He's a player, so no. That would be an awful idea."

Charity frowned. "That's a shame. Have you been missing him lately?"

Yeah, they definitely thought it was someone from back home. She felt a flare of guilt.

"Kind of. But I need to just get over it."

Faith winked. "The best way to get over him is to get under someone else."

Gabby laughed, but in her heart, she knew it wouldn't be that simple.

EIGHT MEN SAT AROUND LOGAN'S DINING TABLE, CARDS IN front of them and a pile of M&Ms in the center. They didn't bet with real money because some of them were loaded and others weren't. Using candy equalized the playing field.

"Call," Logan said, adding a few more M&Ms to the pile.

"Call," Kyle, his brother, said from his right.

"Fold." Michael placed his cards face down and reached for his beer.

Everyone waited for Shane. And waited. Until it became obvious he was lost in his own world.

"Shane." Michael nudged him with his elbow.

"What?" He jerked to life, quickly realizing he'd been holding up the game. It wasn't the first time and probably wouldn't be the last. Shane was absent-minded and easily distracted. But he did seem unusually preoccupied today. "Fold."

"Is everything okay?" Logan asked as Tione called the bet.

Shane smiled wryly. "Probably. I'm just worried about Gabby. She's been unusually quiet lately, and she sounded a bit down in the dumps when I talked to her before I came over here."

Logan's heart squeezed. He'd been craving news of Gabby, but now he felt uncertain about what to do with it. If she wasn't happy, it was none of his business, but try telling that to the mushy organ in his chest that wanted to fix whatever was bothering her.

"Was she upset?" he asked.

Shane shrugged one shoulder. "Maybe. It's hard to tell, which is unusual in itself because she usually shares anything and everything that goes through her head."

"Do you know why?" He sensed Kyle glance over, his curiosity piqued. Logan didn't usually ask many questions when the others talked about their families, so digging for details was out of character for him.

"That's the thing." Shane sipped from his beer bottle and set it down. "She says it's just about being single, but I think there's more going on. Maybe she's missing her ex, or he might have tried to get in touch. I just wish she'd let me in."

Logan scowled. "From what little you've told us, he sounds like a cheating asshole, and she's better off without him."

Not that they knew much. The entire Walker family had been close-mouthed about the situation. They were protective of their own. Especially after what had happened with Shane's ex.

"He is, and she is," Shane replied. "But sometimes the heart wants what it wants."

Logan didn't like the idea of Gabby missing her douchebag ex, but he had no business getting invested in her love life so he told himself to cut it out. He shouldn't be feeling anything toward her. Not concern. Not even the frustration he'd experienced when he realized she'd been avoiding him as much as he'd been avoiding her. Yes, it was childish, but he'd wanted her to catch his gaze across the room or drop by The Den just to see him. Now, hearing that she wasn't doing well, he wondered whether he should check up on her. Maybe stop by her place to say hi.

And take her to bed? his subconscious asked skeptically.

He sighed. Yeah, he should leave her alone.

4

ON THE FIRST MONDAY OF APRIL, GABBY COULD BARELY convince herself to get out of bed. Even Thomas's begging to be fed didn't do the job. It was only when her bladder was full to bursting that she realized she had no choice. She dragged herself to the bathroom and answered the call of nature, then fed the cats and dogs. She didn't have enough oomph to go outside and put out alfalfa for the goats and grain for Princess, the beautiful palomino mare. Instead, she headed for the kitchen and started making scrambled eggs.

Unfortunately, the smell turned her stomach. She rushed to the toilet, fell to her knees, and retched until her gut felt hollow. Sweaty and wrung out, she wiped her mouth clean. Then, with difficulty, she got back to her feet, washed her mouth out, splashed her face, and returned to the kitchen. She threw the eggs out the window and washed the frying pan, ignoring the churn of her stomach as it threatened another mutiny.

Okay, no eggs. Perhaps she'd try a piece of toast. That usually went down all right when she had a tummy bug. She fixed the toast and flopped onto the sofa while she ate, warding off Mouse, who wanted to curl up on her belly.

Mouse was the smallest of the cats and usually Gabby would love to cuddle with her, but she didn't need any pressure on her stomach right now.

When she'd managed to get the toast down, she called her boss and said she wouldn't be in. She hated to call in sick. She couldn't even remember the last time she'd had the flu, but something was clearly not right with her today. Although, to be fair, she hadn't felt great for a few days. It had just come to a head this morning.

Knowing that she needed to take care of the other animals, she tugged on a robe and left the house. It only took a few moments to put alfalfa down for the goats, check they had fresh water and that each of them looked healthy. She sighed, already exhausted, and trudged around the house to the barn. It was dim inside, the mornings getting darker now that it was halfway through autumn. She opened the large door at the end of the building and went to Princess's stall.

"Hey, beautiful." She stroked the mare's neck and slipped her an apple. "You ready to get some sunshine?"

Princess snickered, nudged Gabby with her nose, and munched the apple.

Gabby smiled and rubbed her affectionately. "You want breakfast?"

Princess followed her out of the stall and waited while Gabby brought her a flake of hay and some oats. When she was eating back in her stall, Gabby quietly returned to the house. Thelma was waiting for her at the front door and followed on her heels as she went to the bathroom. Perhaps she'd been working too hard. A day off and a nice spa routine might put everything right.

Her skin felt disgusting, so she opened the medicine cabinet, looking for one of her clay facial masks. Instead, her eyes fell on the box of tampons on the top shelf. Her stomach dropped. She stared at them. When was the last time she'd had her period? It must have been a while because she could remember expecting it weeks ago but putting the lateness down to the stress of the breakup, selling her house and buying this one, the move, her new job, and everything else she had going on. Now, she mentally counted backward and swore.

Two and a half months.

Either something was majorly wrong, or she was pregnant.

Complicated emotions twisted inside her. Fear, and excitement. Despite the bad timing and the sad state of her love life, she'd always wanted a baby. Confusion. Sure, she wasn't on the pill, but she never had unprotected sex. In fact, the *only* sex she'd had in months was with Logan.

Oh, shit. What if she was pregnant, and Logan was the father? He'd be furious. He'd made it very clear that he didn't want children or a relationship. If she was pregnant, that meant she'd taken away his right to choose, because if there was a baby growing inside her—and it was a big if—there was no way she'd give it up.

Slow down.

She tried to think it through. What were her symptoms? She hadn't had her period for months. She'd been feeling tired for weeks. Now she was nauseous and the smell of eggs had made her throw up. It was certainly possible that those things could add up to pregnancy.

She hadn't used an oral contraceptive or any contraceptive device other than condoms for a couple of years because she hadn't wanted them to impact her ability to have a baby once she'd found a partner and decided to go for it. Still, condoms were effective. Although... how old had that condom in her purse been? She squeezed her eyes shut as she did the mental arithmetic. It had been there for months. Maybe even a year. It could have gotten damaged during that time.

She rubbed her temples and took a few deep breaths, trying to slow her heart rate. Thelma brushed against her leg and whimpered.

"It's okay, girl."

Everything would be fine. First, she needed to know for sure whether she was pregnant. That meant taking a test. She didn't own any, and she had no intention of purchasing one from the minimart. She could only imagine what might happen if she showed up there and bought a pregnancy test. Word would spread around town in minutes. She'd have to go to the pharmacy in Te Awa Tui, the next town over. But was she up to driving that far? She felt like crap.

Was there even an alternative? She supposed she could ask Faith or Charity to buy one, but she couldn't handle their curiosity yet. She'd just have to do it herself.

She stumbled out of the house, only realizing she was still dressed in a robe when she was halfway to the car. With a muttered oath, she hurried back and changed into jeans and a sweater and grabbed her purse. She put the dogs outside and drove to Te Awa Tui in a stupor, a thousand thoughts buzzing through her mind but none of them settling for long enough to examine them. Once there, she parked on the roadside by the pharmacy and glanced around to make sure nobody was paying her any attention before she entered. No one was, of course. That would be crazy.

"You're paranoid," she muttered under her breath. Or maybe she wasn't, because two steps inside the pharmacy, she nearly bowled into Betty.

"Gabrielle!" Betty lit up at the sight of her. "I didn't expect to run into you here."

Gabby silently cursed her bad luck. "I didn't think I'd see you either."

She should have anticipated running into one of the older generation from Haven Bay though. There was no local pharmacy, so they all used the one in Te Awa Tui.

Betty frowned. "Are you okay? You look very pale."

Gabby latched onto the opportunity to divert attention away from her real reason for being there. "I've got a tummy bug. Need to pick up some medication."

"Oh, dear. That's no good." Betty backed up a step, probably worried Gabby might be contagious. "You'd better get onto that then. Nasty things, those stomach viruses."

"Have a nice day."

Gabby waved until Betty had left, then breathed a sigh of relief. She beelined for the pregnancy tests, snatched one of each brand off the shelf, and paid for them before anyone else she recognized could turn up. On the journey home, the paper bag drew her eye over and over again. When she arrived, she went straight to the bathroom and used one test after another.

They were all positive.

<hr>

LOGAN WAS PERCHED AT A TABLE NEAR THE BAR IN THE DEN, checking the bookings for his afternoon surfing class, when Betty and her friends Mavis and Nell claimed the table behind him and started chatting while they waited for Corinne, his mother, to take their order. Logan was officially off the clock, which meant that Corinne was playing waitress and bartender. They kept a small staff. Just the two of them, a cook, and a couple of casuals they called in for busier evenings, mostly during the height of summer.

"Guess who I saw at the pharmacy in Te Awa Tui this morning," Betty was saying.

"Well go on, tell us," Mavis said, never one for mincing words.

Betty gave her a reproachful look. "Gabrielle Walker. And let me tell you, she looked dreadful." She pursed her lips, visibly worried. "I don't say it lightly, but whatever she's got, we'd better hope it's not catching. The poor thing was absolutely miserable."

Logan felt a pang of guilt. He should have checked on Gabby a week ago after Shane said that she'd not been her usual self. Instead, he'd opted not to, just to avoid the discomfort of talking to her for the first time since their night together. He needed to do better. *Be* better.

"Did she say what it was?" Nell asked, her voice full of concern. Such a sweet lady.

"Just some kind of tummy bug," Betty said. "But I got the feeling she wasn't telling me the full story."

Mavis snorted. "You're probably reading too much into it. You do love drama, Bets."

Betty narrowed her eyes. "I'm telling you, something is off with that girl."

Logan wondered how much weight to give to her words. Mavis wasn't entirely wrong. Betty did thrive on drama. But she also wouldn't make such a fuss if she didn't think there was a reason to.

He grabbed his phone from the tabletop and found Gabby's new number, which he'd got from Shane's contact list while he wasn't paying attention, and fired off a quick message.

Unknown: *This is Logan. I heard you're sick. Can I visit, or are you going to give me the plague?*

He put the phone down and tried to refocus on his

emails, but the instant it pinged with a reply, he checked to see what she'd said.

Gabby: *Thanks for checking in, but there's no need for you to come over.*

His lips parted in surprise. Their exchanges were always a back-and-forth of snarky banter. The fact she'd been polite worried him far more than Betty's comments had.

Logan: *You thanked me. You've clearly been possessed by an alien. I'll be there soon.*

He stood and closed his laptop, but his phone pinged again almost immediately.

Gabby: *I'm serious. Don't come. I don't want any guests.*

Logan: *Not even little old me?*

Gabby: *No.*

The rejection shouldn't have hurt. He and Gabby weren't exactly friends. But that didn't stop the sting of knowing she didn't want to see him. He considered turning up on her doorstep anyway, just to see with his own eyes that she was okay, but he couldn't handle it if she told him to get lost, so he sat down again and went back to working through his inbox.

It's better this way, he told himself. But he didn't believe it.

5

OVER THE NEXT TWO DAYS, GABBY LIVED IN DENIAL. SHE called in sick to work, moped around in her bed surrounded by a furry huddle of love, and ate only chocolate hazelnut spread on toast because that was what she'd discovered she could keep down. She couldn't continue like this forever, she knew that, but nor could she decide what to do next. She'd have to return to work. She didn't have any more sick leave. But with how tired she'd been, and her temperamental stomach, working would be difficult.

On Wednesday morning, she brushed Princess until her coat shone a glorious shade of gold and let Thelma and Louise loose in the empty paddock attached to the property so they could burn off some energy since she didn't feel up to walking them. That done, she curled up on the sofa with a blanket and a chocolate bar and watched re-runs of McLeod's Daughters, a show about sisters running a cattle ranch in southern Australia.

She was three episodes deep when someone knocked on the door. She considered ignoring them, but if it was one of her family members, that would only make them worry. She paused the show and tidied her hair, hoping that whoever it was wouldn't notice what a mess she was. When she opened the front door, she was surprised to find Charity standing there. While she got on well with Charity, they'd never spent much time together one on one.

"This is an intervention," Charity announced. "You're not answering anyone's calls and we're worried. Shane wanted to give you another day, but I decided I don't like seeing him and Faith stressed so I'm here to figure out what's wrong with you." She brushed past Gabby, pausing to say hello to Thelma and Louise, who'd climbed through the fence to see who'd come to visit, and continued through to the living area. She stopped in the doorway, scanning the blanket on the sofa, the crumb-covered plates, and the empty chocolate wrapper. She pivoted to face Gabby. "Seriously. What's going on?"

With a sigh, Gabby flopped back onto the sofa and wrapped the blanket around her shoulders. She'd known she'd have to tell everyone eventually. She'd just hoped to have more time to come to terms with the situation. It was hard to know how to break the news when she wasn't sure whether she was thrilled or terrified to be carrying Logan's baby.

Charity sat cross-legged in an armchair and patted Thomas when he jumped onto her lap.

Gabby pursed her lips. "I can tell you, but I need you to promise you'll keep it to yourself for a day or so. It involves someone else, and I haven't spoken to them yet."

"Scandalous." Charity's tone was dry, but Gabby could tell she was intrigued. Maybe having her here wasn't so bad. She needed to practice telling people, and Charity was sensible and pragmatic. She'd be a good test run.

Gabby was grateful when Mouse, who'd been lingering at the door, trotted over and made herself at home on her lap. She'd be a good distraction. Gabby stroked her with one hand while figuring out where to start. She decided that getting straight to the point would be best.

"I think I'm pregnant."

Charity's eyes widened, but other than that, she didn't show any visible reaction. "With your ex?"

"No. I got my period shortly after we broke up."

Charity cocked her head. "So, who is the dad?"

Gabby bit her lip. "Logan."

"Well, damn." Charity gave her a look she couldn't interpret. Surprise, but also something else. A hint of approval? "So, he's the person you need to talk to before the news gets out?"

"Yeah." Gabby buried her face in Mouse's soft fur until she'd gotten control of her emotions. "And he's who I mentioned to you and Faith a while ago, the one I was having a hard time getting over."

"Wow." Charity blinked. "I didn't see that coming. Are you...dating him?"

"No." She sighed. "We've never dated, just had some really great sex. I have no idea how he's going to react." Probably not well.

Charity's expression softened. "It will be okay. I'm not going to lie and say he'll be pleased. He's probably going to lose his shit for a little while. But if there's one thing Logan is, it's loyal. He'd do anything for his family, and I'm sure it will be the same for your baby once he gets over himself." She hesitated. "Are you keeping it?"

"Yes." Gabby raised her chin and silently dared her to comment. She didn't. Gabby turned over what she'd said. She hoped Logan would be someone she could rely on, as Charity had suggested, but she also didn't want to put too much on his shoulders. He'd never asked for this. In fact, the opposite was true, and she didn't want to tie him down if it would only make him miserable and resentful. She needed to hope for the best, but prepare for life as an independent single mum, because that was where she'd probably end up.

"Did I ever tell you what Logan did when Kyle and I started dating?" Charity asked.

Gabby struggled to follow the change of topic. "No."

"Logan was sure that I would hurt Kyle, so he stuck his nose into our relationship in a way that caused problems for us."

"I'm sorry."

Charity shook her head. "That's not the point. The point is that Logan thought Kyle was in trouble and he did whatever it took to protect him, even if it was underhanded. Once you have Logan's loyalty, he'll be fiercely protective."

Gabby's heart squeezed. "But what if I never get it?"

Or what if she did, but for all the wrong reasons? She couldn't stand to be an unwanted obligation.

"You're having his baby." She looked Gabby dead in the eye. "That will outweigh everything else. Trust me."

"I hope you're right." She knew she had to tell Logan soon. He deserved to know. But she dreaded it. What if he blamed her, or asked her to terminate the pregnancy?

"I am," Charity said. "You need to rip off the Band-Aid and tell him. It'll be better that way."

She was right. But...

"I should do a blood test first. Just to be sure."

Charity raised an eyebrow. "How many at-home tests have you taken?"

"Four." She looked away. "But I want to be certain."

Charity sighed. "Just as long as you're not using it as an excuse to delay. After all, with four positive tests and the fact you look like a dog's breakfast, how much doubt is there really?"

She probably was delaying, but it would be terrible if

she announced the pregnancy to the world and then learned she had some stress-induced hormonal condition that mimicked the symptoms.

"I'll do the test today," she said. "As soon as I get the results, I'll tell him, and then we can figure out how to let our families know."

AFTER SHARING A LUNCH OF MORE TOAST AND A FEW crackers with Charity, Gabby drove to Serenity Cove, a town about an hour north along the coast. She'd made an appointment at the medical laboratory there, rather than the closer town of Te Awa Tui, to reduce the risk of running into anyone she knew. Besides, she'd been meaning to visit Serenity Cove. She'd heard good things about the sleepy coastal town from Marley, who had lived there briefly after college.

Gabby entered the waiting area and took a number from the desk. She picked up a health and wellness magazine and skimmed until she found an article about good nutrition during pregnancy. Apparently, she'd been doing everything wrong. She was supposed to be eating more vegetables and lean protein.

Tell that to my stomach.

At least the wholegrain bread she'd been using ticked one box.

When her number was called, she followed a short, plump nurse down the corridor to a small private room and sat on the patient bed while the nurse prepared the needle.

"Have you been trying for a baby?" the nurse asked as she lined the tip of the needle up with a vein in Gabby's elbow.

Gabby grimaced as the needle jabbed into her but didn't

flinch. Years of being a veterinarian had made her immune to needles and other tools of the trade. "No, but I've always wanted one."

The nurse smiled as she removed the needle and capped it. "Let's hope for good news then."

Good news. Was that what it would be when the test came back with the result she knew it would? Maybe.

For the first time, she allowed herself to feel excited without guilt. Sure, this might not be the way she'd have preferred to do things, but she was having a baby. She placed her hand over her flat stomach and for a moment, joy overcame her, so intense that tears filled her eyes. A little boy or girl was being created inside her, and that was incredible.

"Let's hope," Gabby murmured, but she knew that no luck was needed. She was pregnant. This test was just a formality.

She smiled, wondering what her child would be like. Would they love animals like she did? Would they have her golden-brown eyes or Logan's turbulent blue-green ones? Her dark hair, or his blond? She was certain they'd have plenty of spirit. Both she and Logan were well-endowed in that department. Most likely, they'd have made a feisty little one who'd have plenty of their own opinions and not hesitate to share them.

She couldn't wait.

When the nurse gave her the all-clear to leave, instead of going straight back home, she wandered down the main street and looked through the shop windows. She stopped outside one called The Stork. Beautiful cribs that had to be hand-carved were displayed in the window, with lush blankets in pastel colors. Further back in the shop, she could see rows of baby clothes.

Before she knew what she was doing, she found herself

standing inside the shop, staring at the tiny outfits. There were so many, and they were all completely darling. She ran her hand down a onesie, marveling at the softness of the fabric. She spotted one with a pink tool belt print around the waist and laughed.

"Hi."

She spun around, and her jaw dropped at the sight of the man in front of her. Blue eyes twinkled out of his suntanned face, with tiny crinkles at the edges from smiling. He treated her to a glimpse of his perfect teeth and smoothed a rogue curl on the top of his wavy brown hair. But that wasn't the best part. He was hand-in-hand with a miniature version of himself, whose hair was more blond than brown, and who was gazing up at her with the most intense blue eyes. Utterly adorable.

"Hi." She tucked her hair behind her ear. "Am I in your way?"

His eyes widened. "No. Sorry. I just wanted to say hello. This is a small town and we haven't met before, so I wondered if you're new to the area."

"I'm just here running errands," she said. "I live in Haven Bay. I moved there a few months ago."

"Oh, right." Was it just her, or had his smile dimmed slightly? He offered his hand. "I'm Tristan, and this is Ollie."

She shook his hand. "Gabrielle, but you can call me Gabby." She bent to the boy's level. "It's nice to meet you, Ollie."

"You're pwetty," he said, staring at her with open curiosity but also a degree of caution. Maybe he was a shy kid.

"Thank you." Perhaps a three-year-old wasn't the type of man she'd wanted to tell her so, but he was unbelievably cute, and she knew she looked pasty and tired so she'd take what she could get. She straightened. "You must live around here then?"

Tristan nodded. "On the cliffs overlooking the harbor, but I work out of town."

She glanced at Ollie. "Not today, though?"

"No, it's one of my off days, and Ollie's best friend is getting a new cousin sometime this week, so we're looking for a gift."

"How exciting!" Gabby loved babies. "A boy or a girl?"

"We're not sure. The parents want it to be a surprise." He smiled, showing those white teeth again. "Who are you shopping for?"

Gabby's hand immediately went to her stomach. Understanding dawned on Tristan's face.

"Congratulations. Is this your first?"

"Yeah." She nibbled her lower lip. "Is it that obvious?"

"No. I was just assuming that if you had others, they'd be with you. Although I suppose they could be in school."

She laughed. "No others. In fact, this little guy or girl wasn't planned, and I'm still not sure how I feel about it."

She pressed her lips together. She could hardly believe she'd just admitted that. What had possessed her to open up to a complete stranger?

His expression softened. "Trust me, even if it doesn't feel like it now, they'll be the biggest blessing you ever have."

Gabby warmed inside, some of the scared voices in her head quieting. "Thank you. I needed to hear that. It's scary, the idea of doing it by myself."

He frowned. "The dad isn't in the picture?"

"We're not together." She forced herself to sound nonchalant. "I'm not sure how involved he'll be."

He reached into his pocket with his free hand and brought out his phone. "Why don't we swap numbers? I'd be happy to chat, or to listen if you need to talk."

Gabby frowned. "That's so kind of you. I hope you don't mind me asking, but why would you make that offer to someone you just met?"

One side of his mouth hitched up. "I've been a single parent for half Ollie's life. Any doubts or questions you have, I've probably been there. I wished I had someone to talk to, so I'm happy to be your sounding board."

"Thank you." Gabby's heart lifted. Perhaps everything was going to be okay. Although she still had to break the news to Logan...

6

"WHEN YOU'VE PUT THE BOARDS BACK IN THE TRAILER, YOU can change out of the wet suits and leave them in the box over there." Logan waved a hand at the blue plastic box he was referring to. "Thank you so much for coming today. I hope you enjoyed yourselves, and that this is only the first of many surfing experiences for you." He smiled at each member of the class, then fielded a couple of questions from the more eager students while the others carried their rental surfboards back across the sand to the storage trailer.

When he was alone, he turned, intending to collect the wet suits and begin his post-class tidy-up, but found himself face-to-face with Gabby. His stomach flipped over. She really didn't look good. Pale skin, dark circles under her eyes, and her cheekbones seemed more angular than usual, as if she'd lost weight.

"Hey," she said, meeting his eyes only briefly before looking down at the sleeve of her sweater, which she was picking at with clumsy hands. "Can I talk to you for a moment?"

"Sure." He shook his knee out, needing to loosen it up after a couple of hours spent wading through the surf, correcting his students. "Do you mind if we head back to the trailer? I don't want to leave it unattended for too long."

Gabby's eyes darted to his again before returning to her sleeve. "I'd prefer for our conversation to be private."

He shrugged. "So we'll walk slowly."

She hesitated, then nodded. "Okay."

He strode toward the wet suit box, limping slightly, his knee throbbing in protest with each step. He looked over at Gabby, who walked quietly beside him. It seemed as if she was working up the courage to say something.

"Are you okay?" he asked. "You don't look great."

She snorted. "Just what every woman wants to hear."

He rolled his eyes. "I mean it. You okay?"

She drew in a slow breath and stopped walking. He paused too, and turned to face her.

She caught his eyes and raised her chin. "I'm pregnant. I just had it confirmed today."

Oh, wow. He hadn't seen that coming. He scanned her up and down. Weren't pregnant women supposed to glow? And gain weight? She looked like she'd eaten bad chicken. And who the hell was the father? He hadn't seen her with any particular man lately. Of course, he'd been going out of his way to avoid her, so it was possible she'd been seeing someone and he didn't know. He doubted it though. Especially after what Shane had said about her being upset about her lack of a love life. Although maybe she'd been emotional about something else entirely. Or just felt like crap.

"Are you sure?" he asked.

"Yes." Her voice didn't waver.

He cocked his head. "You don't look happy. Haven't you always wanted a baby?"

"Logan." She spoke slowly, her tone pointed, but he had no idea what she was getting at. "You're the father."

What?

He laughed. This had to be a joke. She was having him on. She was probably just sick and knew she could use that to scare the bejesus out of him.

But her expression didn't falter.

"I'm serious," she said. "I'm pregnant, and you're the dad."

His smile faded, and he stopped laughing. She really seemed to mean it. "You're not kidding?"

Her lips thinned. "I wouldn't joke about something like this."

His gut hollowed out. Fuck. No. It didn't make any sense. Dread crept up his spine.

"What makes you think it's mine?" His voice sounded alien. Tight, strained, and detached.

"What do you think?" she snapped, a flush working up her cheeks. "You're the only man I've been with since my ex."

Her ex. That must be it. He grasped at the straw. "Surely it's your ex's."

"I've had my period since we broke up, but not since you and I slept together."

Holy shit.

Logan's head swam. It felt as though his world was caving in around him. He couldn't become a parent. Fuck, no. He'd sworn to himself that he'd never mess up a kid the same way his dad had messed him up. He was careful with contraception—always.

"I wore a condom," he said.

Gabby cringed. "In hindsight, it had been in my purse for a while. It might have been compromised."

"Shit." He dragged his fingers through his hair, not even caring that twinges of pain exploded over his scalp from where they caught in the windblown saltwater tangle. He should have used one of his own condoms. He'd only grabbed hers because she suggested it. A whisper of suspicion tickled at the back of his mind. It had been her useless condom, and she'd never made a secret of the fact she wanted kids. She'd lost her chance at having a blissful family life with her ex, so had she decided his sperm would be as good as anyone else's? He'd heard of women poking holes in condoms but he'd never imagined it might happen to him.

"Did you do it on purpose?" he asked. "Did you know this would happen?"

Smack!

Her palm cracked across his face before he saw it coming.

"How dare you?" she hissed, her eyes full of hurt.

He touched his cheek. It throbbed. Shame filled him. She hadn't deserved that. He was angry and upset, but he trusted she wasn't the sort of person who'd do that to him. She was honest. Sometimes too honest.

"I'm sorry. I deserved that."

"Yes, you did." Her face was red. "For what it's worth, I'm sorry too. Not about slapping you. Fuck you for even thinking I'd be capable of what you implied. But I'm sorry for what's happened. I know it's not what you wanted, and to make sure there's no doubt, I'll get a paternity test done. I don't want you wondering for the rest of our lives whether it's really your child."

"You don't have to do that," he said immediately. If she said there was no possibility anyone else had gotten her pregnant, he believed her. Even though he'd rather not.

"But I will," she insisted. "For both of our peace of mind."

Logan took a few steps toward the wet suit box, needing a distraction, but then her words from a moment ago really hit him. *The rest of our lives.* If she was pregnant, it wasn't a temporary inconvenience. Everything from now on would change. He'd be a father. He no longer had the choice to opt out of fatherhood, as he'd always intended. He could either follow in his absentee father's footsteps or try to be a decent dad even though he worried he'd end up letting his child down the same way he had been.

His jaw tightened. He couldn't leave his son or daughter to wonder why they weren't enough for their dad to hang around. He'd gone through that, and he wouldn't wish it on anyone. But what was the alternative? He wasn't cut out to be a father. He hardly knew anything about kids, and even less about babies. He wasn't responsible enough to even keep one alive and healthy, let alone raise them to be well-rounded and mentally stable. For fuck's sake, he owned a bar and surfed in his free time. What part of that said, "parent material"?

He felt a hand on his arm.

"I can have papers written up for you to sign away your parental rights," Gabby said softly. "I know this is a lot, and I don't expect anything from you. I earn a good income and my family will be supportive. I'm not afraid of being the sole carer for the baby. It's not what I always dreamed of, but life rarely turns out the way we hope."

Logan shook his head. He didn't want that, but she was bombarding him with too much at once. First the news she was pregnant, then the offer to make it all go away. "I need to think. Can you give me some time before you ask questions like that?"

"All right." She dropped her hand from his arm. "Is there anything I can do to help?"

"Not now." He stared blindly at the pile of wetsuits, his plans for a quiet afternoon completely shot to shit. "I'll call you. I just need to get my head around this."

"Fair enough."

They stood together for a moment longer, and then Gabby turned and walked away, leaving Logan alone to process the bombshell she'd dropped on him.

WELL, THAT HAD GONE ABOUT AS WELL AS SHE'D EXPECTED. Although she hadn't anticipated that he'd accuse her of having gotten pregnant on purpose. The nerve. But she understood where it had come from, and even though it hurt to know he'd thought that, she reminded herself that he was dealing with a shock. At least he'd apologized when she called him on his bullshit.

As she walked back to her car, she realized he'd never asked her whether she wanted to keep the baby. Perhaps he knew her well enough not to bother. She unlocked her car and sat in the driver's seat, gazing blindly at the steering wheel. Tears burned at the backs of her eyes and a tremble ran through her, but the relief of having gotten the secret off her chest outweighed everything else. She'd done the hardest thing now—at least until the birth itself—so she could handle whatever else came her way.

Still, she didn't like the thought of returning home just yet. There would be too much silence and plenty of opportunities to second-guess herself. Maybe she could visit a friend, but most of them would still be working. She could pop in to see Charity at the library. Not for long, just enough to calm her mind and get some of the moral support she craved.

Decision made, she drove to the town square and parked on the side street nearest the library. As she approached the main entrance, the scent of coffee wafted over from Cafe Oasis next door and she covered her mouth and hurried inside before she gagged. As the doors swung shut behind her, she looked around. Kyle was seated at a desk behind the counter, and the place was relatively quiet, with just a few patrons searching the shelves or reading quietly. Gabby strolled along the ends of the aisles until she found Charity in the G-J part of the fiction section.

"I did it," she said as soon as she was close enough for Charity to hear without having to raise her voice.

Charity cocked an eyebrow. "You'll have to be more specific."

Gabby rolled her eyes. "I told Logan."

She put down a book and gave Gabby her full attention. "How was it?"

Gabby glanced back at the counter to make sure Kyle wasn't paying them any attention before answering. "Not bad, but not great. Pretty much how I thought it'd go."

"That's good." Charity smiled encouragingly. "So, what next? Tell the family?"

"First I need to wait until Logan comes to terms with the news, and who knows how long that will take." Hopefully not more than a few days because with how sick she'd been, she might not be able to hide the truth for much longer.

"He's quick," Charity said. "It might be faster than you think."

"I hope so."

An elderly man in a hand-knitted sweater sauntered into their aisle.

"I'd better let you get back to work," Gabby said. She trusted Charity not to spill the beans, but the gossipy residents of Haven Bay—including whoever this old guy was— couldn't be trusted not to open their mouths.

"Call me if you need to," Charity said. The remark reminded Gabby about Tristan's number, and the fact she hadn't gotten in touch with him yet. Although he had hers too, so the onus wasn't on her to reach out. It felt wrong turning to another man for support when Logan had only just found out about the pregnancy, though, so she'd resist the urge to pick his mind for now.

"Thank you." Gabby kissed Charity's cheek. Her friend pretended to wipe it off, but Gabby could tell she secretly liked it. Charity had never been particularly comfortable with affection.

Her thoughts were more in order as she drove home. What she needed was a nap and then an outing with the dogs. She let herself into the house and dropped onto the sofa, where she fell asleep almost immediately. When she woke, Mouse was curled on her chest and Thomas was tucked against her side. She took a moment to fuss over each of them, and then to scoop up Karen, who'd been sitting nearby wearing her usual slightly disgruntled expression. She kissed the top of Karen's furry head despite her mews of protest and went to the back door to find Thelma and Louise.

She tried not to think about Logan. She was mostly unsuccessful.

7

AFTER LOGAN HAD CLEARED AWAY EVERYTHING FROM HIS class, he took his surfboard out to catch some waves. He knew it wasn't a smart idea considering the pain in his knee, but right then he didn't particularly care. Unfortunately, his timing was off, his balance seemed to have vanished, and no matter how long he bobbed on the waves under the cloudless sky, the clarity and calm he'd been searching for remained out of reach.

His emotions were in turmoil, his thoughts bouncing all over the place. Even though he knew the pregnancy wasn't Gabby's fault, he was angry. At her, at the stupid condom, and at the universe, which felt like it was laughing at him. As if some cosmic dictator had thought it would be karmic justice to spit in the face of his desire to remain childless by not only creating a pregnancy but by binding him to a woman who desperately wanted a family and who absolutely deserved it. As if it weren't enough for him to have brought an unborn child into existence, he'd now doomed Gabby to a lifetime of being tied to someone who didn't share her dreams, which might put off the men who did.

He growled and paddled toward another wave, but he

got the pacing wrong and the swell passed beneath him without sweeping him along on its journey. He realized his jaw was clenched and tried to release it. Getting frustrated would only make things worse. He paddled again, this time with more success, but not enough to sate the urge inside him to go to that place of oblivion where nothing mattered except riding the wave.

What would happen now?

He'd already decided that, given what choices remained, he'd have to suck it up and try his best not to fail his baby —*his* baby, God, what a foreign concept—like his own father had. Jonathan and Corinne had divorced when Kyle was only a toddler, but Logan had been old enough to remember. His dad had promised to be around. He was supposed to take Logan and Kyle every other weekend and on school holidays, but within six months he'd moved overseas and hadn't been back since. He'd sent a few Christmas and birthday cards, and for the first handful of years he'd called once a month, but Logan had stopped accepting those calls as a teenager and now he honestly couldn't remember the last time they'd spoken. He had no idea where his father was or what he was doing, and he liked it that way.

Knowing Jonathan, he was probably married to some girl in her twenties. He liked remarrying younger and younger women. Even though he wasn't rich, he was decent looking from what Logan could recall and he'd had a knack for convincing women to love him. That was one of the reasons Logan was so careful to spell out his intentions toward women before anything happened. He didn't want to leave a trail of broken hearts behind.

All his life, people had commented on how similar he and his father were. How Logan had grown into his mirror image. How they were both just so charming. He hated it, but he also couldn't deny it. He was like his old man in a lot of ways.

"But not in this," he murmured to himself. "Please, not in this."

He could do better than Jonathan, right? Hell, it wasn't as though the bar was high. But none of his past actions supported that idea. He'd always been Mr. Love 'Em and Leave 'Em. Never Mr. Right, just Mr. Right Now. And he'd steered well clear of any women who had children or wanted them—except for Gabby. He wasn't responsible, or patient, or any of those things dads needed to be. He was doomed.

But then, as he paddled out to deeper water, another thought occurred to him. The reason he'd kept Gabby at arm's length was gone. He hadn't wanted to get involved with her when they had such different goals in life, but now there was nothing stopping him from pursuing something with her. Except for the possibility of making things awkward with the mother of his baby. He grimaced. Or one of his best friends.

Okay, so maybe more thought was needed there.

He stayed on the water until the sun dipped to just above the horizon, then he dragged himself back to The Den on leaden legs. His friends would be arriving for poker soon. How could Logan look Shane in the eye knowing what he'd done? He'd knocked up his friend's little sister.

Did Shane already know? Logan racked his mind but he couldn't recall Gabby saying who she'd told, so he sent her a message to ask. The phone pinged in reply as he entered through the rear of the building, past the door that led to the bar where Corinne would be hard at work.

Damn, what would she think of him? Would she be disappointed in how careless he'd been? Would she feel let down by her son pulling the same kind of crap her husband might have? Or would she be excited to have her first grandchild on the way? She'd been dropping hints about them for years, but he'd always assumed Kyle would be the one to give them to her. Kyle had a partner. He was responsible, and good to his core. He wasn't scarred by their dad's broken promises the way Logan was. He'd be a good father.

Logan... yeah, he didn't have the makings of a super dad, but he'd try, and hope for the best.

When he was safe in his apartment, he checked the reply from Gabby. Apparently, she'd told Charity, but other than that, no one knew. He stripped off his clothes and got into a hot shower, mulling this over. Gabby was certain that Charity wouldn't say a word, and she was probably right. That woman had proved herself capable of keeping plenty of secrets, but he felt guilty she'd been put in this situation. Especially considering she'd no doubt want to talk it over with Kyle but wouldn't be able to.

He buried his face in his hands as the water sluiced over his back and shoulders, and groaned. This was a nightmare, and he couldn't see any way it could end well.

Fortunately, Shane wasn't the first to arrive at poker. It had been ridiculous to think he would be, considering he was almost always the last to turn up, but Logan's mind hadn't been rational as he tried to figure out how the hell he'd endure being alone with Shane without breaking the news. Somehow, he simultaneously wanted to confess everything to his friend but also never ever tell him. It was a strange dichotomy and he wasn't sure what to make of it. When Kyle strolled through the door, Logan was so relieved, he almost hugged him.

"Hey, man. How's things?" Logan asked, mixing a bowl of dip to keep his hands busy.

"Good." Kyle looked at him strangely, and Logan wondered whether Charity had told him about the pregnancy. Couples told each other everything, didn't they? But if she had, surely he would have mentioned it, or their mum would know and they'd have cornered him for an interrogation. "Is everything okay? You look stressed."

"I'm fine." Maybe if he said it enough times, he'd believe it. Or everyone else would, and they'd stop asking questions. He worried he'd crack the moment anyone pushed for details as to why he wasn't his usual carefree self. Fortunately, at that moment Tione and Sterling walked in together, Sterling chuckling at something Tione had said.

"Ready to lose?" Logan asked, pasting a fake smile on his face.

Tione scoffed. "You wish."

Sterling raised a haughty eyebrow. "I think we all know who'll be taking the pot home tonight."

Logan grunted. Sterling had a point. He did tend to come out on top. Occasionally, Logan or Michael would steal the win, but Tione played too conservatively, Jack was reckless, Shane was distracted, and Kyle didn't have a killer instinct. Logan suspected Gray would give them a run for their money if they changed venues to his place. He suffered from extreme anxiety—although it was gradually improving —and being away from home consumed a lot of his focus.

Jack sauntered in and helped himself to a beer from the fridge, then passed out drinks to the others. Logan eyeballed his to make sure the lid hadn't been tampered with. Jack wasn't above slipping spirits into people's beer to gain a competitive edge.

"Relax," Jack said. "It's just beer."

"It better be," Sterling grumbled, clearly recalling the

first time he'd joined their game. Logan had sneakily refilled his glass each time he looked away. He'd been drunk off his ass, but he'd still beaten them.

They sat around the table, greeting Michael as he entered looking every bit the school principal. Shane was right behind him, rumpled as always. The sight of him was like a punch to Logan's gut. He sucked in a breath.

Tione thumped his back, and he coughed. "You okay? Sounded like you choked on something."

Just my guilt.

"Went down the wrong pipe," he croaked.

Michael and Shane took the two remaining chairs, then Shane pulled a container of carrot sticks and one of hummus from his backpack and placed them on the table. He was such a dad. Always making sure they had a healthy option.

Logan frowned. Damn, he was going to have to think of things like that soon too. It would be up to him to help ensure the health and safety of a helpless baby. He so did not have the right instincts. He'd be more likely to feed them sugary cereal and chocolate. Perhaps he'd ask for Shane's advice—after he'd been forgiven, and who knew how long that would take?

Kyle dealt the cards and the game began. Logan tried to focus, and to behave normally, but he caught several of the men glancing at him, then catching each other's eyes. Communicating silently. At least he knew that whatever was going through their minds couldn't possibly come close to the truth.

"How's Gabby?" Kyle asked Shane as one hand ended and Tione grabbed the cards. "Is she feeling better now?"

Logan forced himself to stare at his cards. If he raised his eyes, there was no telling what they'd see in them.

Shane dunked a carrot stick in hummus. "She's still not

herself. I'm starting to wonder if she's going through a health scare but doesn't want to tell us."

Logan coughed. Sterling narrowed his eyes at him.

"Do you think so?" Kyle asked, his expression awash with concern.

God, how was Logan supposed to stay silent when they were so genuinely worried about her?

"Whatever it is, I'm sure she'll tell you soon," Logan said. "You just need to let her know you're there for her."

After all, she'd need whatever support she could get.

Shane smiled. "You're right. I have to trust that she'll let me know when she's ready to talk."

Thankfully, the conversation went in a different direction after that, and Logan managed to make it through the rest of the night with no incidents. When his friends had left, he sat alone at the table with a bottle of beer and contemplated the one-eighty his life had taken in only one day. His phone beeped and he checked the display.

Gabby: *I'll tell Shane once you've had time to process.*

Ah, it was a follow-up text from their previous conversation. He sent a reply.

Logan: *We can do it together.*

He dreaded it on so many levels, but acting as a team was the right thing to do. He was just as responsible for this pregnancy as she was.

8

ON SATURDAY MORNING, GABBY WAS BLESSEDLY FREE OF nausea. A relief, since she'd spent the day at work yesterday running to the bathroom every half hour. She got up to take care of the animals, then returned to bed and snuggled beneath the blankets with a notepad and a pen. Raising a baby required a lot of stuff she didn't have. A crib, clothes, diapers, a stroller, formula, toys, and who knew what else? Even though it was still early days, she should think about getting what they needed. With the help of the internet, she compiled a basic list. She separated the items into necessities, nice to haves, and super cute but totally impractical.

That done, she needed to assign a room to be the nursery. Fortunately, her house had three bedrooms. She'd taken the largest, sunniest room for herself. The other two bedrooms were smaller but still nice. The one at the front of the house had a beautiful view of the paddocks and the sun would stream through the windows when the weather was fine. That could be the nursery. She'd repaint and redecorate. Perhaps in white, cream, or a light shade of blue-gray. She'd put a patterned trim around the skirting boards and maybe stick some glow-in-the-dark stars to the ceiling.

She grinned, excitement flickering in her gut. She was going to make the best nursery Haven Bay had ever seen. Even Logan wouldn't be able to deny how cute it was. She pursed her lips, some of her excitement fizzling out. She wondered how he was feeling today. Was he still upset? Did he think the sky was falling, or had he come around to the idea? She suspected the former. Logan was not only averse to being a father, but he also had a flair for the dramatic.

Her stomach rumbled. She rubbed it and considered making toast for breakfast, but she didn't feel like that. Hmm, a nice cinnamon bun, perhaps. Yes, that would do.

She made the short trip into town and bought a cinnamon bun from Cafe Oasis, then sat on the edge of the fountain in the center of the square to eat. Her eyes wandered to The Den. Was Logan inside, or was he out on the water? What was going through his mind?

Cool it.

She needed to talk to someone, but he'd made it clear that he'd come to her when he was ready, so she wouldn't hunt him down now. She could call Charity, the only other person who knew the truth, but it wasn't fair to burden her with so many secrets. Shane was her usual go-to for advice on anything except the romantic. He'd married a she-devil prior to finding Faith, so she didn't put much stock in his dating tips. There was always Marley. She hadn't spoken to her best friend as much as she'd like since moving to Haven Bay, and Marley would be furious if Gabby didn't share something so monumental with her.

She relaxed, licking cinnamon sugar from her fingers. That was it. She'd call Marley as soon as she got home. She drew in a deep breath and got a whiff of something meaty. Even on good days, she didn't like the smell of cooked meat, but now it turned her stomach. She launched off her seat on the edge of the fountain and ran for the nearest trash can, throwing up violently into it. She gripped the edges and panted as her stomach tightened and rolled. Another retch. She sucked in air. Released it. She was fine. Everything was under control.

"Um... are you okay?"

Gabby released the trash can and turned slowly. She hated to think how she looked. Probably splotchy and sweaty. A petite brunette stood behind her, wearing a form-fitting dress and designer sunglasses. She shifted the sunglasses to the top of her head, revealing warm brown eyes full of concern. Gabby vaguely recognized her, although they'd never met. Mikayla Talbot, a friend of Charity's and the town's elected councilwoman. The man beside her, clad in jeans and a cashmere sweater, was gorgeous and startlingly familiar.

"You're Anderson Gray!" she exclaimed, cringing as soon as the words were out of her mouth. People probably fangirled over him all the time, and she doubted it was something he enjoyed.

"Yup." He shoved his hands into his pockets, visibly uncomfortable. "I prefer to go by Gray."

"I'm Gabrielle. Shane's sister."

Mikayla smiled. "I thought you looked familiar." She reached into her purse and pulled out a tissue. "Here. It looks like you need this."

"Thanks." Gabby's face burned hotter as she took the tissue and wiped her mouth clean. "I'm sorry you had to see that."

Mikayla rolled her eyes. "Somehow, I don't think seeing it was nearly as unpleasant as experiencing it. Seriously, are you okay?"

Gabby took another long, slow breath, double-checking the current state of her stomach. It seemed to have settled again. "I think so. I must have eaten something that didn't agree with me. I'll be all right as soon as I get home."

"Hmm." Mikayla's eyes narrowed. "Are you sure it was the smell of Lana's chicken and bacon waffles? It seemed like you made a run for it as soon as someone came out with a plate of them."

Gabby's stomach dropped. Mikayla had noticed that? She pursed her lips and scanned the other woman's face surreptitiously. Had she put two and two together?

"Do you need a ride home?" Mikayla asked.

Gabby gave a weak smile, relieved she wasn't pushing the waffles angle. "No, I drove in."

"We can get your car back to your place," Mikayla said. "I'll drive while you ride shotgun, and Gray can follow in our car to pick me up after."

Gabby shook her head, immediately regretting it as something throbbed at the back of her skull. "I'm really okay. I'd hate to put you out like that."

Gray smirked. "Just agree. There's no point arguing with her."

Her shoulders slumped. She really would like to get home, and she felt a bit shaky. Driving probably wasn't the best option, but she also didn't want to spend more time around Mikayla, who seemed too perceptive for Gabby's liking. She'd just have to put on a good face.

"Okay, thank you."

"No problem." Mikayla turned to Gray. "You're all right to drive behind us?"

"Yeah." They exchanged a tender glance and Gabby looked away. Why did everyone have to be so gloriously in love except her?

"Where's your car?" Mikayla asked.

Gabby led her to it and handed her the keys. She gave

directions while they drove, and when Mikayla parked outside her house, she expected her to get out and go straight to Gray's car, but she didn't.

"You have goats?" She sounded excited.

"Six of them," Gabby explained. "And a horse, four cats, and two dogs."

Mikayla laughed. "Wow, that must be chaos."

"It definitely is, but in a good way." She'd never be without her fur babies.

Mikayla smoothed her hands down her dress. "Could I meet them?"

"Sure." She could hardly say no when the other woman had been so kind. "But I have to warn you, they'll leave fur all over your dress."

Mikayla waved her hand dismissively. "Not a problem."

Gabby hoped not. The dress looked expensive. Mikayla strode over to Gray's car and spoke to him through the window. He got out and they both joined Gabby. She introduced them to the goats first, since Mikayla had seemed so interested in them, before taking them to the corral to visit with Princess, and then inviting them into the house for coffee. Well, tea for her. Coffee was a no-go now.

She noticed Mikayla's eyes narrow as she served herself lemon and ginger tea and tried hard not to breathe in the scent of coffee. She must be being paranoid. Mikayla couldn't possibly know. But her spine prickled with dread anyway. What would she do if people started figuring out she was pregnant? She'd avoided it so far by staying home, but she couldn't do that for much longer. She didn't want to risk rumors getting back to Shane before she told him, but she'd promised Logan she'd give him time to process. What was she supposed to do?

She jerked in surprise, drawn out of her introspection,

when Mikayla exclaimed in delight as the dogs fought for her attention. At least they were an effective distraction. She didn't want Mikayla paying any more attention to her than she already had.

Gray sat quietly in an armchair with Luna on his lap. He was obviously more reserved than his girlfriend, but he seemed gentle and good-hearted. Luna wouldn't have gone near him otherwise. She was well-attuned to people's character.

When they left—thankfully without Mikayla having said anything else to make her worry—they exchanged numbers. Gabby was torn between being grateful for the chance to make a new friend in town versus worrying that Mikayla might text her the questions she hadn't asked face-to-face. Her mind wouldn't quiet down, even after they were gone. The only way to get her thoughts off Mikayla, and what she may or may not have guessed, was to think about Logan. She wanted so badly to call him, and use him as a sounding board, but she'd wait until he was ready, provided no one outed her first.

In a bid to distract herself, she video called Marley.

"Gabs!" Marley cried as her face filled the phone screen. "It's been way too long! What have you been doing that's kept you so busy?" Her eyes narrowed. "Have you met a sexy beach bum?"

Gabby laughed, her mood lightening. Marley did that to her. Her friend was such a vibrant, present person. She also wasn't far off the mark. It was thanks to a gorgeous surfer that she was in this situation. Well, technically it was her own fault, but he could share the blame for being annoyingly irresistible.

"Oh!" Marley's eyes widened comically. "There *is* someone, isn't there? You've got this weird look on your face."

Gabby snorted. "That's just my face."

Marley shook her head. "It's a nice face. Although a bit pale, come to think of it. Are you getting enough of that fresh sea air?"

"Plenty," she assured her. "But..." She pressed her lips together, her stomach twisting with nerves and excitement. "I'm pregnant."

Silence.

Marley's mouth opened, then closed.

"Holy crap!" she shouted. "Are you for real? You're having a baby?"

"Yeah." Gabby allowed a smile to creep through. "I'm nearly three months along."

Marley shrieked. "I can't believe this is the first I'm hearing of it!" she exclaimed. "Who's the lucky guy? What does he do? Is he treating you right?"

Gabby laughed and held up her hand. "Whoa. One question at a time. First, I found out recently, and I only broke the news to the father yesterday. You're the third person to know, other than me."

She pouted. "Who was the other?"

"A new friend here who turned up during a weak moment but as far as I know, she's kept it to herself."

"She better not have replaced me," Marley said.

"Of course not. You're irreplaceable."

"Hmph." Her eyes twinkled. "So, the father?"

Gabby grinned. "He's a super-hot former pro surfer who owns the local pub."

"Ooh. Photos?"

Gabby tapped a few buttons on her phone. "I just sent you a link to one of his social media profiles."

She waited for Marley to open the page and scroll through a few photos.

"He's like sex on a stick," Marley said after a moment. "I can see why you went there. Are you dating him?"

Gabby was relieved Marley hadn't just assumed they were together. No doubt plenty of other people would, and she'd have to correct them.

"No. We had a one-night stand." She paused, then corrected herself. "More like a series of one-night stands spanning the last few years."

Marley's lips twisted mischievously. "You naughty girl. I'm impressed. How did he react when you broke the news?"

Gabby pulled a face. "About as well as you'd expect from a notorious playboy who has outright said he never wants to settle down and have a family."

"Ugh." She grimaced. "Gotcha. That's rough. Do you think he'll support you if you decide to keep it?"

Again, no assumptions, even though Marley probably suspected she'd want to keep the baby. This was why she loved Marley. She never assumed or judged, unless someone hurt one of her friends. Then she was fierce. Gabby grinned, recalling the way she'd keyed an insult into the driver's side door of Henry's Mercedes. Of course, Gabby had been right there with her. They both had hot tempers. But they'd stopped short of smashing the window with a cricket bat. She'd thought it would be karma, but Marley had pointed out how much more likely they were to get caught if they made a scene.

"I'm keeping it, and I think he will be supportive, but it might take a while for him to stop freaking out. I offered him the option of signing away his rights."

Marley nodded, her expression turning serious. "If he does that, you can't ask for child support, can you?"

Gabby shrugged. "I should probably check, but honestly, I get paid well. I can afford to support a child. It's just that working out childcare would be easier with two of us. Not to mention that I have so much to learn. I love babies, but it's different when they're your responsibility." At least, she assumed it was since she hadn't actually gotten that far yet.

"Are you excited?" Marley asked.

"Yes!" Gabby let out a girlish squeal that she'd deny to her dying day. "You know I've wanted kids forever. It's just harder without having exclusive access to a willing penis. But maybe I should have thought of this option sooner. Not getting pregnant to my brother's friend, but doing it myself. Just going for it. Other women have, so why not me?"

"Maybe because you want the whole kit and caboodle?" Marley said softly. "The man and the baby."

Gabby ignored the pang in her heart. "Yeah, well, the baby part of the equation is on a biological countdown timer, but the man part isn't. There's no reason it can't happen in reverse for me."

"There's not." Marley looked thoughtful. "You could at least see whether Logan would be open to trying a proper relationship though." Gabby started to protest, but Marley held up a hand. "Hear me out. You're obviously attracted to him, hence falling into bed with him more than once. You probably like him well enough too, or else it wouldn't matter if he was a supermodel, you just wouldn't want to touch him."

Gabby wrinkled her nose. "He's all right. Annoying as hell, but that's only on the surface."

"See." Marley pointed at her. "You're stuck with him now. You have chemistry and at least some level of mutual admiration. Why not give it a shot? Maybe he's your white picket partner."

"Uh, no. I don't think so." Logan wouldn't settle down. How many times had he said that? Marley raised some valid points, but even if Gabby were willing to take the chance, she doubted he would be open to it. She hadn't even been worth being the sole focus of a man who actively wanted a wife and family. He'd made her the other woman and given her dream to someone else. There was no way she could entice a guy who'd never wanted to settle down to be with her. Even if it were possible Logan would give up his playboy lifestyle for a woman, it wouldn't be her. She was nobody's exception.

9

LOGAN SPENT SUNDAY MORNING RIDING THE WAVES. IT WAS raining on and off, so he was the only one out there. All the better to try to seek the clarity he desperately needed. There were questions he had to answer. He was taking it for given at this point that they'd be keeping the baby, and that in order to avoid following in his irresponsible father's footsteps, he'd have to man up and do his best for them, however little his best might be worth. It was difficult to get his head around all the ways his life would change. This wasn't a little thing. Everything would be affected. Their child would have to factor into every decision he made from now on.

Yet he had no idea what it would mean for him. Would the baby live with Gabby since she was the one who could breastfeed, or would they alternate and he could use formula? He didn't like the idea of leaving her to handle the baby on her own. He'd seen what Shane was like when the boys were young, and how much Bex had struggled as a new single mother. It wouldn't be fair to expect Gabby to take that on herself. But he didn't want sole responsibility for the baby for so much as five minutes either because he'd mess it up somehow. Give the kid too much food or too little. Forget to change their diaper. Not be able to comfort them when they were crying.

How were they supposed to make this work if he didn't want to leave her alone but didn't trust himself to care for the baby properly without her? Should he move in with her while the baby was young so he could provide support but know that she would be there when he got it wrong? If so, at what point should he move out again? He didn't want to find himself as part of a couple by default. Gabby deserved better than that. She deserved better than *him*.

Not to mention the broader issues raised. He'd gone thirty-four years without getting a woman pregnant—to his knowledge—but now that it had happened, he didn't want to run the risk of it happening again. Did that mean he should give up his flings and one-night stands with women vacationing in the area? Could he handle a life of celibacy? He'd never tried, except in the aftermath of his knee injury, when he'd been too depressed about losing his sporting career to worry about anything else.

It would be respectful to Gabby if he stopped playing the field. But then, there hadn't been many women lately anyway. He'd already been growing tired of flirting and games. If he did stop seeing people, would Gabby feel obligated to do the same? He didn't want her to feel like she couldn't date, even though the thought of seeing her with another man made him want to punch something.

Poor Gabby. Recalling the cruel words he'd thrown at her on Friday, he felt a pang of guilt and shame. He'd reacted badly, and said things he didn't mean. He knew she'd never want to be stuck in this situation with him. If she'd wanted to get pregnant with someone, she sure as hell wouldn't have chosen him. He couldn't think of a poorer candidate for Dad of the Year.

When the rain became heavy, he trudged to shore, dried himself, and returned to his apartment. He got the heater going, showered, and emerged to a warm living area. He glanced at the heater. It was nice, but he'd always wanted a fireplace. He'd never gotten around to having one installed, and perhaps he wouldn't now because fire would surely pose a risk to their baby. He made himself a coffee and reheated leftover pizza, deep in thought. He needed someone to talk to. There was only so much internal debate he could have over the same questions. But he wasn't ready to see Gabby. He wanted to get his thoughts in order first.

He blew across the surface of the coffee. He could call Charity. She already knew, and unless he wanted to break the news to Kyle or one of his friends, he didn't really have other options. With a groan, he grabbed his phone and sent her a text, asking her to come over if she was free. This must be karma. After he'd been a shit to Charity, he was now relying on her to be his confidant. Fucking hell.

She replied almost immediately and said she'd be there soon. Thank God. He released his breath. Even months later, he still felt bad for how he'd treated Charity when she and Kyle started dating. In his defense, she'd been awful to Kyle when they were teenagers. He'd asked her out, and she'd turned him down—not only publicly, but with maximum humiliation. Logan had been out of the country at the time or he'd have given her a piece of his mind.

Somehow, despite their rocky start, Charity and Kyle were strong now. She'd been through a lot and emerged as a decent person. Snarky, perhaps, and prickly as a hedgehog. But decent at her core. He regretted the problems he'd caused them, but he'd always do what he could to protect his family.

He ate the pizza, put the dishes away, and prepared a pot of tea. He kept a particular brand he knew Charity liked.

One of his ways of trying to make up for interfering between her and Kyle. A few minutes later, she knocked on the door. He let her in and she sat in an armchair, her feet tucked beneath her, while he took the couch.

"So, what do you want to talk about?" she asked after he'd tried to do the polite chitchat thing. She wasn't much for small talk.

He met her eyes, trying to read whatever was going through her mind, but she was a closed book. If he didn't know she knew about Gabby, he'd never have guessed because she wasn't giving anything away.

"It's about Gabby," he said, his stomach flooded with nerves. "And the pregnancy."

"Oh?" She arched an eyebrow. "What about it?"

"I need to discuss it with someone objective."

Her other eyebrow flew up. "And you think that's me?"

He shrugged. "You're smart, and you're not going to go easy on me. Plus you already know."

"That's true." One side of her mouth curled with amusement. She sipped her tea. "So, what would you like to discuss?"

"Everything." The word burst from him on a wave of emotion. "I'm so lost right now. I have no idea about pregnancy or babies, and everything I know about raising a child comes from watching Bex and Shane."

Charity's expression softened—something he wasn't used to seeing from her. "I'm not an expert either, but I think a lot of new parents are the same. From what Shane has said, all the knowledge in the world doesn't matter much without experience. It's just one of those things you figure out as you go along."

Logan made a sound of frustration. That wasn't what he wanted to hear. There was plenty he was comfortable with winging, but going into fatherhood without a plan seemed like a surefire recipe to end up as a deadbeat dad. This wasn't the time for her to basically tell him to be himself. "Himself" was a promiscuous flirt and a generally unreliable guy. Not the type of man who'd be the parenting partner Gabby—or their baby—deserved.

He sighed. "Okay, putting aside the baby thing for a moment—"

Charity snorted, and he couldn't blame her.

"Putting that aside," he continued, "I don't know what to do about Gabby either. What's the proper protocol for when you accidentally get someone pregnant? Should I move in with her? Offer to marry her?" Even the thought made him break out in a cold sweat.

Charity's eyes narrowed. "Whatever you do, do not propose. She won't appreciate it, even if it's coming from a good place. Gabby may come across as tough, but she's a romantic. When someone proposes to her, it should be because they want to marry her and nothing else. Do not ruin her first proposal by offering her a ring out of a misguided sense of duty. Trust me, no woman wants a guilt ring."

"See?" He slumped in relief. "I have no idea about this stuff." He was going to mess it up.

She rolled her eyes. "I know your motives are good, but you're not talking about this with the right person. You should be saying all of this to Gabby."

He buried his face in his hands and groaned. He knew she was right.

GABBY RAN THE BRUSH OVER PRINCESS'S LEFT SHOULDER, admiring the golden gleam of her coat. "You're such a beautiful girl," she murmured. Princess nudged her pocket, looking for a treat, and Gabby slipped her a piece of apple. "Such a smart girl, too."

She hadn't been riding much recently because the jostling worsened her nausea, but she hoped she'd be through the worst of her sickness soon, and then she'd be able to get out more. Although she still needed to weigh the risks of riding. It was rare for her to come off, and Princess was a dream—so smooth and even-tempered—but there was always a chance of it happening, and if it did, there was no saying what damage might be done to her unborn child.

Perhaps she could stick to the road and the trails she knew were safest. Alternatively, she could walk Princess or ask Dylan if he'd like to take her out for some exercise. He was an outdoorsy kid, and he came over every couple of weeks to visit her, even though his afternoons and weekends were usually busy with friends or sports games and practices.

A car crunched up the drive and an anxious buzzing sensation started in her gut. Princess nuzzled her, probably sensing her abrupt change in mood, and Gabby gave her a quick rub of reassurance.

"Everything is all good, sweetheart."

She finished grooming Princess, put the gear away, and strolled toward the house. It was afternoon, and it had been raining, so the dogs had opted to stay inside while she spent time with Princess. On other days, they often joined her. She couldn't say the animals were friends, but Princess certainly didn't seem to mind Thelma or Louise and the dogs were fascinated by her.

She reached the back door just as Logan came around the side of the house. He must have knocked at the front and then come looking for her.

Her insides stilled. "Hi."

"Hey." His smile was strained. He lifted an arm, as if to

wave or invite her into a hug, but then dropped it again. "Have you been with Princess?"

She cocked her head. "You know my horse's name?"

She couldn't recall ever having told him.

He lifted his shoulder nonchalantly. "I probably heard Shane mention it. Or maybe Dylan."

That made sense.

Silence fell.

Gabby gestured toward the door. "Would you like to come in for a hot drink?"

He nodded. "That would be great."

She removed her boots, which were caked in mud, and peeled off her socks. "Just let me find a dry pair and I'll be right out."

"I'll start the kettle."

"Do you know where it is?"

"I'll find it."

Yes, she supposed he would. Logan seemed like the type of person who managed to make himself at home in most situations. She headed for her bedroom, grabbed a fresh pair of socks, and hesitated. She sniffed her shirt. She smelled of horse and wet hay. She stripped off her top and jeans and donned a clean outfit, telling herself it was because her clothes were damp rather than because of vanity. She darted to the mirror to check her hair. It was plastered to her head. She fluffed it up, but it wasn't much of an improvement. Her complexion was pale, too, as it often seemed to be lately.

She drew in a deep, slow breath, and held her own gaze. "You've got this."

When she went to the kitchen, Logan had already helped himself to the coffee. Thelma was happily sniffing his feet while Louise eyed him warily from the door through to the living area.

"I wasn't sure what you'd want," he said apologetically. "You usually have coffee, but…"

"Yeah." She grimaced. "I'm not a fan of this whole minimal caffeine thing. According to the internet, I'm probably okay to have a cup each day, but until I've spoken to an actual doctor, I'm steering clear. The smell isn't great for me anyway."

She found a box of lemon and ginger tea, placed a teabag into the empty mug beside the kettle, and filled it with steaming water. That flavor of tea seemed best for her nausea. Anything else was too strong at the moment. She took the mug to the living room and sat cross-legged on the couch, placing her tea on a coffee table so she could help Louise onto the cushion beside her.

Apparently sensing her need for space, Logan sat in the armchair and was immediately set upon by both Mouse and Thomas. She tried not to appreciate how gentle he was with her pets as she watched him rubbing beneath Mouse's chin and stroking Thomas as the cat settled on his lap. Thelma leaned against the side of the chair and gazed up at him longingly.

I get it, girl. He's irresistible.

"You have a lot of pets," he said. "Are they always inside?"

"The cats and dogs often are. You don't have allergies or something, do you?" God forbid he pass a cat allergy on to their baby.

"No, I'm just not used to it." He smiled, but it didn't reach his eyes. "I haven't got any pets. Obviously. You've been to my place."

"Do you not like them?" She thought he seemed comfortable enough with them.

"I do, but I always figured I wouldn't take care of them well enough, and besides, having animals near the pub would be a recipe for disaster in terms of hygiene and food safety." He cleared his throat and cupped the coffee between his palms. "Anyway, I didn't come here to talk about pets. I wanted to say that I'm sorry about the other day. I reacted badly and accused you of something I know you'd never do."

"You were shocked." As was she, by his apology. Perhaps she shouldn't have been though. He was a decent man. But she'd understood how much her news had rocked his world, and he was entitled to lose his shit for a while. Even if she didn't like the things he'd said.

"That's no excuse." His expression was sheepish. "I hope you know I really don't believe you tricked me."

"I do."

"Good." He nodded to himself, gnawing on his lower lip. "Look, we have a lot to work out, but I'll support you and I want to be involved in raising our baby."

Something inside her eased. A tension she hadn't even known she was holding. It felt like taking a deep breath after days of surviving on shallow gasps.

"Thank God."

His lips twitched. "Glad to know you had faith in me."

She rolled her eyes. "It's not every day you have to tell a guy you're pregnant with his baby. I have no experience with it, so how should I know how you're going to respond?"

His eyes warmed. "I know, and I'm sorry you went through that on your own. It's crap that men get to go on with their lives while women are left to deal with the roller-coaster of figuring out they're pregnant on their own."

"Right?" Not that this was a common occurrence for her, but it would be nice if, for once, it was the man who had to feel sick and get hormonal crying jags and figure out how to tell some poor woman he'd slept with once that they were having a baby together.

He flashed her a grin. "I'll do whatever I can from now on, but I'm a complete beginner as far as pregnant women go, so you'll probably have to tell me what you need."

"I can do that." Did that mean he was planning to be there for her, as well as for their baby? Because a lot of men would probably assume they had no responsibility until the baby was born. Then again, Logan had been raised by a single mum, so perhaps that affected his attitude. It certainly couldn't be because he was interested in her. After all, they'd slept together several times over the years and he'd never given any indication he wanted her for more than that.

"I have no doubt." He winked. "You haven't had any trouble telling me your opinion before."

Despite herself, she laughed. If Logan was one thing, it was entertaining. Infuriating sometimes, but always entertaining.

"I'm going to start dinner soon," she said. "Why don't you stay and we can talk?"

He stood. "I'll help cook."

She waved him down. "Finish your drink first."

She could use the delay. For all the thinking she'd been doing over the past few days, they still had a lot to discuss and there was no need to rush. It would be better if they took their time and thought everything through properly. Since Logan was impulsive, she'd have to be the one to make sure they didn't end up in a mess. She also needed to remember that anything he promised now might go up in smoke as soon as he was faced with the reality of a baby. She could hope for the best, but she needed to prepare for the worst.

10

LOGAN WAS METAPHORICALLY SHITTING HIMSELF. IT WAS Easter weekend, a little more than a week after Gabby had told him they were expecting a baby, and they were visiting Shane and Faith to break the news. For the first time he could recall, he'd canceled poker last night. He couldn't stomach the idea of spending the evening with Shane when he'd agreed not to confess anything until he and Gabby could do it together. It would have felt too much like lying, even if it was a lie of omission, and Logan may not be boyfriend material, but he liked to think that when push came to shove, he was a good friend. He certainly hadn't been that to Shane.

"Are you sure we should have brought the Easter eggs?" he asked Gabby, who was riding shotgun while he drove them to Shane's home a couple of blocks away from the beach.

"Yes." She awkwardly patted his hand where it rested on the steering wheel. "This way, Hunter and Dylan are distracted and hopefully the fact they're happy will put Shane in a good mood."

"Unless they end up with a sugar high he has to deal with later," Logan grumbled. Giving kids treats was always a risk. He generally did it anyway because he loved to see their big smiles and he found it funny as hell when their parents had to deal with the fallout. Now *he'd* be the one dealing with the fallout. He winced. No doubt his friends with kids would be paying him back for that as soon as they could, and he'd deserve it. He'd been an irresponsible ass.

"He's going to be furious," he muttered. His heart felt like it was hammering out the William Tell Overture, and as he parked outside their house, he was slightly lightheaded. What if he lost Shane's friendship? He should never have been so cavalier and assumed that his bad behavior wouldn't catch up with him. Shane was one of his favorite people. Steady, reliable, kind. All things Logan wasn't.

Shit.

"Just breathe," Gabby said, twisting to face him. "In and out. It's going to be fine."

She was full of positivity for someone who looked even paler than usual. Maybe she'd been throwing up again. She'd shared with him during their dinner last Sunday that she'd been struggling with morning sickness. He hated that she had to deal with feeling physically awful on top of the emotional stuff they were going through. He'd read up on morning sickness after he left, to see if there was any way he could help, but it seemed like she was doing most things right and he just needed to be there for her. Not that she'd tried to lean on him at all. He'd told her to call for anything she needed, but so far, she hadn't asked anything of him. He wished she would, so he'd feel like he was contributing.

"Logan?" she prompted. "Are you okay?"

"Yeah." He pushed the car door open. "Let's get this over with."

She searched his eyes quickly, then nodded. "All right."

When she got out of the car, he took the two large Easter eggs from her, along with a packet of caramel-filled eggs for the family to share, and waited for her to head up the path first. Gabby knocked on the front door and Hunter opened it.

"Hey, buddy." Gabby knelt to give him a hug. "Shouldn't your Mummy or Daddy be answering the door?"

He dipped his head guiltily, giving away the fact that one of them had likely told him to wait and he'd gone ahead anyway. "Mummy said—"

Faith appeared behind him, her eyes narrowed. "Hunter, what did I say about waiting for me?"

He squirmed. "Sorry, Mummy."

Logan's heart warmed. He loved to hear Hunter call Faith "Mummy." She was such a better parent than the she-devil who'd given birth to him and abandoned the whole family to seek her fame overseas. Dylan wouldn't call Faith "Mum," because he said he had one of those, but he'd taken to calling her his O.P., short for Other Parent, and considering how rocky their relationship had been at the start, he knew it meant a lot to her.

"Hey, Faith." He kissed her cheek. She was flushed and smiling. Beautiful, but also happier than he'd ever imagined seeing her. It was strange because he used to think of her as a kindred spirit, and assume that they'd grow old being the only singletons in the bay. Then she'd fallen for Shane, and it had felt like the end of an era. He'd realized that it would just be him carrying the mantle, and honestly, it had probably been around then that he'd stopped sleeping around so much. His previously blissful existence had begun to feel unfulfilling. Not that he'd admit it.

Faith looked at him quizzically. "Hi. Did you drop by to see Shane?"

"Yes, and no." Logan tried to sound casual and failed. "Can we come in?"

"Of course." She stepped aside to let them in and closed the door behind them as they stooped to take their shoes off. Logan only wore flip-flops so he kicked them off while Gabby battled with her lace-up farm boots. Faith glanced at the Easter eggs. "Are these for the boys?"

He nodded.

She smiled. "What do you say, Hunter?"

The little boy's eyes widened as Logan handed him one of the eggs. "Thank you, Uncle Logan."

He winced, almost imperceptibly, at the reminder of his closeness with the family, and Faith's sharp gaze seemed to catch it. She looked intrigued.

"This one is for Dylan," he said, thrusting it into her hands to distract her.

"Brilliant." She knocked on Dylan's bedroom door. When he opened it, his eyes bleary from sleep, she handed it to him. "This is from Logan."

"And Aunt Gabby," Hunter piped up.

"Hmm, yes," Faith mused. "Apparently." She jerked her head toward the living area. "Come on. I'll make us coffee."

"Just water for me, please," Gabby said.

Faith's lips pursed. "Curiouser and curiouser."

Logan pretended not to hear. He had a sneaking suspicion that she at least had some idea of why they were there. Either Charity had dropped a hint, or they looked guilty as hell.

"Hey, Gabby." Shane looked up as they entered, then did a double take as his gaze fell on Logan. "Logan. Are you feeling better this morning?"

"I'm not a hundred percent," he said truthfully, feeling a prick of guilt for lying about being sick last night. "But I'm not contagious."

Shane glanced at Hunter. "You'd better not be."

"Cross my heart." He made the motion over his chest.

Shane relaxed and folded the newspaper he'd been reading. "What are you doing here?"

"We need to speak to both of you." Logan took the lead. This was Gabby's family, and he knew she wanted to do most of the talking, but he wasn't going to let her go out on a limb by herself.

"We?" Shane clasped his hands together, his usually friendly face tightening with suspicion.

"Hey, Hunter," Faith said. "Why don't you go and play with Tinkerbell? She looked lonely on our bed all by herself."

"Okay," Hunter said happily and jogged out of the room on little legs, carrying his easter egg.

Logan sat at the table opposite Shane, and Gabby took the seat beside him. They waited in charged silence while Faith made drinks and served them. Then she sat next to Shane and propped her chin on her palm, her eyes twinkling.

"What's going on?" Shane asked.

Gabby straightened her back and raised her chin. Logan felt a burst of pride at her strength. Crazy, when it had nothing to do with him. "Logan and I have something to tell you."

Logan held his breath, terrified that her next words would spell the end of his friendship with Shane.

"Are you dating?" Faith blurted out.

"No," Gabby said, so quickly it felt like a slap. She wasn't wrong. They weren't dating. But did she have to be so eager to shut off any mention of that possibility? It hurt more than he'd like to admit that she clearly knew he wasn't good enough for her.

"We're pregnant," Gabby continued.

Silence dropped like a bomb between them. Logan heard a clock tick. Shane made a quick intake of breath. Faith's eyes widened. The clock ticked again.

"You're *what*?" Shane demanded, staring at Gabby as though she'd just announced her intention to become a traveling circus performer.

Her posture grew even stiffer. "I'm pregnant, and Logan is the father."

"But... what?" Shane looked lost.

Faith glanced from Logan to Gabby. "So, you're having a baby, but not dating?"

"That's right," Gabby said, reaching for his hand under the table. He intertwined his fingers with hers and squeezed.

Shane jolted upright and launched himself across the table.

Logan shoved his chair backward and let go of Gabby's hand, trying to get out of the way. Drinks spilled, and he hit the floor as he tripped over his own feet. The landing knocked the air from his chest and he struggled to haul in a breath. Shane didn't land on top of him, which was fortunate, but a moment later he loomed above, glaring down at him.

"You seduced my sister and got her pregnant, but you don't even want to date her?" He sounded furious. Logan had never heard him like this.

"I—"

"Shane!" Gabby grabbed his shoulder and spun him around. Her eyes were flashing furiously. Absolutely stunning. Logan staggered to his feet while Shane was distracted and stood at Gabby's side for moral support. "Logan did *not* seduce me."

I kind of did, he thought, recalling the way he'd approached her after that failed date. He should have resisted that magnetic draw he felt toward her, but he'd intentionally pushed her buttons and hoped they'd end up in bed.

"I'm not some virginal miss from a Regency romance novel." Gabby squared her shoulders. "We had sex. It was mutually enjoyable. But obviously, the condom didn't work properly and here we are."

"Here we are," Faith repeated faintly. Logan glanced at her. She didn't look as upset as Shane did. She wrapped her arm around Shane's waist and kissed his cheek. His glower softened temporarily but then reappeared as he focused on Logan.

"You're going to be an uncle, sugar," Faith said. "Isn't that exciting?"

He blinked rapidly, and his forehead furrowed. Shane loved kids, and that love must be battling with the anger burning inside him.

"Was this a one-time thing?" Faith asked. "How far along are you?"

Logan met Gabby's eyes, silently communicating with her. They'd decided to be completely open about their history so there wouldn't be any more lies between them and their families, even if it meant going through some uncomfortable moments.

"We've been together several times over the last few years," Logan said.

Shane paled.

"I'm three months along," Gabby added. "Give or take a couple of weeks."

Shane pointed at Logan. "This has been going on behind my back for years?"

He nodded. "I'm sorry."

He wouldn't make excuses. He deserved any censure he got.

"But you're not in a relationship?"

"No." Gabby's tone brooked no argument. Again, he felt a pang at her unintentional rejection.

Shane's expression twisted with hurt, and guilt churned sickeningly in Logan's gut.

"Now you're pregnant?" Shane asked. "Seriously, Logan? I thought you'd have had enough practice wrapping it up not to land in this situation."

Logan flinched as the barb struck true. Yes, he'd had plenty of casual sex. No, he shouldn't have touched Shane's sister. But there wasn't much he could do about that now.

"It was an accident," he said.

"I'll say." Shane shook his head. "Do you even want to be a dad?"

Logan kept his mouth shut. If he said yes, Shane would call him a liar, but if he told the truth, he'd hurt Gabby. There was no way to win.

"You're the fun uncle," Shane continued. "You don't know what to do with a baby."

He still didn't reply, this time because his doubts were choking him. Shane was right. He had no experience with babies. He didn't know what to feed them, how often to change them, or even how to hold them properly. He had no place being a father.

"Don't talk to him like that," Gabby snapped. "Even if he doesn't, he can learn."

He was tempted to tell her not to bother standing up for him. It was nice that she wanted to defend him, but Shane had a point. He'd more than likely let both Gabby and their child down.

"Why don't we all sit down?" Faith suggested. "You can talk us through everything that's happened, and what your plan is. We're all friends here." She gave Shane a meaningful look.

Again, Logan appreciated the support, but he didn't want to cause a rift between Faith and Shane too. He'd already done enough damage.

"We never meant for any of this to happen," he said softly.

Shane's eyes narrowed. "Well, it did. So you'd better figure it out."

———

During the trip home from Shane's house, Gabby's nerves were ping-ponging all over the place. She'd known Shane wouldn't be happy, but she'd underestimated how upset he'd be—and it wasn't all because they'd lied to him. She'd sensed his doubt when they told him they intended to raise the baby together. He didn't believe Logan would do his part. He knew Logan better than she did, so his reaction made her nervous. She'd already told herself she needed to mentally prepare to be a single mum, and her brother's behavior reinforced that decision. She had to face reality. Logan didn't want this, and when it got to be too much, he probably wouldn't stick around.

"Do you feel like a kid who got caught with their hand in the cookie jar?" she asked Logan, to lighten the mood in the car.

He glanced over. "Worse. I feel like Mum just told me she's disappointed in me."

She winced. They were due at Corinne's house for dinner this evening. They figured that in a gossipy town like Haven Bay, they'd better break the news to all the most important people in one day, before they discovered it via the grapevine.

"She won't, will she?"

He hesitated. "Honestly, I don't know, but she won't say anything like that to you."

That didn't reassure her. She didn't know Corinne well, but from their few encounters over the past months, she liked her. She was a warm, friendly person, and Gabby didn't want to upset her.

"God, we're a mess," Gabby said.

"At least after today, we won't have to tell anyone else. The news will be around town by the end of tomorrow."

"True." She gave a small smile. Even though there were pitfalls to living in a place where everyone knew everyone's business, she liked it. It made her feel like part of the community in a way she never had before. Although she supposed it also meant she'd have to break the news to her boss ASAP.

Logan pulled down her drive and parked outside the house. "Does it still work if I come by at six to get you?"

"Yes, although you know I could drive myself."

He patted her knee, then seemed to realize what he was doing and carefully removed his hand. "It's good to put on a united front."

She sighed. "I know." She leaned over and kissed his cheek. "Thank you for coming with me this morning. I appreciate the support."

"We're all in this together," he said wryly.

She snorted a laugh and clapped a hand to her mouth. "Did you just quote High School Musical?"

He rolled his eyes. "What? It's a classic. Those kids knew how to sing."

She grinned behind her hand. "It's so cheesy. I watched the first one because my friends made me, but I refused to see any of the others." She smirked. "I'd never have guessed you were a fan of musicals."

He narrowed his eyes. "Don't mention it to a soul or I'll tell Betty we're naming our baby something like Herbert."

She gasped. "You wouldn't!"

If Betty heard that, the entire population of Haven Bay would have made them customized baby goodies with "Herbert" monogrammed on them in no time.

He winked. "I guess my secret is safe then."

"For now. But I'm never, ever watching a musical with you." She pushed the door open and got out. "For the record, this is blackmail."

He didn't look sorry. "Pick you up at six."

She stepped away from the car, mouthing "blackmailer." He waved flippantly as he turned the car around and left. Gabby watched him go, noting the little trip in her heartbeat. That couldn't be good.

Don't go getting a crush on your baby daddy.

If she let herself have feelings for him, she'd only end up heartbroken. Men weren't to be trusted. Especially when they flirted as easily as they breathed. Logan reminded her of Henry in that way. Henry, who hadn't cared about her nearly as much as she had for him. She'd only been his backup girl. His also-ran. She needed to learn from that and not expect anything different from Logan. If she couldn't be Henry's number one, she sure as hell would never be Logan's.

She gritted her teeth. Even Henry's fiancé hadn't seen her as a threat. She'd tried to tell Vanessa that Henry was a cheating dickhead, but the other woman had said she was delusional and slammed the door in her face.

"Don't get yourself hurt again," she muttered to herself as she walked toward the front door. Her phone vibrated in her pocket, and she was grateful for the distraction. She drew it out and paused, her curiosity growing. It was Faith.

"Hello?" she said hesitantly after she accepted the call.

She half-expected it to be Shane on the other end, ready to ask her more questions about what she'd been thinking when she slept with Logan.

"Hey, gorgeous."

She relaxed. Just Faith. Not Shane to express his disappointment. Her sister-in-law seemed to have taken the news better than he had. "Did I leave something behind?"

"No." Faith's voice was quieter than usual. Gabby actually had to concentrate to hear her. "I just wanted to say congratulations."

"Really?" Gabby felt herself smile.

"Yeah." There was a muffled sound, and then Faith was back. "I know you want kids, and you're going to be a wonderful mum. Shane knows that too; he's just upset about who the father is."

Gabby scoffed. That was putting it mildly. "Thank you for calling. It means a lot."

"I thought you should hear it." Faith's tone grew sly. "Plus, think what a beautiful baby you and Logan will make. They will be genetically blessed. However it happened, I know the both of you will do everything you can to raise them well."

To her surprise, Gabby felt her throat constricting and realized she was choking up. "That's so sweet of you."

"It's just the truth." Faith sounded dismissive. "Logan isn't as bad as Shane makes him out to be. He'll do the right thing."

Gabby's heart squeezed. She appreciated what Faith was saying, especially given Shane's reaction, but even as she felt a pang of relief, guilt swelled within her once again. Both Charity and Faith had now said that Logan would "do the right thing" and she was grateful for their reassurances, but it only made her more aware of the fact that Logan was doing this out of a sense of duty. She and their baby were an obligation.

Given his choice, he'd probably rather spend tonight at The Den, picking up a pretty tourist, than sharing dinner with her and his mum. She'd turned his life upside down, and she was thankful to him for going along with it, but she couldn't let herself forget that none of this was what he wanted.

"I'll work on getting Shane to come around," Faith continued. "He needs time to work through his emotions. This isn't what he'd choose for you, so he's having a hard time accepting it."

Gabby heard a scratch against the inside of the front door and crossed the last few yards of gravel until she reached it. "Thank you." Tears prickled her eyes. She was so glad she had Faith. "I have to go tell my parents now. Wish me luck?"

"You won't need it." Faith sounded confident. "June and Dennis will be thrilled to have another grandchild on the way."

Gabby slotted her key into the lock. She knew Faith was partially right, but she suspected her parents would be scandalized by the fact she wasn't even dating Logan. She'd always been sensible and level-headed—except when someone messed with her family—so she doubted they'd ever expected her to end up in this situation. Hopefully, they wouldn't focus on the negatives.

"Talk soon," Gabby said. "I'll update you on how it goes."

"Great. Love you lots." Faith blew her a kiss and then ended the call.

Gabby rested her forehead against the door and groaned. She really wasn't looking forward to this. One of the dogs barked, so she opened the door and bent to greet them both. "Hello, you two."

She spent a few seconds plying them with love, then tossed them each a couple of treats and opened the back door in case they needed to answer the call of nature. She made herself a mug of lemon tea and settled on the couch with her drink. Thomas climbed onto her lap and rested his paws possessively over her chest, his nose only inches from hers.

She chuckled. "How am I supposed to drink my tea now?"

He held her gaze steadily, clearly communicating that it wasn't his problem. Knowing it couldn't be put off any longer, she selected her father's number from her phone and made a video call.

An hour later, she'd gone through all the same questions about their relationship status that she'd already faced with Shane, followed by muttering along the lines of:

"I thought Logan was dating that blonde girl?" This came from her mum. "The one we met last Christmas. Or... wait. Was it a redhead? I seem to remember a redhead with him when we were in town for Hunter's birthday party."

"Probably both and neither," her dad replied, sotto voce. "From what Shane says, I don't think Logan is the type of man who dates, if you know what I mean."

Mum frowned. "What do you mean? Of course he dates. He's always surrounded by women. Oh." Her face twisted. "*Oh*."

Gabby grimaced. She knew Logan had been with his share of women, but the fact that even her parents had noticed made her want to sink into the carpet and disappear. She supposed at least they'd taken it better than Shane had, although they obviously had reservations. She couldn't blame them. She had reservations too. Especially after having been reminded of exactly how many beautiful women Logan had taken to bed. There was no reason to believe she meant more to him than any of them. She wasn't anyone special.

Backup option.

Before they hung up, Dad promised they'd visit next weekend. He claimed it was so they could celebrate properly, but she knew the truth: he wanted to size up Logan.

This was going to be so much fun.

11

Logan arrived at Gabby's place at six sharp and jogged to the door just as it opened. He stopped, momentarily taken aback. She had gone to the effort of dressing in a pretty purple dress that showed off her figure, and her hair was loose around her shoulders. The sight of her stole his breath. She'd been looking unwell lately and he'd forgotten how gorgeous she usually was. Pregnancy had stripped her of her vitality, but she'd temporarily restored it with the assistance of makeup and a clever outfit choice.

"Do I look appropriate for the mother of Corinne's grandchild?" she asked, smoothing her hands nervously down the front of her dress.

Logan leaned over to kiss her cheek but stopped at the last minute because he didn't want to mess with the makeup she'd obviously spent time doing. "You look great."

Honestly, he thought his mum would be thrilled to have Gabby as her substitute daughter-in-law. She'd be more upset with him for not locking her down in a relationship. After all, Gabby was smart, pretty, kind to animals, and Corinne knew her parents. He suspected that made her ideal daughter-in-law material in his mum's eyes.

Corinne would certainly take it better than Shane had. He could still remember the way his friend's expression had darkened right before he'd lunged at him, and it hadn't improved during the course of their conversation. His reaction had forced Logan to face an unpleasant truth.

"Shall we go?" Gabby asked, and he realized he'd been caught up in his own thoughts.

"Yes. Great idea." He placed a hand on her lower back and guided her to the car. He opened her door and glanced down as she entered, frowning when he noticed her defined collarbone. She'd definitely lost weight. Shouldn't she have gained it? He rounded the vehicle and got in his side. "Have you seen a doctor about your morning sickness?"

"Not yet. If it doesn't stop this week, I'll make an appointment."

"Good." Although in his opinion, she should see one as soon as she could. It was her body though. She knew it better than he did. Hell, she probably knew a lot more about pregnancy than he did too, even if he'd been reading up on it in his free time.

They drove to the home Corinne and her boyfriend, Lawrence, shared a few miles outside of Haven Bay. The house was right on the coast, with walking access to the beach. Lawrence had bought it earlier in the year, and Logan knew he'd probably chosen it because of how much Corinne loved the sea. Like Logan, she enjoyed being out in the surf, and now she had access to a beautiful, nearly unused stretch of sand and water.

Logan had been wary of Lawrence at first. He was the only man Corinne had seriously dated since their father left. But seeing how Lawrence loved to spoil Corinne had soothed Logan's protective nature.

"Wow, this place is impressive," Gabby said, her gaze flitting over the fountain in the center of the parking area and the pristine gardens around the white stone house, which must be cared for by a gardener because Corinne didn't have a green finger in her body.

"It is nice, isn't it?" he said with satisfaction. He'd watched his mum be forced to make do with less than she deserved for years to ensure he and Kyle were well taken care of. It made him happy to see her so content with her new home and partner.

Charity's car was already parked near the entrance, so Logan pulled up alongside it and got out. He intended to assist Gabby, but by the time he'd made it around to her, she'd already climbed out and shut the door.

"If you'd waited a few seconds, I'd have given you a hand," he said.

She smirked. "I'm perfectly capable of standing up all by myself."

"Still." He wanted to make things easy for her. That wasn't too much to ask, was it? "Are you ready?"

She pulled a face. "As I'll ever be."

"Come on." He took her hand and rapped on the door, then pushed it open. Corinne never stood on ceremony. He kicked off his shoes and steadied Gabby when she leaned down to undo the fastening on her heels.

Corinne breezed into the foyer, bringing with her the scent of seawater and flowers. Her blonde hair, the same shade as Logan's, was tied back and her blue-green eyes sparkled with delight. "Logan. Gabby. What a pleasure to see you."

Gabby straightened and smiled. "You look lovely, Corinne. Thank you so much for having us."

"It's no problem at all." Corinne beamed and glanced knowingly between them. She probably thought they'd come to tell her they were dating, as Faith had. Unless, of course, she'd already heard the news, but Logan didn't think so.

"Good evening, Logan." Lawrence appeared behind his mum. He rested a hand on her hip. "Dinner is ready. Charity and Kyle are at the table. Why don't you head through while we bring the meals out."

Corinne laid a hand on Gabby's forearm. "We made fried rice with tofu for you. I hope that's okay."

Gabby smiled. "Sounds lovely, thank you."

Logan hoped there was no egg in it too. That seemed to be the food that set her off most, from what she'd told him.

"This way." He guided her down the hall and through to the dining room. There was a more casual dining area by the kitchen, but Corinne liked to use the formal dining room for full family dinners because it gave them more space and meant no one felt like they had to rush to do the cleanup.

"Exactly how rich is Lawrence?" Gabby murmured as they passed by a painting that must be worth five figures.

Logan shrugged. "I've never asked, but I guess the answer is rich enough. He always seems to have however much money he needs."

Lawrence owned a renewable energy company and had his finger in the pie for a few other business ventures as well, but he'd taken a step back over the last year and hired Mikayla Talbot to run the day-to-day management of the company.

Logan and Gabby entered the dining room and sat opposite Charity and Kyle. The way Charity studiously avoided their gazes after a brief greeting told Logan she'd guessed the purpose of the dinner and didn't want anyone to know she had any idea what was going on.

Corinne and Lawrence brought in the plates. They'd cooked a roast. Logan glanced at Gabby out of the corner of his eye and noticed her eyeballing the pork. Her nostrils flared, but she let out a slow breath and seemed to come right.

"Okay?" he whispered.

"Yeah."

When they were all seated, and everyone had complimented the chef, an expectant hush fell. Logan bumped his leg against Gabby's beneath the table and she leaned slightly closer in a silent display of support.

He drank half his glass of water and set his cutlery on the side of his plate. "Gabby and I have news."

Kyle looked confused. Charity studied her meal as if it was the most fascinating thing she'd ever seen. Lawrence arched an eyebrow. But Corinne... she leaned across the table, looking more excited than Logan had ever seen her.

"We're having a baby."

Corinne's mouth fell open. Whatever she'd been expecting, it wasn't that. Meanwhile, Kyle seemed to be choking on something. Charity thumped him on the back and murmured soothing words. Lawrence's face remained impassive.

"I'm three months pregnant," Gabby interjected. "Give or take."

Corinne's hand flew to her mouth and her eyes gleamed with emotion. "Really? You are?"

Logan nodded.

"I didn't even know you were together," Lawrence said.

"We're not," Logan replied, for what felt like the dozenth time.

"But you're having the baby?" Corinne asked. "I'm going to have a grandson or granddaughter?"

"Yes, Mum."

"Oh, my God." She got slowly to her feet and then, before he had time to react, she raced around the table and pulled him into a fierce embrace. The moment she let him go, she grabbed hold of Gabby and hugged the shit out of her. "I'm going to be a nana." She drew back, her face alight with joy. "I can't believe it. I'm finally going to have a little one to spoil." She kissed Gabby's cheek. "You have no idea what a gift this is."

His heart warmed and his muscles loosened. After the tense meeting with Shane and Faith, his mum's reaction came as a relief. Gabby's eyes darted to his and she sent him a small smile. He smiled back. Nobody else had reacted so positively. It was nice. He should have known Corinne would see the good in the situation.

"Thank you," Gabby said.

"Congratulations, darling." Corinne gave her another hug before returning to her seat. "You're going to be a wonderful mother. And Logan." She shook her head, her smile turning mischievous. "You're a bag of surprises. Who would have guessed you'd be the one to give me grandchildren first?"

He grinned. "I live to please."

"How long have you known?" Kyle asked, a furrow between his brows that suggested he was doing some mental arithmetic.

"A bit over a week," Logan said.

"Have you made a pregnancy and birth plan yet?"

Logan cocked his head toward Gabby, wondering if that was a phrase he ought to know. "Um, no."

Kyle smiled. It wasn't as wide as Corinne's, and there was a degree of caution in the way he held himself, but he wasn't nearly as upset as Shane had been. But then, the situation wasn't the same. "I can help with that."

Logan winked. "We know how much you love your lists."

Kyle colored. His love of lists had become famous after the Bridge Club had circulated a literal Love List he'd written with his ideal traits for a romantic partner. Some-how, while Charity didn't fit many of the things he'd thought he wanted, they were perfect together anyway.

"That would be great," Gabby said quickly. "Wouldn't it, Logan?"

"Absolutely." He felt like a weight had been lifted from his shoulders. There had been no intense discussions. No interrogations. And best of all, no accusations or hurt feelings. He knew it wouldn't all be smooth sailing, but they were off to a good start.

The conversation for the rest of the meal centered around the pregnancy, and his and Gabby's "relationship," such as it was. Still, Logan was feeling more at peace with himself as he drove Gabby home at the end of the night.

That was, until she turned to him and said, "By the way, my parents are coming next weekend. They want to meet you properly."

The nerves returned, along with a hefty dose of "oh shit."

GABBY FELL INTO AN EXHAUSTED SLEEP AFTER GETTING HOME from Corinne and Lawrence's house. Confessing her pregnancy to three groups of family members on the same day had taken it out of her. The next morning, when she woke, she still felt like crap. She got out of bed for long enough to feed the indoor animals and grab an Easter egg—yes, she bought those for herself; she was a grown woman and allowed to do as she pleased—then burrowed in bed while she worked her way through nearly the entire chocolate egg.

At ten, Faith messaged to ask if she was coming over for their Easter egg hunt. Gabby groaned. She'd have loved to, but she really didn't think she was up for it, so she let Faith know she wasn't feeling well and continued her pity party. Half an hour later, she heard a car outside and wondered if it would be childish to hide beneath the covers and pretend she wasn't home. She needn't have worried though, because Logan strode into her bedroom without her even having to move.

"How did you get in?" she demanded, pulling the blankets up to her chin. She didn't want him to see her in this state. She was a mess.

"Faith told me where the spare key is." He sat on the edge of the bed, placed a paper bag beside her, and drew several items from it. "I have anti-nausea medication that the pharmacist at Te Awa Tui says is safe for pregnant women, or if you'd prefer, a medicinal tea from Bex's mum. And here we have...snacks." He showed her a box of plain crackers and a block of her favorite chocolate. Gabby stared at him in shock.

"You... How did you know what I'd want?"

He looked embarrassed. "Faith told me you weren't feeling well—which, by the way, you should have told me yourself. You said you'd let me know if you needed anything."

"There's a difference between needing something and just feeling sorry for myself," she pointed out.

"Not as far as I'm concerned." He handed her both items of food. "Eat up. You're too thin. It can't be good for the baby."

She rolled her eyes. "I'm trying to keep food down. It's not easy."

He stood. "That's why I'm going to make this tea and we'll see if it helps. Now, when I come back I want you to tell me any chores you need done because you can't be cavorting around the stable in your current condition."

Gabby snickered. "Cavorting? You sound like a nine-teenth-century chaperone."

He sniffed. "This is what I get for being helpful."

She stopped laughing. "Sorry. Thank you for coming. Really."

She was touched. He cared for her, even if he tried to hide it behind bossiness and teasing.

Don't get used to it, she told herself. *It won't last forever.*

His expression softened. "I'm partly responsible for the way you're feeling, so I'd better do what I can to help, even if it's not as much as I'd like."

"Aww." Emotion stuck in the back of her throat and she blinked rapidly, her own warning fading from her mind. "You're just a big old softy."

"Nope." He backed away, raising his hands defensively. "No tears, woman. That was not part of the deal."

Sniffling, she grinned. "It was in the fine print."

As he left, her heart filled, and she wondered if maybe she could have something real with him after all. Could she be brave, as Marley had suggested, and take a chance on him? Or would he inevitably want to move on to someone new and more exciting?

12

GABBY'S PARENTS WERE DUE TO TURN UP IN TIME FOR DINNER, so Logan arrived a few hours early. It was a sunny day, and they sat in the paddock with dogs frolicking around them and Princess out enjoying the sun. Gabby had set up a picnic table with soda water, lemon tea, coffee for Logan, and an array of snacks. She'd opted for foods that had only a faint smell and tasted bland because those were what she could keep down. Well, those and chocolate. Although her morning sickness had definitely improved this week, and she'd found herself able to enjoy a few larger meals too.

She'd regained a little weight, which seemed to please Logan. Every time she turned around, he was there with something for her to eat. He'd even dropped by at work once with a meal for her. It was a bit ridiculous but she hadn't told him to cut it out because it was sweet and, frankly, made her feel special. She reminded herself not to read anything into it, that it wouldn't last, but she couldn't seem to help indulging in it for as long as it did.

"What do we need to sort out before your parents get here?" Logan asked as Thelma bounded over with a tennis ball in her mouth.

Gabby sipped a mug of lukewarm tea. "I don't think we have to make any hard and fast decisions now, but they're the type of people who love organization—a bit like Kyle—so it will help if we can show we've at least talked about some of the important issues."

He took the ball from Thelma and threw it, watching as she raced across the paddock and snatched it up a moment after it landed. "Such as?"

Something nudged her leg, and she glanced down and saw that Louise was trying to get her attention. She patted the dog's head and scratched behind her ear.

"Such as where the baby will live."

He turned back to her. "Here would be the obvious answer, but it depends on what you want. I can have them some of the time at my apartment if that would help."

Gabby sighed. "If we did that, it would mean two homes we'd have to fit out with baby gear."

"So, we'll keep them here," he said.

Gabby smoothed a hand down Louise's back, enjoying the way she leaned into the touch. "That's not fair on you though. I don't want to compromise your ability to see them just because it's less convenient."

Logan's lips twisted. "Wherever they are, I'll make sure to see them."

Gabby's heart warmed and her insides melted.

Don't get used to it. He might bail once they're born.

"Besides, you have that lovely bedroom at the front of the house," he added. "My spare room is dark and cramped. It's fine if there's no better option, but in this case, we do have a better option so I think we should take it. But,"— he glanced down at his hands, an unfamiliar note of anxiety entering his voice— "if the baby is going to live here, then I'd like to stay here too. At least in the beginning. I want to be available for support and to share those early days with our baby."

Damn, why did he have to say things like that? It made him difficult to resist. She had to remember that they weren't a couple. He wasn't the man she'd dreamed of starting a life with. And this wasn't what he wanted, no matter how good he was at putting a pretty face on it.

"You can have the other spare room," she told him. "It's not so nice but—"

"It'll be fine," he cut in, smiling. "Are you sure?"

"Yes." She'd already considered the possibility. She just hadn't expected it to become a reality. *It still might not. It's early days.* "Maybe you can move in a couple of weeks before the due date so you're around in case the baby comes early, and then we can reevaluate after three months?"

His smile turned wry. "I should have known you'd need a concrete plan rather than a vague agreement."

"Is there a problem with that?"

He shrugged. "Sometimes it's easier to play things by ear."

"Agree to disagree." She felt like she was floundering when she didn't know what came next. She was already in over her head. She needed plans, steps, and lists, so she could keep stable during what was sure to be a turbulent time.

He cleared his throat. "Speaking of planning, I want to be there for as many medical appointments as possible."

"No problem." She'd hoped he'd say that. While she was perfectly capable of taking care of herself, it was always scary to go through a massive physical change, and it would be nice to have him there to distract her. She bit her lip, knowing what else she needed to say but dreading how he'd react.

"Spit it out," he said good-naturedly. "I can practically

see steam coming out your ears from how hard you're thinking."

Her eyes narrowed. "I don't want you bringing any flings home once you move into my place. I don't care what you do elsewhere, but there won't be any random women parading through my baby's life."

Okay, that first bit was a lie. She did care. She didn't like to think of him with anyone else. But she knew who and what he was, and they weren't together. She could hardly expect him to be celibate. One day, she might want to date too, although she doubted it would be for a while yet.

"Fine," he said easily. Too easily. He was probably thinking he could just pick them up in the bar and take them to his apartment instead. Even if he lived with her, she assumed he'd keep the apartment for later. Why did the image of him and some unknown woman hurt?

Because you're an idiot who wants more than he can give.

That brought her neatly to her next point.

"No sex," she said.

He frowned. "Excuse me?"

"Between you and me," she clarified. "Obviously I don't get to dictate your sex life, but you and I should avoid doing anything that might muddy the waters."

"Is that right?" An unholy light entered his eyes. "I've heard some women get horny during pregnancy. I won't make any moves on you, but if you ask me for it, all bets are off."

"Logan." Her voice was flat.

He shrugged. "It's not my fault if you can't resist me, and I refuse to turn you down if you need me."

Gritting her teeth, she sighed. It wasn't the answer she'd hoped for, but she supposed she'd just have to make sure she held onto enough self-control to keep her distance.

Yeah, because you exercised so much self-control when you got yourself into this mess.

LOGAN WOULD NEVER ADMIT IT TO GABBY, BUT THE THOUGHT of sitting down to dinner with her parents made him break out in a cold sweat. He used to have nightmares about accidentally getting a woman pregnant, and now his dumb ass had actually done it. He doubted Dennis and June were thrilled with him. Somehow, it seemed even more difficult to face them because they weren't strangers. They knew him —at least a little—and their opinion of him had probably taken a sudden plunge off the edge of a cliff.

He was uncharacteristically quiet while they prepared dinner. Gabby had cooked a creamy tomato pasta bake and steamed vegetables, while he'd been in charge of the chicken. She'd also arranged for Shane and Faith to join them, although the boys were having sleepovers with friends. That was probably for the best because Logan wasn't convinced Shane wouldn't take another shot at him.

Dinner was nearly finished cooking when Gabby's parents arrived.

"Would you like to keep an eye on this while I go and let them in?" she asked.

"You stay here." He squared his shoulders. "I'll get them."

Even if he was silently shitting himself, he'd own up to his part in this and not let her act as a shield. The sooner they got through the worst of it, the sooner they could move on. He marched to the front door, Thelma bouncing wherever he tried to put his feet. He hesitated for only a few seconds before plastering a smile on his face and opening the door.

Dennis's scowling face appeared before him. "Oh. It's you." He looked Logan up and down disapprovingly. "The man who defiled my beloved daughter."

Logan fell back. Ah, shit. He thought he'd been prepared for the worst, but he wasn't. He was thinking furiously about how to respond when he saw the twinkle in Dennis's eye.

"I'm having you on, son," Dennis said with a hearty laugh. He patted Logan's arm. "Let an old man have his fun."

Logan finally dared to breathe again. "You got me." He nodded respectfully. "That was ruthless."

Fuck. He forced himself to take a long, slow inhale and the pinch in his chest lessened. God, he'd really thought Dennis had meant it for a minute. Not that he blamed the guy for taking a potshot. He'd just been so wound up he hadn't considered the possibility Dennis would try something like that.

"That's it," June urged, her kindly face brimming with concern. "Nice and easy." She shot a dirty look at Dennis. "Don't mind him. He doesn't get out enough."

Logan shook his head. "It was a good one." He clasped Dennis's hand firmly. "Great to see you, sir."

Sir? Seriously? He mentally rolled his eyes at himself. But what was he supposed to call the grandfather of his baby?

Before Dennis could reply, Shane's car rolled up the drive. Shane was behind the wheel and he parked beside his parents. He and Faith got out, wearing identical expressions of interest, obviously curious to know what they'd interrupted.

"It's so lovely to see you, Faith," June said, hugging her daughter-in-law when they reached the doorstep.

Faith beamed. "You, too, June. It's been a while."

"Since Christmas," June said.

The Walker family congregated at one of their houses

for Christmas each year, and since both Shane and Gabby were in Haven Bay now, the parents had opted to visit them here and use it as an opportunity to throw Gabby a house-warming party. Of course, Gabby hadn't invited Logan. Shane had asked him to come along, but he'd known she wouldn't want him there.

"Logan," Shane said curtly.

"Shane," he replied, his heart squeezing again. Clearly, his friend hadn't gotten over anything.

"So." Faith glanced from Shane to Logan. "Who's running the pub tonight?"

"I asked Mum to fill in." She'd been happy to once she heard where he needed to be instead. He knew she hoped that the Prides and the Walkers could eventually have joint family events, which meant smoothing over any ruffled feathers. She'd given him strict instructions to do just that.

"Of course." Shane greeted June with a hug, and then Dennis.

Dennis kissed Faith's cheek. "You look beautiful, as always."

Faith preened. Logan knew she went to a lot of effort, especially when it came to impressing her in-laws. The first time they'd met, she'd made a less than stellar impression thanks to Shane's spiteful ex, so she loved any indication of their approval. As if they'd ever withhold it. Shane was clearly happy with her, and the boys adored her, so why would they be any different?

"Dinner smells wonderful," Faith said, winking at Logan. "Does Gabby need help?"

"Everything is pretty much done. We'll dish up in a few minutes."

"Perfect." She sashayed past him, and Dennis and June followed, but Shane lingered behind. Logan's stomach clenched.

Shane shifted from one foot to the other, his expression taut.

"What's up?" Logan asked.

Shane met his gaze. "Don't lead Gabby on."

The words hit him like a punch in the gut. "What?"

He tugged at the ends of his hair. "As Faith keeps telling me, you're trying to do the right thing, but I know how my sister thinks. She's a romantic. She wants kids, but she also wants a partner who'll always put her first, and she deserves that, especially after the last asshole." He grimaced. "Having this baby with you might make her think you're going to be that partner, but we both know you're not, so don't confuse her or get in the way of her finding the man she really wants. You owe me that much."

Logan gaped at Shane, shocked speechless. He'd always known his friends thought of him as a carefree playboy, but to hear that Shane thought he was capable of hurting Gabby that way... he was gutted. Not only that, but Shane didn't think he was good enough for his sister. Of course, he knew he wasn't—he couldn't give her the white picket fence she wanted—but knowing that subconsciously and having someone say it to his face were two different things.

"I... I won't," he said after a long moment. "You probably don't believe me, but I care about Gabby."

Shane studied him closely. "Maybe. But how about you care about her from a respectful distance?"

"I'm not going to leave her to deal with this pregnancy without my support."

Shane rolled his eyes. "I'm not asking you to. Just don't make her think it means more than it does."

"I'll do my best not to." He turned away, his stomach sinking to his shoes. "Come on. Dinner is probably ready."

They headed inside, and Logan felt like he'd found solid ground only to have it snatched out from beneath him.

Fortunately, Shane left him alone after their conversation. Faith was obviously trying hard to bridge the divide between them, but it was getting her nowhere, and even Dennis and June seemed to have noticed. He was relieved when they finished, and it was time for him to return to The Den.

He'd just pulled up outside when his phone pinged. He glanced out the window at the pub, which was brightly lit and giving off a cheerful hum of conversation, then checked his phone. He'd received a message from one of the women he'd hooked up with in the past.

Em: *I'm in town overnight and thought we could catch up. *winky face**

Another message arrived a few seconds later.

Em: *I'm at The Den. Where are you? And why does your mum keep glaring at me?*

Logan grimaced. From what he could recall, Em had been a nice girl and they'd had fun, but even if he'd been in the mood, he had no desire to see her tonight. He sent a quick reply to let her know he was busy and then snuck in the back entrance, locking his apartment behind him.

13

GABBY WAS EXHAUSTED, BUT AT LEAST SHE'D GONE ALMOST A full day of work without being sick. She slumped into her car and closed her eyes to rest them for a few seconds, then rapidly blinked them open when her head started to droop and she realized she was about to nod off.

She drove into town and parked outside The Den. Logan had said he'd close the pub until after their doctor's appointment because Corinne wasn't available to keep an eye on things. Gabby felt a bit guilty about affecting his livelihood, but he was determined to accompany her and had said he'd rather lose an hour or two of revenue than miss seeing their baby for the first time. She had to admit, hearing that had made it difficult to remind herself that they were, in fact, not a couple. They were just two people who, as he'd say, were all in this together. At least until shit got real.

She hadn't even left the car before Logan appeared on the front steps and locked the entrance to The Den. She opened the car door and clambered out, her weary legs not getting the memo that they were expected to do their job.

"Do you mind driving?" she asked. "I'm tired."

"I'd be happy to." He accepted the keys from her and she circled the bonnet and flopped with a sigh of relief onto the passenger seat. "How have you been today?" he asked.

She closed her eyes and let her muscles relax. "Exhausted, but I haven't thrown up."

"That's great."

She winced. "Can you dial down the enthusiasm?"

He chuckled. "It's like being with someone hungover."

Her eyes slitted open and she glared at him. "Except the hangover is from your dick, and it's lasted way longer than is fair."

His lips twitched. "What can I say? It's a talented dick."

"Ass." She closed her eyes again. When she next opened them, the car was stationary but they were no longer outside The Den. Instead, they were in the parking area behind the small hospital in Te Awa Tui, and the afternoon light was beginning to dim. Logan wasn't in the driver's seat and she jolted in surprise, looking around for him. Her door opened and she exhaled with relief.

"Here." He offered her a hand. Reluctantly, she took it and let him pull her to her feet.

She strode toward the clinic, then had to stop as her head spun. "Whoa. Got up too quickly."

He steadied her. "You have to be careful."

"No shit, Sherlock."

He sighed in exasperation. "Just let me help you."

"Fine."

She allowed him to wrap an arm around her waist and escort her into the clinic. He gave the receptionist her name and they were directed to the waiting area.

"This reminds me of when I went to get the blood test," Gabby said, looking around. As with the medical laboratory, there were stacks of magazines on a nearby table, but these ones were all about pregnancy and parenthood. She reached for one and flipped it open.

"Were you scared?" Logan asked softly.

She stilled, staring hard at a pregnant brunette on the page she'd stopped at. "Yes, but I was excited too, and I felt guilty about that because I knew you'd be upset."

He leaned closer, still speaking quietly. "You're allowed to be excited, Gabs. Babies might not have been part of my plan, but they're part of yours and I don't want to ruin that for you."

She looked at him and smiled hesitantly. "You won't."

At least, not if he kept going the way he had been. More likely, he'd make her want things he couldn't give.

"Gabrielle Walker?" an accented voice called, snapping the thread of tension between them.

"That's me." She stood, relieved when Logan immediately tucked her against his body because once again, she'd gotten up too fast and her head was spinning. They followed the doctor into her office and sat on a pair of chairs facing the desk.

The doctor perched on the edge of an ergonomic chair and crossed one leg over the other. She addressed Gabby. "Nice to meet you, Gabrielle. Is this the baby's father?" Her accent hinted at a European background. Dutch, perhaps.

"Yes." Gabby reached between the chairs and grabbed Logan's hand. "This is Logan."

"Brilliant." The doctor pushed her small, round spectacles off her nose. Her smile was wide and friendly. "I'm Doctor Vink. Today, we'll do some basic checkups and use the ultrasound to get our first look at your little one. All right?"

They both nodded.

"Okay, then. First, I'd like to hear how your pregnancy has gone so far. I understand it was unplanned and you were most of the way through the first trimester before you realized you were pregnant?"

Gabby blushed. Put like that, she felt stupid for not having opened her eyes to what was going on sooner. "Yes. Logan and I spent a night together in February and it was about three weeks ago that I suspected I might be pregnant instead of just stressed or sick."

She explained what she'd experienced to the doctor and answered questions about her medical background and family, listening with interest when it was Logan's turn. Finally, Doctor Vink asked her to lie on the bed while she prepared the ultrasound.

"This might be a bit cold," she warned before spreading a jelly-like substance on Gabby's abdomen. It wasn't as bad as she expected. Logan was completely silent, watching the screen intently as Doctor Vink started the device.

"We'll record it and email you a copy," the doctor said, also concentrating on the screen.

Gabby tried to ignore the strange sensation and studied the image that appeared. She'd seen enough ultrasounds from pregnant animals to make out the basics. Then she saw something that made her breath catch. Doctor Vink seemed to have spotted it too.

"Congratulations," she exclaimed. "You're having twins."

"Twins," Logan breathed. Holy crap, there were *two* babies?

Gabby's wide eyes met his and he hoped he didn't look as scared as he felt.

"Yes, twins," Doctor Vink confirmed cheerfully. "And both look to be perfectly healthy so far."

"Good." His voice sounded weak so he swallowed and

pulled himself together. "We've got this, Gabby. Our babies are healthy, and everything is fine."

Just fine. They were having not one baby, but two. Two tiny humans who'd depend on him. No big deal. Why was it that twins felt exponentially more terrifying than a single baby?

He stared at the image on the screen. Honestly, he couldn't tell what he was supposed to be looking at. It all looked like blobs to him. But Gabby could obviously see the details, and she'd gone white.

"They're going to be beautiful," he told her. "Just like their mum."

Provided he didn't screw them up first. There would be so many opportunities for him to make mistakes, and he'd never been good at getting the important things right. But the stakes had never been so high either. He wanted to protect these little lives. Even if they looked like blobs, he wanted to care for the tiny humans developing inside Gabby.

Warmth surged through him. Not just for his babies, but for Gabby too. She was carrying these new lives. Supporting them. Giving them what they needed to thrive. How incredible was that?

"Twins," Gabby murmured. "I didn't see that coming."

He snorted. "I doubt anyone did."

"It'll be all right." She sounded as though she was convincing herself as much as him.

"It will be," he agreed, hoping it hadn't crossed her mind that she'd now have to give birth to two babies. Although maybe that wouldn't bother her, considering her job. She'd probably participated in plenty of births, even if they weren't human.

Doctor Vink wiped Gabby's skin clean and put the device away. They set the date for their next appointment and Doctor Vink jotted it on a card along with their expected due date. Seeing the numbers in black and white made it real. These babies weren't a concept or something that would happen in the distant future. They were less than six months away.

Holy shit, he was so unprepared.

He kept an arm around Gabby as they left the hospital. They were passing through a corridor near the waiting area when a man coming the other way glanced at Gabby and stopped abruptly. He clearly worked at the hospital as he was wearing scrubs and a hairnet. He smiled at her in greeting, his eyes startlingly blue as they swept over her and lit up with approval. Logan resisted the urge to glare at him.

"Hi, Tristan," Gabby said, smiling back. "I didn't know you worked at the hospital."

"I'm a surgeon." He looked more delighted to see her than Logan would like. How did they know each other? It wasn't as if Gabby had lived in the area for long, and she was usually working. Could Tristan be one of the men she'd dated earlier in the year, when she seemed to be out with a new man every second night? Jealousy bubbled inside him. He had no right to it, but couldn't seem to tamp it down.

"This is Logan," she said, nudging him with her elbow. "We're here for our first prenatal appointment." She looked up at Logan. "I met Tristan after having blood drawn for the test. He has the cutest little boy."

Logan relaxed. If the good doctor had a son, he was probably married. "Nice to meet you, mate."

"You, too." They shook hands. Tristan's grip was firm but not tight. Another good sign. He wasn't trying to get one up on Logan. But then Tristan turned back to Gabby and said, "I haven't heard from you."

Logan scowled. Perhaps he wasn't married.

"Everything has been crazy," Gabby said. "But I'm definitely keen to talk."

They smiled at each other, and it was just a bit too mutually adoring. He'd bet Shane wouldn't be opposed to the good doctor dating his sister. Tristan had a son, so he knew how to be a dad. He had a well-paying, respectable job. He was everything Gabby had been looking for, and all that she deserved. But Logan couldn't stand there and watch them make eyes at each other.

He placed a hand on Gabby's back. "We'd better get going. She's worn out and needs her rest."

Tristan's eyes met his, assessing him, then he nodded. "I'll talk to you later, Gabby."

Gabby called a quick goodbye as Logan steered her away.

"What was that about?" she demanded once they'd rounded a corner and Tristan was out of sight.

"Nothing," he grumbled.

"Uh-huh." Her tone was rich with disbelief.

Logan's stomach churned. "Did he ask you on a date?"

"What?" She sounded shocked. "No. He's a single dad and he said I could ask him any questions I have about parenting. That's all there is to it."

Somehow, he doubted it. More likely, Tristan had seen her pregnancy as a way to get close to her. He knew how men thought. The guy had definitely been interested in her as more than a fellow parent. Logan should be happy for her, but he hated the thought that she might already be imagining Tristan as the doting husband in her happily ever after. His fingers curled into his palm.

She's not yours.

14

—————

GABBY ROLLED UP TO SANCTUARY, THE BED AND BREAKFAST BY the beach, late on Saturday evening. She'd managed to get through another day without being sick, and Dylan had come to take Princess out for a ride, which had been a weight off her mind.

Now, she was here for the cocktails and cupcakes night that some of the local women held sporadically. Charity had invited her. At first, she'd declined, because being around alcohol wasn't really what she felt like, but when Charity said that Megan, the local cupcake maker and one of the sweetest women on the planet, wanted to throw a mocktails-themed event in her honor, she couldn't say no.

She tucked the cranberry juice and tropical fruit juice she'd bought under one arm and let the dogs out of the back of the car. Megan and her partner Tione, the B&B's cook, had four dogs that Thelma and Louise loved playing with. Gabby led her girls around the back of the sweeping early 1900s villa and left them happily sniffing the three largest of Tione's dogs while she entered the kitchen through the side door.

"Gabby!"

She was engulfed in a warm embrace that smelled faintly of cream and sugar. Faith.

Her sister-in-law drew back, her hazel eyes dancing with excitement. "What's this I hear about twins?"

Gabby glanced around, noting that Kat, who owned the lodge, was leaning against one of the counters beside Bex, the local artist and gym owner. A younger blonde Gabby had met once or twice in passing was chatting with Megan, who looked as pretty as ever. Charity and Mikayla hovered behind Faith, their expressions curious.

"It's true," Gabby said loudly, so she wouldn't have to repeat herself. "For anyone who hasn't already heard, Logan and I are pregnant and we're having twins."

Faith squealed and wrapped her in another hug. As soon as she released Gabby, Charity moved in.

"You're going to rock it," Charity said quietly. "I know you're probably freaking out, but you have nothing to worry about."

"Thanks." Gabby gave her friend a quick hug, not lingering for too long because she knew Charity wasn't always comfortable with displays of affection.

"Is this why you were puking in the rubbish bin the other day?" Mikayla asked, one well-groomed eyebrow raised.

"Yeah," Gabby admitted. "The morning sickness has been tough. It's starting to get better, but I actually lost weight over the first few months rather than gaining it. Hopefully that will change soon."

Doctor Vink hadn't been too concerned when they'd told her about it. She'd just said to eat what she could, drink plenty of water, and make another appointment if the sickness didn't continue improving.

"How is Logan handling it?" the blonde, Brooke, asked. "I'm pretty sure I've heard the words 'I will never have a wife and two point five children' come directly from his mouth."

Gabby squinted at her, considering whether to ask if she'd heard that right before Logan took her to bed. It was part of his usual spiel, after all. But she knew that Brooke had been dating Logan's best friend Jack for a couple of years, and she'd have been quite young before that, so it was unlikely they'd ever been together. That was just her insecurity rearing its head.

"He's doing well, considering," Gabby said. "He was upset when I first told him, but he calmed down after a couple of days and he's been nothing but supportive since."

There had been a moment in the doctor's office where she'd thought he might even be excited about the babies, although she'd been careful not to ask because she didn't want to make him self-conscious or scare him off. She'd also been aware that there was a possibility she'd seen what she wanted to, and not what actually was. She couldn't afford to read too much into his behavior without confirming anything because that would only lead to heartache.

"I'm not surprised," Bex said. "He's always been great with Izzy. Although he does love to pump her full of sugar."

"The boys love him too," Faith said. "He taught Dylan how to talk to his crush, and now they're 'going out.'" She grinned. "It's adorable. They hold hands and play video games together. Shane doesn't know what to make of it."

Gabby grimaced. She knew Faith meant well, and it was cute to think of Logan having a man-to-man talk with Dylan, but he'd picked up his knowledge of flirting by doing it himself with dozens of women, and she'd rather not think of that.

"It's a pretty big change though," Gabby said. "Having kids is different from spending time with other people's kids, and it's not like he signed up for it."

"I know what you mean." Bex's expression was sympathetic. "When I first heard the news, I was shocked that Logan—of all people—had gotten someone pregnant. I thought he'd be clinging to his bachelor status until the day he died, but in hindsight, I'm surprised it didn't happen sooner." Her eyes widened and she clamped her lips shut, obviously surprised that last part had popped out of her mouth. "I mean, because—"

"It's fine," Gabby said, wanting to avoid whatever excuse Bex had been about to deliver. Gabby knew what she meant. It was amazing it hadn't happened sooner because Logan had a new woman every weekend. He liked variety. He'd no doubt been with people more experienced and sexier than her. She got it. But it still sucked.

"I really do think he'll come up to scratch," Bex said, her expression apologetic. "Like I said, Izzy loves him."

"She's right," Faith chimed in. "He likes to make people think he's flippant, but he's made of strong stuff. You should have seen how difficult things were for him after the accident that hurt his knee, but he got through it and now he's thriving."

"He's like a cat that always lands on its feet," Charity muttered.

"A big old tomcat," Brooke giggled.

Gabby forced herself to smile. She wished that fatherhood wasn't something for him to "get through" but rather something he looked forward to, and that she meant more to him than a duty to take care of, but she had to be realistic. He was not her happily ever after, and it was foolish of her to ever dream he could be.

Kat slanted a look at Brooke. "Do I need to tell Jack you think he and Logan are old?"

Brooke narrowed her eyes. "You wouldn't."

"She wouldn't, but I would," Mikayla said with a grin.

Gabby caught Megan's eye across the room. She was watching with interest, but hadn't volunteered any of her own thoughts yet. Gabby would love to know what was going on in her head. Megan struck her as being unusually wise. She didn't ask, though, because she didn't want to put her on the spot.

"So, tell us how this fling between you and Logan started," Faith said, passing Gabby a pink drink in a tall glass. Gabby sniffed it suspiciously. "No alcohol," Faith promised. "Just cherry goodness."

She sipped. It was a great balance of sweet and tart. "Nice." She raised the glass in a toast. "Logan and I didn't really have a fling. It was more a series of one-night stands."

She explained their history while the others listened, rapt.

When she finished, Bex whistled. "It sounds like you have serious chemistry," she said. "It's not like him to be with the same woman more than once, so there must be something about you that draws him in."

"I don't think so." Gabby's heart leaped at the possibility, but she shut down the flicker of hope as soon as it appeared. "It was just a matter of being in the right place at the right time." She'd tell herself that until she believed it. Better to be disappointed now than heartbroken later.

On the last Sunday of April, Logan was behind the bar at The Den when he received a call from Gabby. He frowned, surprised. She was babysitting Hunter tonight, while Shane and Faith went on a date night and Dylan was at a friend's, so he hadn't expected to hear from her.

"My head is killing me," she complained when he answered. "I've thrown up so much my abs feel like I've been doing planks. Is there any chance you could come over and keep Hunter entertained?"

"Hold on a minute." He scanned the bar, noting it was almost empty, and turned to Corinne. "Gabby needs help with Hunter. Are you okay to hold down the fort here?"

"Of course." She smiled. "It'll be good practice for you to spend some time with Hunter."

Yeah. He supposed so. Although now that she said it, he felt a whole lot more pressure to do well.

"Thanks, Mum." He put the phone back to his ear. "I'll be there soon."

He hugged his mum, grabbed his jacket, and hurried out to the car. It didn't take long to get to Shane and Faith's place. He parked outside and debated whether to knock, but went ahead and let himself in. Hunter thundered up the hall toward him, his mouth turned down.

"I'm hungry," he complained. "Aunt Gabby won't leave the bathroom to make dinner."

Oh, dear.

"Go to the living room, buddy," Logan said. "I'll be there in a minute and we'll get you something to eat."

"Really?"

"Yes, really."

Hunter reluctantly walked away, looking back over his shoulder. Logan made his way down the hall, stopping when he glanced into the bathroom and saw Gabby leaning over the toilet. She raised her head to look at him; her eyes were glassy, and her complexion was gray.

"You're a lifesaver," she said. "Thank you."

"No problem." He winced. Her position didn't look comfortable. "Have you had your anti-nausea pills?"

"Yeah, but I keep throwing them back up."

"Ah." There wasn't much he could do about that.

She struggled to get to her feet. "If you keep Hunter busy, I'll make him something to eat."

"Uh-uh." He scowled. "No way. All you're going to do is lie down and rest."

"But he needs dinner."

"I'm sure I can figure something out." How hard could it be to feed a six-year-old? "Is there a bucket around here?"

"In the laundry."

"Okay." He wrapped his arm around her back to steady her. "Let's get you to bed." He steered her into Shane and Faith's bedroom and helped her sit down. "Get comfortable. I've got everything under control."

She looked at him with way more trust than he deserved. "Thanks."

He nodded, and headed to the laundry to get that bucket in case she needed to be sick again. He poured a glass of water, gathered her purse, which hopefully contained her medication, and found a box of chocolates in the pantry. He carted it all to the bedroom and set each item on the nightstand, except for the bucket, which went on the floor.

"If there's anything else you need, just call for me."

"I will." She lay against the pillow and closed her eyes. "Are you sure you're all right with Hunter?"

"Absolutely," he assured her. He left, closing the door behind him, and went to find Hunter.

Fifteen minutes later, he was worried he'd massively overestimated his own abilities. He'd offered several different meal options, but he hadn't been interested in any of them. He wanted meatballs. The only meatballs Logan had ever cooked came in a box from the minimart, and there were none of those in the fridge. He would have run down to the shop to buy some, but they'd closed an hour ago.

"What about breakfast for dinner?" he asked, hoping to divert him. "We could have your favorite cereal."

"I want meatballs." He was persistent, Logan would give him that.

"Okay, buddy. I'll see what I can do."

Even if he'd never made them from scratch before, he was sure there was a recipe on Google, and he was a good all-round cook. Surely it wouldn't be that difficult. He found a recipe online and searched the kitchen for ingredients. Fortunately, there was ground beef in the freezer, which he put in the microwave to defrost. He searched the pantry. Luckily, everything he needed was there, except for bread-crumbs. He also found an onion, a few cloves of garlic, and some parsley. There was no ready-made sauce he could use, but there were fresh tomatoes, so he could make a sauce from that if he added basil and perhaps some spices.

He turned and almost tripped over Hunter, who was standing right behind him. "Damn."

"That's a bad word," Hunter said.

"Yes, it is. I'm sorry." He ruffled Hunter's hair.

"Are we having meatballs?" Hunter asked.

"Yeah, little man. We are."

"Yay!"

Logan followed the recipe, and the resulting meatballs looked pretty good. The sauce smelled great as it simmered on the stove. He cooked a pot of spaghetti and when he put it all together, he was happy with the final product.

Hunter ate one mouthful and his face crumpled. He stuck his finger into his mouth and pulled out a partially chewed piece of onion.

"What's that?" he asked.

"It's onion." Logan answered with a sinking feeling.

"I don't like it," he whispered. "And the s'ghetti is lumpy."

Oh, shit. Logan cringed. He was probably referring to the hunks of tomato in the spaghetti sauce.

"The meatballs aren't right," Hunter continued. "There's no crumbs. It isn't how Mummy makes it."

"It's different from Mummy's meatballs," Logan said quickly. "It's Uncle Logan's meatballs."

Hunter sniffled. "But I want Mummy's meatballs. Not these."

Logan's heart plummeted as the little guy began to cry, tears and snot streaming down his face. Fuck, Gabby had asked one thing of him—to keep a single boy alive and happy—and he couldn't even get that right. How was he supposed to manage with his own kids?

"Mm." He scooped up a mouthful and chewed it, making loud noises of appreciation. "So good."

Hunter only cried harder. Damn. What the hell was he supposed to do?

"Hey, buddy. It's okay." He got up and rounded the table, squatting beside Hunter. "No need to cry. You don't have to eat the onion or the lumpy bits. We can pick them out."

Unsurprisingly, that didn't make him stop. Panic tightened Logan's chest. He didn't know what to do. He had no experience with crying kids. He was only used to being the fun uncle. The guy who shared treats and played games. This was above his pay grade.

He could wake Gabby, but she clearly needed sleep. There was only one other thing to do. He called his mum.

* * *

A WHILE LATER, HUNTER HAD BEEN FED, BATHED, AND PUT TO bed. Logan had watched in awe as Corinne became Super Mum, first consoling Hunter and then turning his mood around with seemingly no effort. He had no idea how she'd done it. He'd been totally lost, and nothing he'd tried had made a damn bit of difference.

He made two cups of herbal tea while Corinne finished tucking Hunter in. His confidence was at an all-time low. In only a few months, he'd be responsible for looking after two babies. They'd be completely dependent on him. If he couldn't get it right when a kid was old enough to use his words, he didn't know how he'd manage with babies. Like his own dad, he just wasn't cut out for this.

"Everything okay?" Corinne's voice jolted him out of his thoughts.

No. But he wasn't going to say that. He pulled her into a hug. "Thank you so much for coming."

"It wasn't a problem. I just closed a little early."

"You saved my ass."

She smiled wryly. "You're exaggerating. It wasn't that bad."

"It felt it." He passed her a mug, then sat with his own and sipped. Corinne dropped onto the chair beside him. "Can I ask you something?"

"Of course." She looked surprised by the question. "Anything."

"Were you surprised when Dad left?"

She frowned, clearly taken aback. "Do you mean when he left the country?"

"Yeah." Had there been signs he'd abandon his children? It felt like it, in hindsight.

"Yes, and no." She sighed. "Did I think he'd go overseas? No. But I wasn't surprised, either. He was a free spirit. He hated feeling stuck."

"That's one way to put it." Logan would phrase it less politely. He'd been a selfish, irresponsible jerk. "Do you know why he went?"

She cocked her head in thought. "Not really. Where is this going?"

"So, it wasn't because of us?"

"No." Her mouth dropped open, then snapped shut. "Absolutely not. I promise, it was never about you. It wasn't even really about me. It was just what he felt like he had to do."

And screw anyone else.

Logan looked down so she wouldn't see his expression. He'd taken off, too. As soon as he'd been old enough, he'd saved his money and left to join the professional surfing circuit. Had doing that made him just like his father? He knew Corinne had missed him, and Kyle had been bullied at school while he was gone. Perhaps a better person would have stayed.

"It means he didn't make any of us a priority though," he said. Jonathan's actions had indirectly told his ex-wife and children that they didn't matter. Their happiness and well-being wasn't important enough for him to bother trying to come up with a solution that enabled him to stay involved in their lives. Logan didn't want to do the same to his children, but he worried he wouldn't be any better at parenting than his dad had been.

"That says more about him than it does about us," she said firmly.

Yeah, it did. But as the saying went, "like father, like son."

"Do you ever have any regrets about him?" he asked.

"Of course not! Being with him gave me you and Kyle, and you're the best things that ever happened to me. Jonathan and I were badly suited, but I like to think I did pretty well for us after he was gone."

"You did." He patted her hand. "We had everything we needed, and most of the things we wanted too. In hindsight,

I realize how difficult it must have been to make that happen."

She smiled. "But totally worth it."

They lapsed into silence while they drank. Logan's mind wandered back to his father. His memories of the man were fuzzy. He couldn't even clearly remember what he'd looked like anymore, which felt wrong considering how much of an impact he'd had on Logan's life. All Logan knew for sure was that he'd been told his whole life how much he resembled Jonathan Pride, and he wanted more than anything for that to be wrong, but after how he'd handled tonight, he wasn't so sure it was.

15

GABBY SET DOWN THE PAINT ROLLER AND STRETCHED. HER back ached, but she'd nearly finished painting the nursery. The walls were a creamy shade of yellow, and the ceiling was white, as were the windowsills and running board. She'd considered painting the ceiling dark blue and decorating it with glow-in-the-dark stars, but had decided it was more important for the room to be light than for it to have a feature ceiling. They could always add the stars anyway and nobody would be able to tell what color the paint was at night.

She heard a scratching at the door and sighed. She'd had to shut the animals out so they wouldn't get themselves covered in paint or smear the neat job she'd done on the walls. She'd opened the windows wide to enable air circulation and it was through the open window that she saw a car come up the drive. She frowned. She'd been expecting Logan, but this wasn't his vehicle. It was too new and shiny. Not to mention white. Only an idiot would drive a car like that in a semi-rural area like this if they wanted to keep it pristine. She squinted, trying to see through the windshield, but either the glass was tinted or the angle of the sun was causing too much reflectivity for her to make out who was inside.

The car pulled up a few yards from the window and the door opened. Henry stepped out. Her stomach flip-flopped sickeningly. Her head spun and she stumbled away from the window. He looked up and spotted her. He propped his sunglasses atop his head and raised a hand in greeting. His stride was confident as he approached the door.

She stared in horror. That absolute bastard. What the hell was he doing here and why did he seem so comfortable about it? She'd never expected to see him again, but whenever she'd let herself consider it, she'd thought he'd at least have the decency to be wary of her.

She lunged for the nursery door as she heard the front door click open and the dogs start barking. The asshole hadn't even knocked. He thought he could just walk straight in. She yanked the door open and stepped into the hall. To her delight, Louise was yapping frantically and Thelma didn't seem inclined to let Henry further into the house.

"Gabby." His face sagged with relief. "I don't know what's got into them." He knelt and reached for Louise, who danced out of reach and continued barking furiously. "Come on girl, we're friends."

"No, you're not." Her voice shook, but hopefully he wouldn't notice. "How are you here? I didn't give you my new address."

He stood and shifted his focus from the dogs to her. "I went to your place but someone else was living there. Your colleagues told me you'd moved to Haven Bay."

Her eyes narrowed. "But I didn't give them my address either."

He shrugged. "I went to the town center and asked an old lady if she knew where I could find you. She gave me directions."

Rage heated Gabby's gut. "So you manipulated an innocent woman into giving you my details so you could stalk me? How dare you."

He scrunched his nose. "I'm not stalking you, babe."

She raised an eyebrow. "You're here, at my house, where you were most definitely not invited, and you walked in without even knocking." She wrapped herself in a growing layer of fury because that was safer than listening to whatever he'd come to say. "I thought I made it clear I don't want anything to do with you."

One side of his mouth lifted in a wry smile. "You mean when you keyed my Mercedes and told Vanessa I was a cheating dirtbag?"

"I don't admit to keying your Mercedes." If not a participant, she'd at least been an accomplice, but she'd never admit it. Who knew what his plan was? Maybe he was recording their conversation so he could try and get the money out of her for repairs. He'd loved that car, and he clearly wasn't driving it anymore, so perhaps it was waiting for work. Although she'd have thought that would have been sorted out ages ago. It had been nearly six months, after all.

"Speaking of Vanessa," she continued. "Shouldn't you be at home with her? You know, the fiancée you never told me about because you didn't give a shit about me—or her—and you're a cheating asshole who only thinks with his dick?"

He took a step closer, shooting a look of surprise at Thelma when she growled. "I left Vanessa." His expression softened and became beseeching. "I realize now that I should have broken up with her as soon as I met you. It's you that I want, Gabby." He hesitated, then added softly, "It's you that I love."

Her breath caught. "Don't say that."

He didn't love her. If he did, he'd never have made her

into the other woman. He'd either have left her alone, or ended things with Vanessa before asking her out. But he knew she wanted a Hallmark happily ever after, and he was flaunting the possibility in front of her. How cruel, to taunt her with what she'd always wanted when she knew it wasn't real.

"Why not?" he asked. "It's true." His gaze swept down her, and for the first time, he seemed to notice the slight roundness of her belly that had developed over the past few weeks. He gasped. "Are you...?"

"Am I what, Henry? Fat? Yes, thank you, I've gained a little weight." She wouldn't tell him about the babies. He didn't deserve to know.

"You're pregnant," he whispered, moving toward her despite the dogs making a fuss between them. "Is it mine?"

He touched her belly, and she jerked away. For some reason, his touch made her feel dirty. He came forward again, but before he could lay another hand on her, he was dragged away from behind.

LOGAN SAW RED AS HE MANHANDLED THE GUY WHO'D LAID HIS hands on Gabby. *His* Gabby. He'd arrived just in time to hear the man ask if the baby was his. Screw that. Logan inserted himself between them, pleased when Louise nipped at the man's calf, and wrapped his arm around Gabby. His heart pounded in his ears as he glared at Gabby's ex. A flash of recognition set in. It was Henry Gosling, the famous cricketer. No wonder the Walker family had been tight-lipped about the relationship. Gosling was engaged, and had been since...

Oh, shit.

Since about the time Gabby moved here. They must

have been dating and he'd left her for the other woman. Now he was here, trying to touch her as if it was his right, and asking if their babies were his. Well, he could fuck right off. He'd had Gabby and he'd crushed her. As far as Logan was concerned, Henry's loss was his gain and now he needed to make it clear that the cheating asshole had overstayed his welcome.

"Who are you?" Henry demanded, his fists balled at his sides. Logan almost wanted him to throw a punch. If he did, it would give Logan a reason to do the same.

"I'm the babies' father," he said. "They're mine, and so is she." Not exactly true, but Henry didn't know that. "You lost your chance. She deserves better than what you did to her."

Beside him, Gabby made a soft sound of surprise. Probably because he'd made it sound as though he knew more about their history than he actually did.

Henry's expression darkened as he looked from Logan to Gabby. "You're really with this guy?"

Logan caught Gabby's eye, hoping she could read the silent message he was sending her.

She turned back to Henry. "Yes. I'm with Logan, and I'm happy. I've got everything I wanted, and everything that you promised me when you weren't in a position to do so. Please take your fancy car and get the hell out of here before I decide to make it match your Merc."

Warmth filled Logan. It made no sense, but he liked standing with her like this and hearing her claim him as her family. It felt right on a gut-deep level that nothing other than surfing ever had.

"But I left Vanessa for you," Henry protested, taking a step toward Gabby and holding out a hand.

"Then you don't know me as well as I thought you did." She raised her chin, and pride surged through him. She was so fierce and strong. "Because I would never get back together with someone who betrayed my trust."

Something flashed in his eyes. "Not even for a big house in the country and a family?"

Logan heard her quick intake of breath and wanted to punch Henry. What a bastard to try to take advantage of her dreams for the future.

"I already have a house in the country," Gabby snapped. "And I don't want a family with you. Get out."

Henry shook his head and sneered at Logan. "Are you sure it's your baby? Do you really want to risk raising my kid?"

"Kids," he corrected. "She's having twins, and they're definitely mine."

He'd believed her the day she first told him—once he'd gotten over the initial shock—and that belief had never wavered. She wouldn't lie about something like that, and the doctor had confirmed how far along the pregnancy was.

"What makes you so certain?" Henry demanded.

Logan intertwined his fingers with Gabby's. "That's none of your business, and as she said, it's time for you to go." He was proud of himself for being civil when what he really wanted was to hit Henry in the face and yell at him to get out of her life and never come back.

"Is that really want you want?" Henry asked Gabby. "If you kick me out, I won't be back. We were together for a year. Are you sure you want to throw that away?"

She hesitated, and for a sickening moment, Logan thought she might reconsider, but then she straightened her shoulders and glared at him.

"I'm not the one who threw us away," she said. "You are."

"You heard her," Logan said. "Get out."

With a flash of real shock in his eyes, Henry backed out of the hall, his hands raised as if to defend himself.

"This is it then," he called. "I won't be back."

"Thank God," Gabby retorted.

Logan shoved the door shut before Henry could say anything else and flipped the lock. Gabby buried her face in his chest. He held her close and kissed the top of her head.

"It's okay, sweetheart," he murmured. "He's gone and you won't have to face him again."

They heard an engine start outside and then the crunch of tires on gravel.

"Good riddance," she muttered into the fabric of his shirt.

He closed his eyes and inhaled her scent. Paint and warm woman. His body tightened with interest and he released her, determined not to make her uncomfortable. He'd always been more attracted to her than was healthy and he hadn't been with anyone else since their night together in February, which was the longest dry spell he'd had in years. It was understandable that he'd react to her nearness, but he didn't want to scare her off. He touched his thumb and forefinger to her chin and tilted her face up.

"Are you okay?" he asked.

She drew in a deep breath and released it with a whoosh. "Yeah." She moved backward and absently tidied her ponytail. "Sorry about that. I had no idea he was coming."

He frowned. "I never thought you did."

Her face was twisted with distress, and she didn't seem to have heard him. "Apparently he found me by asking someone in town. I hate that he was able to track me down so easily."

Logan froze. "Were you hiding? Did he hurt you?"

She sighed. "Only emotionally. But I liked the idea of being somewhere he wouldn't find me. It made me feel free."

"He won't bother you again," he told her. He'd seen the look in Henry's eye. The other man wasn't accustomed to rejection and Logan doubted he'd be lining up for more. But even if he did, Logan wouldn't allow it to happen. It would only take a few words in the right ears and Henry would regret ever showing his face in Haven Bay again. "We'll keep him away."

Gabby pressed her lips together. "Sorry for the drama."

"Never be sorry for something someone else did. It's one of my personal philosophies."

To his relief, she smiled. "Sounds about right."

He resisted the urge to tuck her hair behind her ear. She'd just had one man making unwanted advances. She didn't need another doing the same. Especially not when that man was him.

"How much do you know about what happened between Henry and me?" she asked, heading to the living room.

He followed. "Not much. Although now that I know who he is, and based on the timing, I'm guessing he wasn't completely faithful."

"Nope." She dropped onto a chair, seemingly heedless of the paint on her clothes. Ah well. He could clean it later if needed. "The awful part is, she wasn't the other woman. *I* was. But I had no idea."

"Of course you didn't," Logan said firmly as he sat on the sofa and Thelma tried to jump onto his knee. "That's not the kind of person you are. It doesn't matter which way around it was. He played you, and her too."

Gabby's face pinched. "I tried to tell her, you know."

He frowned. "Who? His fiancée?"

"Yeah." She pulled her knees to her chest. "I told her who I was and that I'd been dating him for a year. She thought I was a delusional fan and refused to listen."

Logan whistled. "Wow."

He'd be willing to bet that despite the dismissal, Henry's fiancée had thought long and hard about what Gabby said. In his experience, women tended to be mistrustful when it came to their partners and other women. Even if she hadn't believed Gabby at the time, she might have changed her mind. In fact, there was every possibility she had, and she'd kicked him to the curb. That would explain his appearing on Gabby's doorstep out of the blue. As if she would take him back. She had more self-respect than that.

"He's a complete loser," he said.

"He's a professional athlete," Gabby said, as if that meant something.

Logan had been a professional athlete. It didn't make him any better of a person.

"He plays with sticks and balls for a living." He met her eyes so she'd know his ensuing words were serious. "You save lives. You're a doctor." She opened her mouth but he kept going. "Don't try to tell me you're just a veterinarian, as if that's less than a doctor. Your patients can't communicate what's wrong with them, and you're expected to be able to treat cows, horses, sheep, goats, deer, and probably a dozen other species too. You're smart, beautiful, and successful, and he was an idiot who deserved to lose you."

16

GABBY STARED AT LOGAN, AT A LOSS FOR WORDS. SHE couldn't believe how fiercely he'd defended her. First, he'd stood by her side and faced down her demons—aka Henry—with her. He'd lied about them being together, which made her feel slightly less pathetic. Then he'd held her as if she were precious, and now he was breathing heavily after a speech that made her want to kiss him. She never knew he saw her that way. It was obvious they were attracted to each other, and they'd been building the foundations of friend ship, but to know that he thought so highly of her came as a shock.

Don't read anything into it, she told herself. *It doesn't mean anything.*

But her heart wasn't getting the message. All it understood was that Logan had supported her. He thought she was beautiful and smart. Her cheeks burned and her stomach fluttered. Even though she knew that feeling anything for him was a bad idea, she couldn't help herself. How was she supposed to resist him when he was gorgeous and protective and caring? All traits she'd been seeking but had never thought to find in him.

"Thank you," she whispered.

"Don't thank me. It's what any damn fool should know." He cleared his throat and looked down at Thelma, who'd laid her head on his lap. "Did you finish painting before he turned up?"

"I did." She accepted the change of subject gracefully. "Although I think I got as much paint on me as I did on the walls."

He glanced at her and his lips twitched. "Are you sure the walls got half?"

She laughed. It felt good, after the intensity of the past fifteen minutes. A much-needed release of tension.

"Oh, that reminds me. I've got something for you." He shifted Thelma off his lap and hurried out of the room.

She trailed behind him as he went outside, wariness warring with the desire to trust him. He opened the passenger door of his car and withdrew a box she recognized from her favorite chocolatier, which she'd discovered on one of her trips to Serenity Cove. He jogged over and passed it to her.

"You said you were craving the double chocolate truffles, right?"

She looked from him to the box in her hands. She opened it to reveal several rows of double chocolate truffles. Her insides flipped over. "Oh, my God. I can't believe you bought these."

He grinned. "So I got it right?"

"You did." She couldn't take her eyes off the chocolates. She popped one into her mouth and moaned in delight. "You didn't have to drive all the way to Serenity Cove just to get these."

His expression softened. "You wanted them, and you're the one carrying these babies, so the least I can do is make sure you have what you want."

Tears stung her eyes. "Thank you."

She couldn't believe he'd done that. She'd never expected it. It was the sort of gesture her fantasy man might make.

Don't get any ideas. He's sweet now because you're a novelty. It won't last.

"Hey, now." He took the box from her and wrapped her in a hug. "It's okay. I'm sorry for everything that asshole did and said. You have my solemn promise never to watch another cricket game. From now on, the pub will boycott all televised cricket matches."

She laughed despite herself. "You don't have to do that."

"I know. But I will."

She rested her cheek on his shoulder. Today was the first time she could recall him holding her like this without any kind of sexual undertone. His touch was comforting, and the embrace was nice. Maybe that sounded weak, but nice was underrated as far as she was concerned. She could happily soak up his strength all day.

Don't get used to having him to lean on. He won't stay.

"You deserve the best," Logan said, and she could feel his lips moving against her hair. "And that is not Henry Gosling." He hesitated, then added, "In all honesty, it's not me either, but I'll do everything I can to treat you right."

She drew back and gazed into his beautiful eyes. He looked at her with an emotion she hadn't seen from him before. It almost looked like affection. Her gut tightened, and before she'd taken the time to think it through, she raised her lips to his. Their lips met, clung, and parted. Then met again. A soft exhale passed between hers.

Logan tensed.

Her insides dropped. Oh God, she'd made a terrible mistake.

"I'm s—"

He kissed her. She clutched his shoulders and went slack with relief. The kiss didn't have the fire she'd come to expect from their hookups, but it had a depth and tenderness that had been missing before. She went onto her tiptoes to kiss him back, totally absorbed in the feel of him against her, ignoring the one thought that flashed through her mind.

Thank God he never kissed me like this before or I'd have fallen for him.

LOGAN POURED EVERYTHING HE HAD INTO THE KISS. He needed Gabby to know how much he desired her. How valued she was. But a voice at the back of his mind reminded him that she was sensitive. She'd just come face-to-face with her cheating ex, the man who'd broken her heart. Was she really in the right frame of mind for this? With difficulty, he separated his mouth from hers and touched their foreheads together.

"Maybe we shouldn't do this," he panted. "Not when you're emotional. I don't want you to regret it later."

After all, if things became strained between them, there was no escaping each other. They'd be stuck with that awkwardness forever.

Gabby's eyes narrowed. "I need it." Her lips were swollen from his kiss, and they tempted him to forget his ideals and steal another taste. "Please, Logan. I need to feel wanted. Don't deny me that."

Okay, there was no way he could refuse her plea. She needed him, pure and simple, and while there was plenty he couldn't give her, he could give her this.

"I've got you," he said, ignoring the pang in his gut that

said he'd like to have her for real, rather than in whatever capacity this was. He wanted what he'd told Henry to be true. Even if he didn't believe he was capable of making Gabby happy, he'd like to try. He kissed her briefly and swept her inside. Her property was relatively private, but he was taking care of her, which meant making sure no one else would see her during her most vulnerable moments. He guided her into the bedroom.

"Lift your arms," he ordered, expecting her to resist—she'd proved she didn't like being told what to do—but she did as he said. He stripped the shirt over her head, baring her torso except for a white bra and a few smudges of paint on her chest. "Let's get you cleaned up."

"I can do that later," she protested.

"It'll just take a minute." If she got paint on her bed, she'd be annoyed with herself after. He went to the bathroom and ran a cloth under warm water, then returned to her and used the cloth to clean the paint smudges from her chest. She stripped off her bra, sweatpants, and panties, and stood before him naked. He didn't see paint anywhere else, so he set the cloth aside and cupped her face between his palms. She murmured in approval as he kissed her. He kept the kiss sweet and light. Something uncomfortable tangled in his chest. A tenderness he hadn't expected. He knew he cared for her, but he hadn't anticipated feeling so raw.

"Logan." She nipped at his mouth, demanding more. He deepened the kiss, tasting her. One of his hands went to the small of her back and he urged her closer, pleasure rolling through him as she rocked against his erection. She grabbed the hem of his t-shirt and tugged it up. He obliged the silent demand, lifting it over his head and tossing it aside. She explored his torso with her hands, tracing the ridges and smoothing over his chest and shoulders. He shivered. No one else touched him the way she did, as if she wanted to learn every contour of his body.

He backed her to the bed and laid her down, taking care to prop a pillow behind her. His socks came off, followed by his jeans and briefs, then he knelt over her and looked his fill. Her breasts were fuller than usual, and the nipples were already peaked. He brushed his thumb over one and she whimpered.

"Sensitive?"

"Very."

He kissed the nipple gently. "Good sensitive or bad sensitive?"

Her answering grin was saucy. "The best."

"Perfect."

He toyed with the nub, using his tongue to tease her until she writhed, squeezing her thighs together as if desperate for relief. He shifted to the other and gave it the same treatment. By the time he'd finished, her fingers were threaded through his hair and she seemed to be simultaneously trying to keep him there and speed him along. He journeyed downward, placing kisses on the slight swell of her belly.

"Gorgeous," he told her.

She rolled her eyes.

"I'm serious." He nuzzled the skin there and pressed his ear to it as if he'd be able to hear their babies' heartbeats. He knew it was impossible but he liked the thought. He moved lower still, settling over her sex. He dropped a kiss on the patch of hair above her, then dipped his tongue into her heat. She moaned and arched her back.

"Oh, my God," she gasped as her hips circled, seeking more. "Why are you driving me so crazy?"

"Because you deserve to feel wonderful."

He could tell from the way her breath caught that he'd

startled her. She most likely hadn't expected him to say anything so honest during sex when he'd always tried to keep things physical in the past. So what? It was time for a change. She deserved to feel special. To be worshiped. He buried his face between her thighs and used his lips and tongue until she was panting and strung tight with pleasure.

"Get up here," she demanded. "I'm so wet. I need you in me."

His cock throbbed at her words. He'd just have to give her what she wanted. He was a gentleman like that. He crawled over her, bracketing her between his arms, and dipped his head to kiss her but then stopped, unsure how she'd feel about kissing him considering where his mouth had just been. She came up on one elbow and sealed their lips together, making the decision for him. Their mouths fused together until he ran out of breath, and then he broke away and looked instinctively for a condom.

Gabby chuckled. "I'm already pregnant. The cat's out of the bag. I'm safe if you want to go bare."

He hesitated, awed by her trust in him. He hadn't been with anyone for months, but she didn't know that.

"I'm good too," he said gruffly. "I promise. I would never risk you."

She smiled up at him softly. "I know."

His heart flipped and his cock grew even harder. Fuck, this was going to feel amazing. He'd never been in anyone without a condom before. He'd always been careful, never taken a chance or gotten too close.

He positioned himself at her entrance and thrust in an inch at a time until he was fully enveloped within her hot, velvet grip.

"You feel amazing," he said. "God, Gabby. So damn good."

He willed himself to calm down so it wouldn't be over

too soon, but she tilted her hips and he somehow sunk even deeper. He groaned and she whimpered and clutched his shoulders. She worked her hips, trying to ride him from below.

He grinned. "You're so needy."

Her eyes narrowed, but the expression was ruined by the flush of her cheeks and the slight parting of her lips. "Fuck off, Pride."

He kissed her. "I don't think you really want that."

"No," she admitted. "But for the love of God, please hurry up or I'm going to explode and it'll be all your fault."

"We can't have that."

He drew nearly all the way out, then slid back in, the glide so exquisite he nearly lost his head. He buried his face in the side of her neck and sucked and kissed his way along the silky skin as he buried himself in her over and over again. She wrapped her legs around his hips, her heels digging into his backside to urge him deeper. He raised himself up enough to reach between them and stroke her clit. Her hips stuttered and she cried out.

"That's it, sweetheart."

She tightened around him and their gazes locked as she came. He thrust again and again, wringing every bit of pleasure from her, unable to look away even though he feared what emotions might be showing in his eyes. A shudder tore through him and he groaned in release. He dropped his forehead to hers, breathing heavily, but kept his weight off her. Her golden eyes were glazed and her cheeks were flushed. So sexy.

He rolled off and flopped onto the bed beside her, drawing her into his arms. She tucked up beneath his chin and he hoped she couldn't feel how hard his heart was hammering. He'd never experienced anything that intense before, and it had left him shaken. Sex was usually good, but he'd never felt so connected to his partner. Somehow, he knew he was standing on the precipice of a massive change, and he wasn't sure whether to be excited or terrified.

17

GABBY WOKE A FEW HOURS LATER FEELING REFRESHED AND pleasantly tingly. She smiled as she recalled her time with Logan and rolled onto her side to face him. Her smile dropped when she saw that he wasn't there. Disappointment flooded her gut. She swallowed against the rising tide of bitterness. She shouldn't have been surprised. He'd gotten what he'd wanted, and he'd never made promises. In fact, she could say the opposite was true. But she thought they'd bonded, and that being together today had meant something, even if they hadn't said the words. She sighed. She knew better, but she'd let herself get caught up in the moment.

With a grunt of effort, she kicked her legs off the edge of the bed and got up. Her back twinged. Even though she hadn't gained much weight yet, it always seemed to be achy. She hated to think how it would be once she was further along. She crossed her fingers that she'd have small babies. If they were big, she was in for an unpleasant few months followed by a birth she'd rather not dwell on.

She washed in the bathroom and paused to pat Karen, who seemed to be watching her judgmentally.

"I know you can't help it," Gabby said. "That's just your face."

If possible, Karen's furry little features became even more disapproving, but that could have been Gabby's imagination.

"Are you talking to your cat?"

She jumped in surprise and banged her knee against the sink. "Ow, shit."

"Sorry." Logan winced. "That looked like it hurt."

"It did." She rubbed her throbbing knee and glanced at the doorway, where he stood holding a tray. He hadn't left. She pressed her lips together so he wouldn't see her smile of relief. "What's that?"

He looked down at the tray and shifted from one foot to the other, suddenly unsure of himself. "I thought you might be hungry after the painting, the confrontation with your ex, and, of course, the awesome sex." He waggled his eyebrows, but she could tell it was all for show. "I've got crackers, nuts, chocolate, fruit, and lemon and ginger tea." He glanced at her and kept talking. "If you don't want it now, I can put it away for later. Only, you were asleep and I thought it would be nice to bring it to you in bed."

Her heart swelled with joy. Not only had he stayed, but he was trying to take care of her. She knew she shouldn't read anything into it, but after the way he'd defended her earlier, it felt significant.

"Thank you." She smiled like a goof. "That sounds lovely. Should we take it to the living room since I'm out of bed and the bedroom smells like sex?"

Mischief glinted in his eyes. "There are far worse things it could smell of. If it bothers you, I'll open a window. But yeah, okay."

They headed for the living room, and he carefully set the tray on the coffee table. He'd found a porcelain teapot in one of her cupboards, and now he used it to pour tea into a delicate cup. He left, presumably to open that window, then detoured to the kitchen and returned with a mug of coffee for himself. Gabby reached for a cracker and munched it slowly. She hadn't felt so nauseous lately, but it paid not to eat too fast or her gut would protest.

He watched her, uncharacteristically serious. "I put the dogs outside," he said. "I figured they could use a run in the sun."

Her heart squeezed. "Thanks."

Don't get attached. It was just sex. He's still not the commitment type.

Thomas wandered into the room and jumped onto the end of the coffee table. Logan swept him off.

"No, you don't, pal. That's our food."

Gabby laughed. "Good luck with that. He's the boss in this house."

"Maybe so, but he can't be touching our food. Or the babies'. We want to make sure we keep them safe from contamination."

She frowned. "I know. It will be fine."

She liked that he was thinking about what was in their kids' best interest, but she didn't like the part where it sounded like he was lecturing her, or that he wanted the animals reigned in. They were her fur babies. She pressed her lips together and didn't say anything. He was probably used to being overly cautious because he worked in the food industry.

Logan bit a piece of apple and reached for more. Silence stretched between them. Eventually, he broke it.

"I hope you didn't mind me intervening when I arrived and saw your ex here earlier. I should have waited to see if you wanted my help before just grabbing him."

"It was fine." She recalled Henry's face. "More than fine,

actually. I don't think he knew how to handle it. He's so used to everyone giving him whatever he wants."

He arched a brow. "Did you do that?"

"Maybe." It wasn't a pleasant thought. "We didn't see each other often, so I tried to make the most of it, and that sometimes meant sacrificing other things. I wasn't a doormat though."

He snorted. "Of course not. You couldn't be a doormat if your life depended on it."

She grinned. "Don't you forget it."

"So..." He drew out the word as Thomas jumped onto his lap and demanded attention, which she was relieved to see Logan give. "Do you miss him?"

Gabby's first inclination was to shut the question down immediately, but she paused to consider because he deserved a proper answer. Did she miss Henry? She missed having someone to love. She missed being part of a couple and looking forward to seeing him whenever he had a few days off. But she didn't miss his arrogance that went a little too far, or his tendency to steamroller people.

"No," she said thoughtfully. "I don't think so. I miss the relationship I thought I could have with him, and the time I wasted on him, but not actually him."

"Good." Logan flashed a victorious grin. "He's not worth your pain."

"That's kind of you to say."

His eyes darkened. "It's true."

"Mm." She nibbled another cracker and reached for her phone. "I'm pretty sure he was lying anyway."

Logan cocked his head. "About what?"

"Leaving Vanessa. That doesn't seem like something he'd do. He wouldn't want to be perceived badly, or for his fans to think he'd failed at a relationship."

She tapped a few words into the search engine and hit

"Go." Sure enough, several news stories appeared, announcing that Vanessa had broken off the engagement due to alleged infidelity. Her heart thudding, she clicked into one of them, wondering if it would mention her. If so, she'd have to brace herself for a lot of public scathing. She skimmed the text, relieved to see that Vanessa had apparently walked in on Henry with another woman.

"Bastard," she muttered. Once a cheater, always a cheater. She'd bet the incident had made Vanessa think twice about what Gabby had told her too. At least Vanessa had ended things before they got married.

"What is it?" Logan asked.

She shook her head. "Nothing. Just thought I'd check Henry's story, and like I guessed, he was lying. He didn't break up with Vanessa for me. She dumped him because he couldn't keep it in his pants."

"Ah." His cautious expression told her he understood where her mind had gone. She was forced to acknowledge, once again, that she wasn't special to Henry. Even though she would never have gotten back with him, she'd liked to believe that he might have cared for her, even if it was deep down. But it seemed she was just the backup option. Once again, she wasn't enough.

Logan's emotions were a mess as he left Gabby's house and drove back to The Den. He wished he could stay with her, but tonight would be busy. There was a large booking for a birthday and both he and Corinne were needed. Still, his thoughts were with Gabby as the scenery flew by. It unnerved him. He'd gotten used to the status quo, but then she'd moved here and gotten pregnant and now everything was in turmoil. He felt so much, and it scared him. He'd gotten used to keeping any strong emotions at a distance with his flippant attitude. He couldn't maintain that with Gabby.

He showered in his apartment, and as he toweled dry and chose an outfit for the night, he couldn't help thinking that his place no longer felt like home. It was a place to crash. A convenient stopping point. But Gabby's house, filled with light and warmth, was a home. He enjoyed spending time there. His soul seemed to lift each time he entered. It was by no means perfect. There was fur everywhere and it smelled faintly of dog, but when he walked in, something inside him longed to stay.

He took the stairs down to the pub two at a time and greeted Corinne with a smile. She was serving customers, so he got started filling the drink orders she'd jotted on the notepad beside the register. The Den was bustling, the large party having just arrived, and time passed quickly. He was mentally elsewhere, and several times Corinne had to repeat herself to him. He could tell she was worried. He was usually tuned into whatever was going on around them so he could participate in any conversations he was dragged into and make sure every patron had what they needed.

Tonight, he'd let himself slip. He was too distracted wondering how Gabby would react if he suggested he move in with her soon rather than waiting until closer to the due date. He didn't know whether she'd read something into the suggestion, or even if he wanted her to. How the hell was he supposed to make her understand his reasoning when he didn't fully get it himself? He still wasn't good father material, and he wasn't the steady, responsible partner she deserved. But he found he cared less and less.

"Is everything okay?" Corinne asked as the bar began to empty.

He rubbed his temples. "I don't know. I'm having all

sorts of weird thoughts and I'm all over the place. Sorry. I hope you didn't have to pick up too much slack."

"Hardly at all," she assured him. "I didn't ask to make you feel guilty. I just want to know what's going on. Is there anything I can do to help?"

"Not really." He glanced at Hugh MacAllister, the former town councilman and a total gossip, who was deep in conversation with one of his cronies. "I'll talk to you after we've closed, if you've got time."

"Of course."

After the last of the patrons left, they did a quick clean, and then he poured them both a glass of lemonade. They sat side by side at the bar.

"Gabby's ex turned up at her place today," Logan said, and explained what he'd walked in on, leaving out Henry's name. He trusted his mum, but Gabby's ex's identity was her business and it was up to her who she chose to share it with.

"It sounds like she's better off without him," Corinne said when he'd finished.

"Yeah." Logan agreed completely, but his feelings about the matter were more complicated than hers.

"What's going on in that head of yours?" she asked. "I can see the cogs turning."

He gulped his lemonade and wished it was something stronger. "I like her, Mum."

"And that's a bad thing?"

"No." He sighed, unsure how to put his emotions into words. "But I'm not sure that I'm any better for her than Henry was." Corinne started to interrupt, but he gestured for her to stop. "I'm not a cheater, but that's only because I've never tried to date anyone properly, so I've never had to stay faithful. I always figured it wasn't in my DNA to be a good partner so there was no point trying. Now, I think I'd like to try, but I don't want to hurt her."

Corinne watched him steadily. "Why do you think it's not in your DNA to be a good partner?"

He grimaced. "You remember Dad, right?"

"And?" Her eyebrows drew together. "Is this why you were asking me about him recently?"

"Maybe," he admitted. "We're alike. Everyone used to say it."

Corinne shook her head. "You are not your father. You might bear a passing resemblance to him, but you're your own man."

He pulled a face. He got where she was coming from, but had she paid any attention to his dating history—or lack thereof?

She raised her chin. "I'm serious. You're a much better man than him. Besides, I like to think there's at least as much of me in you as there is of him, especially considering I raised you."

"I hope there is." God forbid every part of him came from Jonathan.

"Do you think I'm incapable of being a good partner?" she asked.

His jaw dropped. "Of course not. You're great with Lawrence."

"Exactly." She leveled him with a look. "If you think DNA plays such a big part in whether or not you can treat someone well, then you need to factor in my contribution to your DNA as well as your dad's. I'm in a healthy relationship. Lawrence and I respect each other, and we're happy. Just like you could be happy with Gabby if you gave yourself a chance."

"Yeah, maybe." He dragged a hand through his hair. He wanted to believe her, but he'd spent a lifetime telling himself differently, and proving himself right over and over again. He drained the rest of his lemonade. If he wanted answers, perhaps Corinne was the wrong person to talk to. Maybe he should go straight to the source. He hadn't spoken to his dad in over a decade, but Corinne had given him Jonathan's email address, and he knew it was saved on his computer.

"I'm going to head upstairs," he said, taking Corinne's empty glass. "I'll wash these. Thanks for the chat."

"You're welcome. I hope it helped."

"It did." He kissed her cheek and gave her a brief hug. "Are you okay to let yourself out?"

"I've done it a thousand times before."

He waved her out, dealt with their glasses, and went upstairs, where he fired up his laptop and composed an email to his no-good absentee father. He read it several times over before hitting "Send." It wasn't perfect, but he'd been polite and asked what he needed to. Now he'd just have to wait and see whether Jonathan would bother to reply. He doubted it. It wasn't as if the guy had been there any other time Logan needed him.

18

WHEN GABBY TURNED INTO HER DRIVE AND SPOTTED LOGAN'S car parked outside the house, she breathed a sigh of relief. It had been an exhausting day, with an operation and an emergency trip out to one of the neighboring farms to deal with an injured horse. It was nice not to return to an empty house. He'd been spending more time at her place since they first slept together again a couple of weeks ago. They'd slipped into an easy relationship where they had sex but never discussed what it meant. Were they heading for the loving family future she'd always wanted, or was this some kind of temporary arrangement that would end as soon as the baby was born?

More likely, the latter. But she was in denial.

Thelma greeted her at the door, her tail wagging frantically, and Gabby laughed. Nothing could brighten her day like her fur babies. Especially Thelma and Louise, who were always thrilled to see her. Dogs were such a balm for the ego. She loved on Thelma, then cuddled Louise, and eventually made it to her bedroom, where she stripped off a t-shirt that smelled of horse and kicked off her muddy pants. She dropped her clothes in the laundry, pulled on a fresh set and followed the scent of tomato and spices to the kitchen.

Logan stood behind the stove, his board shorts lovingly cupping his ass. He glanced over his shoulder and smiled. "Big day?"

"Do I look that bad?"

"No-o." He schooled his expression, rested the handle of the spoon against the edge of the pot, and crossed to her. He kissed her gently and smoothed her hair off her forehead. "You're beautiful."

She rolled her eyes. "You charming liar."

"It's the truth." His smile softened. "You're always beautiful to me."

She melted inside. Damn, he was good at doing that to her, but she never knew how seriously to take him. He was a pathological flirt. "How were your classes today?"

"Good," he said. "Everyone seemed to enjoy themselves. It's definitely on the edge of too chilly though. I think we'll be wrapping up for the year soon."

"Until spring?"

"Yeah." He padded back to the stove and stirred the pot of whatever was simmering. "I'll keep going as much as I can over winter, but not everyone is as committed as me. Beginners tend to only want to learn when it's warm and sunny."

"Funny that." Gabby had surfed a few times, and she was with his students on that one. Surfing was definitely an activity for the warmer months. "What are you cooking?"

"Pasta." He removed the pot from the stove and ladled its contents into two bowls, then gestured at a pair of frying pans at the back of the stove that she hadn't seen yet. "I chopped up veggie sausage if you feel like it."

"Thanks." She came closer and inhaled the scent. "Smells good."

She could get used to this. Coming home to dinner and a handsome man.

This is not your future, she reminded herself. *It's temporary. If anything, you'll be coming home to a pair of babies who need you to feed them, and you'll fall into bed exhausted only to wake up and have to do it all over again.*

"You're welcome." He kissed the tip of her nose.

Seriously, how was her protective layer of cynicism supposed to survive when he did that?

He took one of the bowls and added sausage from one frying pan, stirring it into the red sauce. Gabby emptied the other pan into her bowl. She was starving. They took their meal to the table. Logan had learned by now that if he sat on the sofa or an armchair, he'd have the animals begging for scraps and trying to climb onto his lap to share his food. He was finicky about hygiene, so they compromised by using the table.

"Oh, hang on a second." He disappeared into the kitchen and was back a moment later with two mugs. He placed one beside her bowl and the other beside his, on the opposite side of the small table. It was lemon and ginger tea. Her heart gave a pitter-patter. She'd never imagined Logan would be so thoughtful, and it was dangerous to her romantic heart.

Don't get used to it.

Yes, he was sweet, but he was also determined not to settle down, regardless of their current arrangement. If any woman were to change that, it certainly wouldn't be her. It would be someone fun and flirty, or a surfer babe with long legs and a golden glow. Not average, nothing-special Gabrielle.

"Dig in," he said.

She scooped a healthy portion of pasta into her mouth and moaned. "That's really good."

"Thanks." He grinned. "I learned to make the sauce while I was surfing in Italy."

She ate more, her empty stomach crying out for all the carbs it could get. "Is it too much to hope that you learned other recipes while you were traveling?"

He smirked. "I have a few tricks up my sleeve."

"I hope to see them all."

He waggled a finger. "If you're nice to me."

She stared mournfully down at the delicious meal. "Then I'm doomed."

He laughed, his expression delighted. "You don't have much faith in yourself."

"I have more faith in your ability to drive me up the wall." She grinned, enjoying the banter. "Don't you remember that I'm the hot-tempered Walker sibling? Shane got all the calmness in our family."

He rubbed his chin. "Come to think of it, I do seem to recall you delivering the set-down of the century at Dylan's twelfth birthday party."

Gabby choked. "You saw that? I didn't realize you were there."

"Only for a little while. I couldn't leave The Den for long."

"Huh." That was the party where she'd met Henry. Shane's ex-wife, a film star, had pulled strings to get two members of the national cricket team to visit for her son's birthday. Gabby and Henry had hit it off straight away. In hindsight, it should have been a red flag that she met Henry through Diana.

"So, I've been thinking," Logan said, when a moment passed with no further comment.

"That sounds dangerous," she teased.

He rolled his eyes. "Have mercy, woman." He cleared his throat and repeated, "I've been thinking. Is it a good idea for me to continue running The Den if I'm going to be a father?" He pursed his lips and put his cutlery down. "It's probably not the best environment or example to set for our kids."

"What?" she spluttered, reaching for the tea to wash down a piece of sausage she'd swallowed too quickly. The tea soothed her throat and she drew in a few breaths before continuing. "How would it be a bad example? You run a business. Two businesses, actually. I don't see how that could possibly be a bad thing."

He fidgeted with his hands and she could see he was really worried about this. "Because of the alcohol. I don't want them to be raised thinking drunkenness is normal."

Gabby bit her lip. She'd had no idea he was concerned about this. "Are drunks around during the day, when a child would be awake?"

"Not usually, no."

"Then we'll just keep the babies away from The Den at night." It seemed a simple solution to her. But then a thought crossed her mind. "Unless there's something else you're worried about exposing them to?" Such as his flirting with other women. She knew he flirted his butt off at work. It was practically a job requirement for bartenders and it fit his personality well too.

"No." He sounded dubious. "But are you sure?"

Gabby looked longingly at her pasta, then followed his lead and put her cutlery down to focus on the conversation. "If you want to sell The Den or hire someone to take over your shifts, then go for it. But if it's purely because you're worried about exposing our children to a few tipsy patrons, then we'll just make sure to keep them away during the times they're at risk of encountering that. Honestly, I can't imagine they'll spend much time there anyway, especially not for the first few months." It was possible he'd have to have them there with him at times in the future, but it seemed like that would be the exception rather than the rule.

"Okay." His expression eased briefly, but then he tensed again. "There's something else I'd like to talk about too."

"What?"

He hesitated. "It's a long story. Just bear with me."

Gabby nodded. Whatever it was, she could already tell this was important to him.

ANXIETY ROILED IN LOGAN'S GUT, BUT HE OWED GABBY THE truth. If he wanted to explore the possibility of a future between them, he'd just have to get over it and blurt out all the embarrassing and ugly thoughts he'd never intended to share.

He pushed his bowl away. He'd eaten enough, and the pasta sat heavy in his stomach. Gabby sipped her tea and picked up her cutlery again, apparently deciding that the need to eat outweighed the need to focus solely on him. That was good. Speaking might be easier without her full attention. Maybe she'd thought of that too.

"How much do you know about my father?" he asked.

She chewed, her expression thoughtful. "I know that you don't mention him, and I assume he doesn't live around here. I guess I figured that you aren't close because your mum got custody when they separated."

He laughed humorlessly. "Not quite. Mum and Dad divorced when I was eight. They'd been fighting for as long as I could remember, and honestly, looking back, I think they would have broken up much sooner if Mum hadn't gotten pregnant."

Gabby winced. "I know people mean well, but I don't

think it's ever a good idea to stay together for the sake of a child. Kids are perceptive. They pick up on the unhappiness and hostility, even if they don't understand it."

"Yeah, well." He didn't really know what to say to that, especially when he was about to propose a relationship with her that he'd never have suggested had she not gotten pregnant. But the circumstances were different, so hopefully she'd at least be open to discussing their future.

"Anyway, they were supposed to have a joint custody arrangement where we stayed with Dad every second weekend and on school holidays, but it didn't take long before he was canceling his weekends because of other commitments, and about six months after they separated, he moved overseas."

"I'm sorry." She'd stopped eating again, sympathy etched in every line of her face. "That must have hurt."

"It wasn't my favorite thing." It had taken him a while to accept that his dad wasn't coming back. At first, he'd just thought it was a long vacation. But when Jonathan started mentioning a new job during their phone calls, it had finally sunk in. "He called every now and then. Most weeks at first, but then only every month, and sometimes he forgot even that. He said life got too busy. When he missed our scheduled call for my thirteenth birthday, and I didn't even get a card, I stopped being upset and got angry. I didn't accept any of his calls after that, and I've only spoken to him once since then, when Mum forced me to because she thought it would help."

"Did it?" Gabby asked gently.

He snorted. "No. He apologized and made excuses. Same old shit. I lost my temper with him, and she didn't push me to contact him again."

His heart hurt at the memory. He no longer cared about having his father in his life, but he'd never stop being upset for the boy who'd waited hours for a call that never came.

"You deserved better," she said.

He raised his head, realizing he'd been staring down at the table. "Every kid deserves better than that." Perhaps he'd never been abused or gone hungry, but he'd still been in pain, and he never wanted to be the reason anyone else felt that way. "When I got older, people started telling me how much I looked like him. Some of my school teachers had taught him, and they commented on how similar we were in class. They said I was a chip off the old block. I hated it because I wanted nothing to do with him, but every time I looked in the mirror, I thought of him." It must have been hard for his mum too, although he hadn't realized that at the time. "When I had my first girlfriend and she broke up with me because she thought I'd been flirting with her friends, people said I was going to be a heartbreaker like Dad."

"Oh, Logan." She scooted the chair around the table and took his hand. He considered shaking her off, unsure how to deal with her sympathy, but in the end, he just gave it a gentle squeeze.

"Dad liked to surf too," he said. "I'm better at it than he ever was, but it was another thing people liked to comment on. Never mind the fact Mum is a surfer and I could just as easily have inherited the love of surfing from her."

He lost his train of thought. Where had he been going with this?

"The point is, all of these people in my life were telling me I was just like Dad, and somewhere along the way, I started to believe them. I thought that if I ever got serious with someone, I'd end up hurting them and abandoning them the way Dad did with us, so I decided it was easier to be single. The longer I stayed single and only had one-night stands with women who knew the score, the more it reinforced everything I was telling myself about my ability to commit to someone."

He sighed and raked his fingers through his hair.

"But then I met you, and even though I knew it was risky, I couldn't help being with you over and over again. I always thought that if there was a woman who'd tempt me to try a relationship, it was you. When you moved here, I hated seeing you date those other men. I wanted you all to myself, but I told myself it was best for you if I stayed away."

She huffed and opened her mouth, no doubt to say something snarky and one hundred percent correct, but he kept going. He needed to get this out.

"When you got pregnant, I realized we're bound together no matter what. My reasons for staying away are no longer valid, and honestly, I don't want them to be." He took her other hand and looked into her slightly narrowed eyes. "I want everything with you."

Gabby watched him steadily. He could see thoughts darting through her golden eyes but couldn't tell what they were or how she'd react to his confession.

"Please say something," he prompted. "I'm starting to sweat."

She barked out a laugh. He relaxed a tiny bit. If she were upset, she wouldn't have laughed like that, right?

She released his hands and propped hers beneath her chin. "You've given me a lot to process, so I'm going to go through it bit by bit."

"Okay." Did that sound bad? He thought it sounded bad.

"First off, fuck your dad. He sounds like a deadbeat who decided too late he'd rather not have kids and you guys paid for that. Secondly, people were wrong to compare you to him. That's a shitty thing to do. They were probably trying to make you feel closer to him because he wasn't around, but I doubt they stopped to think about the effect they were having on you. As for you failing someone the way he did, I don't know him, but I do know that you've been beside me every step of the way throughout this pregnancy. You've given me someone to lean on, even when I didn't expect it, and you've helped me in ways I didn't know I needed." She glanced across the table at her discarded bowl. "Do you know how happy I was to see you here, because I knew it meant I wouldn't have to do everything myself?"

He shrugged. "It's just dinner."

"No, it's a sign that you care. You were here for me when I needed you. You stood up for me with Henry, and you comforted me. All along, you've given me everything I need and asked for nothing in return."

"Well, it is my fault you're pregnant," he mumbled.

She shot him a look. "My point is that you're a good man. Do I think you're an idiot for spending years avoiding a relationship because of some misconception that you're version two-point-oh of your father? Maybe a little. Do I think it's high-handed of you to make decisions for people about what risks they're willing to take? Yeah. But deep down, you're kind and decent."

"You're really selling me," he said wryly.

She leaned closer and brushed her lips over his. He closed his eyes and breathed in her earthy scent. "What I'm saying is: yes, Logan. I want a relationship with you. We don't have to make any promises, other than that we'll both do the best thing for the babies at all times. Other than that, let's just take it day by day."

19

"Reporting for duty, sir."

Logan glanced up from wiping down the bar top and grinned at his new bartender, Peach, who stood on the other side of the bar with her blonde curls loose around her shoulders and a sultry smile on her lips. He scanned her, noting the tight pink tank top and small denim shorts that revealed tanned legs. If she was angling for tips, she was going about it right.

"Hi, Peach. Are you ready for your first shift?"

"Absolutely. Where do you want me?"

"Come around here." He kept his eyes determinedly off her as she sashayed closer. He recalled her being more businesslike in the interview, but he supposed people always were.

The door opened and Betty and Mavis walked in, scarves wrapped around their necks and matching gloves on their hands. They'd probably been knitted by their friend Nell, given the bright shades of pink and green. Nell had never met an improbable color combination she didn't love.

"Perfect," Logan said. "Why don't you serve these ladies while I prep the coffee machine?"

"On it." She flashed him another provocative smile and turned to face Betty and Mavis. He busied himself but listened while she greeted them and took their orders. She was friendly, polite, and poured just the right amount into their glasses. When they took their drinks to a table, she approached him with an eyebrow raised. "Did I pass the test, boss?"

He chuckled. "You did well."

Another customer entered and he hovered nearby while Peach got their drink. When she finished, she returned to him.

"We'll make sure someone is here with you for all your shifts this week," he told her. "After that, if you're feeling confident, we can trial you on your own, although we'll be available by phone if you need us."

"Who's us?" she asked. "You and Corinne?"

"That's right."

"Cool. I'll be fine though. I've worked in a lot of bars over the years."

He frowned. He would have thought she was too young for that to be true. "How old are you?"

"Twenty-three. But I have plenty of experience." She winked.

"Uh...okay. Great." He turned away. That had felt like flirting, but perhaps he'd imagined it.

A few hours later, he decided he definitely hadn't. All night, Peach had been bumping up against him, dropping innuendo with a seductive smile, and generally putting herself in his way. He gritted his teeth. He hadn't anticipated this when he hired a part-time bartender, and he wasn't sure what to do about it. If he called Corinne, she'd just tell him he was making a big deal out of nothing, but he wasn't okay with it.

He'd been dating Gabby exclusively for two weeks now,

and allowing a young blonde to get away with touching him flirtatiously screamed of disrespect toward his relationship. He couldn't let it slide. But he also didn't want to alienate Peach when she was obviously good at her job, and they needed her if he wanted to ease back on his hours to have more time for Gabby and the babies.

When the last patron had left, and Logan locked the door behind them, his gut knotted with uncomfortable emotion. It seemed like life was one emotional extreme after another these days, and he didn't enjoy it. He talked Peach through the closing-down routine and showed her where he'd printed out everything that needed doing at the end of the day on a checklist she could refer to each night.

"If I don't know, I can always come upstairs and ask you." She batted her long eyelashes. "You live up there all by yourself, right?"

He sighed. *Please don't screw this up.* "I'm not always there," he said. "Sometimes I stay at my girlfriend's place."

"Oh." She frowned. "I didn't know you were seeing someone."

"Yeah." Best not to give her any room for misinterpretation. "I am. It's new, but we're serious."

"Okay, then." She shrugged one shoulder. "I guess I'll call if I need you and you're not upstairs. See you tomorrow?"

"Yes." He held the side door open for her and waited until she got into her car and drove away. Haven Bay didn't have much crime, but he was still responsible for ensuring his employees were safe when they left.

He closed the door and trudged up the stairs to his apartment, wishing he was staying at Gabby's instead.

GABBY COULDN'T SLEEP. LOGAN WAS WORKING TONIGHT, SO HE was staying at his apartment because he'd said he didn't want to interfere with her rest. Unfortunately, there wasn't much to interfere with at the moment. She was fidgety. Couldn't stay still. She'd been tossing and turning for hours, and then she'd dozed off and been plunged into an erotic dream only to wake up again before it ended. Now she was horny, tired, and frustrated. She checked the time. One a.m. Would Logan be finished at The Den? If so, would he want to fall straight into bed, or would he be interested in helping her burn off some steam?

She moved back and forth between the options a few times before deciding just to message him and see.

Gabby: *Are you finished work?*

She didn't have to wait long for the reply.

Logan: *Yeah, just got upstairs.*

Gabby: *Do you want to come over?*

Logan: *It's late. You should be sleeping.*

Gabby: *Believe me, I know. But I'm sexually frustrated and can't.*

Logan: *Be there in ten.*

She grinned. "Yay for sex."

Mouse stirred on the pillow beside her head. Her eyes glowed as she blinked sleepily. She wasn't going to appreciate being kicked out.

"Sorry, Mousey, but I'm not having you watch our naked fun time."

Gabby switched the light on and waited a moment for her vision to adjust. She picked up Mouse, ignoring her mewl of complaint, and carried her into the hall. Thelma jumped off the bed and followed. Gabby beelined for the kitchen, where she got the pet treats from the pantry. The sound of crinkling bags brought the other animals running and she dispensed enough treats to keep them occupied, then hurried to the bathroom to spritz with perfume and make sure everything was clean and tidy before darting back to the bedroom.

She yanked off the ragged, overlarge t-shirt she'd been sleeping in and sifted through her clothes until she found a black silk nighty. She held it up to herself, wondering if it would still fit. The bottom was loose and flowy, but the lace bra might be too tight. She pulled it over her head and discovered, to her satisfaction, that it was tight in the best possible way. Her breasts spilled over the delicate lace neckline, making it look like she had a spectacular cleavage when she'd only ever had average-sized boobs.

"Oh, yeah." She grinned. "He's going to lose his mind."

Her gaze sunk lower, to the swell of her stomach, and she grimaced. So far, he hadn't seemed put off by her belly, and hopefully he'd be too distracted by her breasts to notice her chunkier midsection.

By the time the car crunched up the drive, she smelled good, looked as nice as she could, and was ready to feel Logan's hands on her body. She sent him a quick message.

Gabby: *Sneak in the back door. The animals are distracted with food out the front.*

Her insides fluttered happily as the car door slammed and she heard him come around the side of the house. She tried not to pay too much attention to those flutters. If she did, she might freak out, and she'd rather just enjoy being with her man. A floorboard in the hall creaked and then her door swung open and Logan slipped inside.

His sea-glass eyes twinkled in the dim light cast by the lamp on the nightstand as he looked her up and down. He whistled low. "Look at you."

Something bumped against the door and there was a scuffle.

"Be quiet," Gabby hissed. "They heard you."

His grin widened. "I don't care. They can't get in here, and they can't see us. You're all mine." He prowled toward her, his eyes darkening with intent. "Have you been lying here like this, unable to sleep because you need me?"

She shivered. God, his words were potent. "Yes."

Okay, so maybe not quite like this, but she'd let him think she'd gone to bed in a pretty nighty rather than a ratty t-shirt.

He knelt on the edge of the bed, curved a hand behind her neck, and took her mouth. The kiss was raw and powerful, with an edge. As if he needed the release as much as she did. He climbed over her and cupped her breasts, then held her gaze while he removed her nighty and lathed her nipples with his tongue. Heat rushed to her sex, and she squeezed her legs together to ease the sensation. She eased a finger in and stroked. Her flesh was already damp and slippery. It had been all evening. Her clit felt swollen and overly sensitive. When she brushed it, she gasped into his mouth. He swallowed the sound and demanded more with his tongue and fingers.

Gabby shuffled sideways on the bed, giving him space to lie beside her, never breaking the kiss. She fumbled with his zipper, mentally high-fiving herself when it gave way. She shoved at the waistband of his jeans, and he lifted his ass enough for her to get them halfway down his thighs. His briefs followed.

"I want to ride you," she said.

"Hell, yes."

He propped his hands behind his head and smirked, clearly expecting her to do all the work. She narrowed her eyes. He wouldn't look so relaxed in a few minutes. She'd set her mind to it. She straddled his hips and settled her slick sex over his erection. She paused astride him, gazing into his eyes. His pupils were blown, and he gripped her hips so tightly, she wondered if he'd leave marks.

Slowly, holding his gaze, she worked her hips, dragging herself along his length from root to tip. His fingers tightened even more on her hips and his jaw slackened. She repeated the motion. Back and forth, the friction eased by her arousal and his precum.

"Fuck, Gabby," he muttered. "Are you trying to torture me?"

A minx-like smile stole across her lips. "Am I succeeding?"

"No." He rolled his hips, encouraging her to go faster. "Torture would be if you put me inside you and let me feel how incredibly tight and hot you are."

"You mean like this?" She lifted herself off him for long enough to position his cock beneath her, then took it inside her bit by bit until she was fully seated on him. She felt completely filled by him, and she loved it.

"Just like that, baby," he agreed. "Pure torture."

She rose up and dropped down, crying out at the exquisite glide of his hard shaft against her channel. She brushed a finger over her clit and bit her lower lip. It was too much. Too good. Or at least, that's what she thought until Logan sat up and wrapped his arms around her lower back, getting even deeper and taking over control of their position. He thrust up into her, and she captured his lips mindlessly, her ability to tease long gone. He stole her breath, made it impossible for her to think, and the tender scrape of his facial hair up her neck as he kissed and nipped the sensitive skin filled her heart to bursting. When he kissed her so sweetly, it felt as if he cared. It felt like making love rather than having sex.

She allowed her head to drop back and he took her from below as thoroughly as if he'd pinned her to the mattress and taken full control. When he bumped her clit just the right way, pleasure tore through her and she clutched his shoulders as she rode out the most intense orgasm she'd ever experienced. He shouted her name and buried his face in her hair, his muscles clenching as he emptied inside her.

Gabby slid off him and collapsed onto the bed, grinning like an idiot. "I'll certainly be able to sleep now."

Logan chuckled, the sound husky. "Glad to help."

He grabbed his t-shirt and used it to clean them up, then lay beside her and patted his chest, indicating she should rest her head on it. She snuggled close and shut her eyes, wallowing in the afterglow. Soft lips brushed her forehead and she smiled, tenderness surging through her. The day she'd gotten pregnant with Logan, she really had gotten lucky. This was everything she wanted.

She kissed his chest and tucked herself under his chin. "How did the new bartender go?"

He stiffened. If she hadn't been sprawled along his length, she might not have noticed.

Her heart leaped to her throat. "Did something go wrong?"

"No, everything went smoothly." He sighed, his body still tense. "But she was a bit flirty."

Gabby's heart sank. Of course she was. Every woman wanted to flirt with Logan. He was too damn gorgeous. And how was she supposed to compete with a cute twenty-something who didn't have a pregnant belly or rollercoaster hormones?

"I told her before I left that I'm seeing someone," he said, when she didn't respond. "She seemed to take it in stride. Maybe she thought flirting would get her on the boss's good side."

"Maybe," she murmured. Or maybe the bartender just wanted him. Plenty of women did, and he'd always been happy to indulge them. Gabby needed to remember that. He wouldn't be here if not for the babies. He'd already made that clear. He might be trying a relationship on for size, but she couldn't count on it sticking. She wasn't anyone's first choice.

20

POKER NIGHT WAS A MUCH-NEEDED OPPORTUNITY FOR LOGAN to catch up with his friends. He had something to run by them, if only he could figure out how to say it. He was afraid Shane would lose his temper, but he also knew that raising it with the group was a way of announcing his intentions publicly, and maybe then Shane would realize he was serious and meant well.

He'd intended to get straight to the point as soon as they sat down, but then Shane started talking about how Faith and Charity seemed to be up to something, and he and Kyle had no idea what. Apparently, they'd caught the sisters having a hushed exchange and they'd been making secretive phone calls.

Logan wondered whether other men might think they were having affairs. Possibly. But Shane and Kyle knew better. He did too. Nobody who looked at those couples could deny the love between them. But the gossip did make it more difficult to raise his own situation. Forty minutes into the game, the conversation petered out and he took his chance.

"I want to move in with Gabby," he announced.

Seven pairs of eyes turned to him, with more than one set of eyebrows raised.

"Isn't it a bit early?" Sterling asked. "She must be, what, four or five months along?"

"I know it's early." He glanced at his cards in an attempt to ignore their scrutiny. "But we've been... involved... for the last few weeks."

"Involved?" Jack teased. "Do you mean sleeping together?"

Logan shot him a look. He didn't want anyone speaking of Gabby disrespectfully, especially when Shane was at the table and he was trying to make a good impression on him. "It's more than that." He huffed. "I know you're all going to mock me, and I don't blame you, but the truth is, I just want to be around her all the time."

"Aww." Kyle smiled goofily. "I never thought I'd hear you say something so sweet."

"Yeah, what happened to being the last happy bachelor in the bay?" Tione asked. "What happened to, 'I'll settle down when I'm dead'?"

He shrugged. "Things change."

Jack grinned. "You're an old dog. You really think you can learn new tricks?"

"I'm willing to try."

"But are you willing to give up all those pretty tourists?" Jack asked.

"Yeah. I am."

They laughed. Except for Shane—and Kyle, who looked uncomfortable.

Tione clapped him on the shoulder. "Best of luck, mate."

Logan's heart sank. They were just ribbing him, the way he'd done to them a hundred times before, but he couldn't help wondering if they were right. None of them believed he was capable of being a good, faithful partner to Gabby. Why should he?

He glanced at Shane. His friend was watching him thoughtfully.

"I mean it," Logan told him. "I care about her. On the nights when I stay here after work instead of going to see her, the place feels too quiet. I never expected it, but isn't that how the best things happen?"

"She's been hurt enough," Shane said. "If you think there's even the slightest chance you might hurt her too, just leave her alone. Things are complicated enough already."

Logan bit the inside of his lip to avoid spitting out a knee-jerk response. He didn't like Shane's lack of faith in him, but he understood it. His friends had had front row seats to his many, many short-term romances over the years.

"Getting back to the moving in thing," Michael said, providing a welcome change of topic. "Have you talked to Gabby about it?"

"Not yet," he admitted. He hadn't broached the subject for two reasons. First, he didn't want to push for something she might not be ready for. Second, he was afraid he'd do something to screw it up.

"Hmm." Michael sounded thoughtful. "I have to ask, would you consider moving in together so quickly if she wasn't carrying your babies?"

Logan sighed. He'd asked himself that same question a dozen times over. He probably wouldn't even be dating her if not for the babies, because he'd still be holding himself back from a relationship out of fear of repeating his dad's mistakes. If, by some miracle, they had started dating, he probably would wait longer before making such a big move. But at the end of the day, the point was moot, because she was pregnant and the babies were coming. They couldn't just pretend that wasn't true.

"None of you are any help," he complained, keeping his tone light so they'd know he was joking.

"Just do what feels right," Gray said, speaking for the first time. "If that's asking to move in, fine. But work on your own timeline, not anyone else's." He flushed and looked down. "At least, that's what the doctor tells me."

By "doctor," Logan assumed he meant his therapist. Whoever the message had come from, Gray had a point. There was no sense in worrying about what everyone else considered acceptable—including Shane. He just needed to do what was best for them.

On Sunday, Gabby returned from walking Thelma and Louise and saw Logan's car parked in front of the house. She knelt to put Louise down—the little dog's three legs had grown weary on their walk, so she'd carried her home—and let them both off their leashes. Thelma immediately bolted toward the goats, eager to sniff them. Gabby paused to make sure the dog didn't startle any of them before she continued inside.

Logan was in the nursery, sitting on one of the wooden chairs from the dining table and just taking it all in.

"Hey." His smile was slow and hot, and an answering warmth crept up her spine. "You ready to do some shopping?"

"Yeah, just give me two minutes to change this shirt and get a bag." She smiled back, pleased when he stood and pulled her into an embrace.

"Take your time," he said. "We're not in a hurry."

She drew away and winked. "You might regret saying that."

Today, they'd made plans to shop for baby stuff in Serenity Cove.

"I can handle it." Somehow, it made the innocent phrase sound dirty. As if they were talking about more than a morning spent exploring the boutiques.

Gabby went to her bedroom and swapped her t-shirt and hoodie for a purple blouse and a jacket, then checked through each room of the house to cuddle its occupants. Luna was the only one she couldn't find. The cat was probably out exploring the paddocks.

"Ready," she said, returning to the nursery. "Are you figuring out where everything will go?"

He laughed and flicked his hair off his face. "Hardly. I have to confess, I might not be much help today. I know the little guys will need beds, clothes, blankets, toys, and nappies, but that's about it. I'm sure there are a heap of other things I have no clue about."

"We'll figure it out," Gabby said. She'd finally gotten around to messaging Tristan, and he'd made recommendations for the basics they'd want to start with, and also suggested she revisit the shop where they'd met, which apparently belonged to his sister and stocked almost everything they'd need. Not that she'd told Logan that. The one time she'd mentioned Tristan, he clearly hadn't been happy. He seemed to view the other man as competition. She didn't know why. Sure, Tristan was handsome and nice, but she'd met him twice, whereas she'd been sneaking around with Logan and breaking her moral rules for him for years.

She held out a hand to Logan and he took it and stood. He kissed her cheek and gave her hand a quick squeeze. Her heart fluttered. He tapped her bum as she started out the door, and she glared at him over her shoulder but couldn't help laughing.

They took his car to Serenity Cove, which meant she was

able to doze during the drive. A couple of times, she opened her eyes and found him looking at her as if he had something to say, but whatever it was, he kept it to himself.

When they arrived, there was a parking space directly in front of The Stork. Logan pulled into it and Gabby clambered from the car and stretched, hoping to wake herself up. As had been the case last time, beautiful hand-carved cribs were displayed in the windows and the interior of the shop was an array of pastel hues.

"This looks expensive," Logan said.

She rolled her eyes. "Babies are expensive, but I want them to have everything they could possibly need, and we can afford it, so why not?" She'd always been good with money, so she had a healthy savings account and she was adding more to it each week in preparation for the twins' arrival.

"Come on, then." Logan's hand brushed hers, and she grabbed hold of it and led him in.

"Hello." A pretty brunette greeted them from behind the counter. Her sky-blue eyes flicked over Logan without lingering and settled on Gabby. Her smile grew. "You must be Gabrielle." She rounded the counter and approached them. "I'm Steph. Tristan told me you might drop by today. It's so nice to meet you."

Logan shot her a look and his hand tightened reflexively around hers. She had a feeling she'd be hearing about this later.

"Nice to meet you too." Gabby hadn't expected Tristan to have said anything, so she was caught off guard. Steph's eyes dropped to Gabby's tummy. "I heard you're having twins."

"That's right. This is their father, Logan."

Steph bobbed her head toward Logan in acknowledgment. "I just had my own little girl a few months ago. I'm home with her most days, but sometimes it's nice to go out for a while. Even just being back at work for a few hours helps me feel like a normal person rather than a sleep-deprived mess."

Gabby nodded. She obviously didn't have any experience with parenthood, but she could understand Steph's urge to have some time to herself. She personally loved her work and hoped she'd be able to return on a part-time basis once the babies had settled. Who knew how long that would take, though.

"So, what do you need?" Steph asked.

Gabby handed her the list she'd jotted on a piece of notepaper. "Let's start with this."

"Great." Steph sounded delighted.

Two hours later, they were loading bags and boxes into the back of Logan's car. They'd bought cribs, blankets, and the cutest little outfits—all in gender-neutral colors—and a few other essentials. Steph had remarked that they were getting organized early, and Gabby knew that was true, but she couldn't help it. She was excited, and based on the way Logan had exclaimed over the sweet little shoes and stuffed toys, he felt the same, although he'd forbidden her from mentioning it to his friends. She'd rolled her eyes. If he'd seen Shane when Diana was pregnant with Dylan, he wouldn't have been so self-conscious. Her brother had been crazy about babies from day one.

When they finished, Logan popped into a cafe across the road and returned with a double chocolate muffin for each of them.

She broke off a chunk and savored it. "This is good."

"Everything in there looked delicious," Logan said. "We'll have to come back sometime."

"I'd like that." Her insides warmed at the way he carelessly spoke as though it were a given they'd be sharing a future of dates and road trips. She loved the idea of it, but didn't want to take the possibility for granted considering his past and how significantly their lives were about to change.

As he pulled out of town, he cast her another of those looks that said he had something to say but wasn't sure how to do it.

"What is it?" she asked.

His lips pressed together. "Tristan, huh? I didn't know you guys had been in touch."

She sighed. "Only a couple of times. He's nice. He's been helping me figure out what we need for the babies."

He raised an eyebrow. "Couldn't Shane do that?"

"Well, yeah, but..." She didn't think her brother had come around to the idea of her and Logan being parents together yet, and she hadn't wanted to force him to face reality too soon. "It's a bit awkward, isn't it?"

He rubbed his temple. "Tell me about it."

"I guess it's our own fault though." They'd been the ones to fall into bed together. Nobody else could take the blame for that, and at this point, she wasn't sure she even regretted it. She was having the babies she'd always wanted, and she had a new relationship that—while she was reluctant to trust in it—was really damn good.

"Yeah. Has Tristan asked you out?"

"No." She glanced at him, noting the hard set of his jaw. "If he did, I'd tell him I have a boyfriend because guess what? I'm not interested."

"He's a doctor," Logan grumbled. "You could have a perfect little medical family."

She gritted her teeth. "It wouldn't be perfect, because I don't want him."

Okay, so maybe there had been a moment when she'd thought he was attractive, but she was too wrapped up in an aggravating bar owner to have eyes for anyone else.

They fell silent for a while.

Logan cleared his throat. "Um, Gabby?"

"What?"

"Do you think you'd be open to me moving in with you now, rather than later on in the pregnancy?"

Her breath caught and she raised her hand to the base of her throat, where her pulse pounded. "Seriously? You're just coming at me with that out of the blue?"

He glanced over and grinned sheepishly. "I meant to ask on the way to Serenity Cove, but you kept falling asleep."

She gaped. "So you decided now was the best time?" She didn't know what to think. She hadn't expected this, especially after his moment of jealousy. "This isn't just to 'lock me down' or something, is it?"

"No." His reply was automatic, and sounded like the truth. "I'm at your place most of the time anyway, and I hate the nights I spend at my apartment. Being near you makes me happy, but if it's too soon, I get it." He hesitated. "What do you think?" His voice was tight with nerves.

"I'm not sure," she said honestly. "On the pro side, you're not a blanket hog, and you can cook." Not to mention that he'd been good with her pregnancy and quick to give her whatever she needed. "But I don't want you to feel like there's a rush because of the pregnancy." If they hurried into something, there was a higher chance she'd end up getting burned by their relationship.

"Oh." He looked deflated. "Well, just think about it, okay?"

Guilt squirmed in her stomach. She could tell he was hurt she hadn't responded with an immediate "yes," and honestly, she didn't know why she hadn't. She was much happier when he was with her. She was just scared. But was fear a good reason not to do something that brought her joy?

"You know what?" She straightened. "Let's try it. You can bring over some of your things and we can take it day by day. If it goes well, we can move over more of your stuff."

Logan's face lit up, making him look years younger. "That sounds great." He raised her hand and kissed the back before refocusing on the road. "For the record, I understand why you're wary, but even if our relationship doesn't work out long-term, I will never ever hurt you the way your ex did."

A sense of rightness swept over Gabby as she studied his profile. From his shaggy hair to his casual clothes and sometimes brutal honesty, Logan was completely different from Henry, and she wanted so badly to believe him. Perhaps it was foolish to give him this chance, but he was offering everything she'd ever dreamed of, and the only way to claim it was to hand her heart into his keeping and hope for the best.

21

LOGAN STRUCK WHILE THE IRON WAS HOT. HE TURNED UP ON Gabby's doorstep the next morning with a suitcase in his hand and a car full of his personal surfing gear, the belongings that mattered to him most. She blinked at him sleepily in her pajamas while Mouse, the fluffy tortoiseshell cat, and Thomas, the ginger tom, twined around her legs.

"I'll make tea," he said, neatly stepping past her, setting his suitcase down, and heading for the kitchen.

She trailed behind him, pausing every few steps to cuddle another of her fur babies. "It's early."

"It's nearly ten."

"It is?" She groaned. "I suppose I'd better get dressed and feed Princess."

"I can take care of Princess," he told her. "You put your feet up."

He poured hot water over two teabags and carried both cups to the coffee table in the living room.

"This isn't you trying to be macho, is it?" she asked with narrow eyes. "You know, telling me to take it easy because I'm a pregnant woman?"

"Psh, no." Although it had crossed his mind that she

looked like she needed rest, not more stress. "I like Princess, and you've shown me what she needs, so just let me have my time with her. I'll be back soon."

Her eyes were still narrowed. "If you say so."

He went out back to the barn to visit Princess and slipped her an extra treat because she had the sweetest brown eyes and nudged his pocket as if she knew it was in there. He dropped by the goats on the way back to the house to put down more hay for them. Thelma trotted alongside him, her tail wagging as she happily sniffed fence posts and clumps of grass. When he returned inside, he noticed that Gabby's tea was still on the coffee table and the shower was running. She must have decided to wash up while the drink cooled.

Luna jumped onto the sofa and Logan scooped her into his arms and nuzzled her, ensuring she could always see him so he wouldn't startle her. Gabby had explained that she was deaf. Apparently, that was an especially common trait among white cats with blue eyes.

The shower shut off. Logan took his suitcase to the spare room, then sat on the sofa and sipped his tea while he listened to the faint sounds of Gabby moving around the bathroom. He hoped he'd be sleeping with her most nights, but it didn't pay to make assumptions.

Luna curled up on his thighs. His phone rang just as Gabby padded into the room, wearing leggings and a loose blouse. He glanced at the screen and, seeing it was his mum, answered.

"Hi, Mum."

"Morning, Logan. What are you up to today?"

"Just shifting a few things over to Gabby's place." Mostly himself.

"Do you have plans for lunch?" she asked.

"No." He glanced at Gabby, who'd tilted her head inquisitively. "I don't think so."

"Great. We're having a family gathering at our place. Be there at twelve. Lawrence is cooking."

"What's the occasion?" They often shared meals as a family, but usually, they'd organize something a few days ahead of time. This was different.

"I have no idea." She sounded a bit miffed about that. "Charity requested it."

"Huh. Weird." Charity wasn't typically the type to want to get the family together for anything.

"Shane and Faith will be there too. Why don't you bring Gabby?"

He grinned at the woman in question. "I'll do that."

"See you then."

"Bye, Mum." He hung up.

Gabby sat cross-legged on the seat closest to her tea. Luna immediately defected from his lap in favor of hers.

"What was that about?" she asked.

"We're invited to lunch at Mum's place," he told her. "The whole family is going to be there."

She frowned. "She wants me there too?"

"You're family now."

Her eyes softened. Maybe he should feel bad for making the most of her love of family, but he'd take whatever advantages he could get.

LOGAN AND GABBY ARRIVED AT THE BEACHSIDE HOUSE A FEW minutes before twelve. Shane's vehicle pulled up beside them and he, Faith, Dylan, and Hunter got out.

"Hey, guys," Gabby said.

"Hi, Aunt Gabby," Hunter said, opening his arms for

a hug. With a massive grin, she bent and embraced him. When she straightened, she bumped fists with Dylan.

Logan nodded to Shane and Faith in greeting, noting that Faith seemed to have made an extra effort to look good today. She always dressed like a fifties pin-up girl, but today her hair was carefully curled and styled and her makeup was more noticeable than usual. Shane, on the other hand, seemed to have missed the memo. He wore jeans and an old university t-shirt.

"Do you know what this is about?" Logan asked as they made their way inside. Hunter ran ahead to greet Corinne while Dylan hung back behind the adults.

"If I did, I couldn't tell you," Shane said. "And not just because I think my sister could do better." He glanced at Faith, who was chatting with Gabby, and his expression was so full of love that Logan had to look away. It felt intrusive to witness. He smiled to himself though, because despite Shane's barbed comment, his tone had been teasing, and that was progress.

He greeted his mum with a hug and Lawrence with a handshake. They gathered in the dining room, where Charity and Kyle were already waiting. He saw Charity and Faith exchange a glance. Kyle was beaming. Logan snorted. His brother had the world's worst poker face. Something was going on, and it seemed like both St. John sisters and their partners were in on it.

They sat. Another table had been connected to the end of the main table so that there would be enough space for them all. Faith and Charity stood and moved to the head of the table.

"Before we eat the delicious lunch that Lawrence has made for us, Charity and I have an announcement," Faith said, her voice loud in the crowded room.

Charity smiled, wide and joyous, so unlike her usual self that Logan couldn't help but stare. "We're pregnant!"

"What?" Corinne gasped. "Who's pregnant?"

Both sisters raised their hands.

"Charity and I," Faith said. "The babies are due in December and January."

"Oh, my God." Corinne looked stunned, then a smile slowly spread across her face until it was alight with happiness.

"Congratulations," Logan said, clapping Shane on the shoulder. "Number three."

"We can't wait." Shane's eyes crinkled at the corners. "The boys are excited to get a baby too. Hunter has already said he wants to teach them how to paint."

"That's so sweet," Gabby exclaimed. "He'll be a great brother. I'm so happy for you." She turned to Charity and Faith, who hadn't returned to their seats yet. "Did you plan for it to happen at the same time?"

"No," Charity said.

"Happy coincidence," Faith added.

Charity's grin spread. "Oh, and Kyle and I are getting married."

"Oh, my God," Corinne said again. "Another grandchild *and* a wedding?" She raised a trembling hand to her mouth, her eyes shining with unshed tears. "I'm the luckiest mum ever." She got up and hurried around to hug Kyle, and then Charity. "This is wonderful news." She drew back and Lawrence put an arm around her shoulder.

"They're going to be the most spoiled babies in the bay," Lawrence said.

Logan snorted. "You can say that again."

He was surprised to realize that he was genuinely excited for his little ones to have cousins to play with and grow up with. He'd always longed for a sibling or cousin his own age.

Gabby leaned closer. "This is epic," she murmured. "It's baby season in Haven Bay."

AFTER LUNCH, GABBY PULLED FAITH AND CHARITY ASIDE, into the conservatory overlooking the beach.

"I can't believe you're both pregnant," she exclaimed, excitement fizzing in her gut. Until now, she'd been experiencing pregnancy alone. Logan had been there to help, but he didn't know what it felt like. These women were both also going through their first pregnancy, and they could share and learn from each other. "How long have you known?"

"Only a couple of weeks," Charity said. "When I started wondering if I might be pregnant, I mentioned it to Faith and she realized she had some of the same symptoms so we both did tests. Sure enough, both were positive."

Gabby felt a momentary pang that neither of them had told her, but she put it aside. What was more important was that she now had someone to talk about pregnancy with.

"Have you had any morning sickness?" she asked.

"I have," Faith said. "Mostly in the afternoon. This lucky bitch has been so healthy she's practically glowing."

Charity laughed. "Hey, it's not my fault my constitution is stronger than yours."

The door eased open and Hunter wandered in, going straight to Faith's side and leaning against her leg.

"Hunter put in a request for a sister, didn't you, bud?" Faith said, ruffling his hair.

"Uh-huh." His expression grew adorably thoughtful. "I

want a sister called Bell, and I can teach her how to paint and use a hammer."

Gabby's heart squeezed at the cuteness overload. Hunter was quite the little artist, and he loved helping with home renovations. "Why Bell?"

Faith's lips quirked. "So she can match Tinkerbell."

"Oh." Gabby muffled a laugh as Hunter nodded. "It's better than Tink, I guess."

Charity sat on one of the cane chairs facing the window and Gabby followed suit. Faith bent and said something to Hunter, who sidled out again. Faith ignored the chairs and sat cross-legged on the floor, leaning back against the wall. Now that Gabby looked closely, she could see that Faith was pale. Maybe that was why she'd used more makeup than usual.

"So," Gabby said. "I have pregnant girlfriends—*and* you're going to be planning a wedding. This is so exciting. I want to hear everything."

They chatted for a while, until Shane stuck his head through the door and said the boys were getting restless, so they'd need to go soon.

"Quick," Faith said once he'd left again. "Before we head home, I have to know: is there going to be a big, romantic happily ever after for you and Logan?"

Gabby's insides turned over. She pressed a hand to her abdomen and sighed. "I don't know. I'd like there to be, and the fact he wanted to move in sooner than necessary is promising, right?"

"Absolutely," Faith agreed. "Logan never does anything he doesn't want to." She winked. "You must be proud to have conquered Haven Bay's most determined bachelor."

Gabby chewed the inside of her lip. *Determined bachelor.* Yeah, she knew that's what he'd always been, and still would be, if not for the pregnancy. He'd never have been willing to try a relationship with her if they hadn't already been bound together. It made her wonder how much of his doting and fussing over her was caused by a sense of duty rather than because it was what he really wanted. She supposed she'd never know for sure.

"He's not just that," she said. "And I'm not exactly sure where things between us are going. I'm adopting a 'wait and see' approach." She desperately hoped it would pay off.

Charity studied her intently. "I think that's smart. Don't leap without looking, but you also need to be careful not to lose him because you're always waiting for the other shoe to drop."

"I'll try not to." But her track record wasn't great, and neither was his.

22

LOGAN TOWELED HIS HAIR DRY, INHALING THE SCENT OF THE ocean that lingered in it, and pulled out a chair at the table in his apartment above The Den. He hadn't rented it out yet, despite the fact things were going well between him and Gabby, because it made a useful office space. Sure, he could have used the tiny room downstairs but, up here, he was able to avoid Peach, who seemed to have decided to view his relationship status as a challenge.

After that first night, he'd expected her to stop flirting and get on with the job but instead, she'd doubled down over the past three weeks. It made him damned uncomfortable. He'd taken to avoiding her rather than discussing the problem with Corinne because he feared his mum would think he'd encouraged her, and it might somehow get back to Gabby. He hated his past behavior for giving him a reputation as a player and intruding on what should be a completely wonderful present. Would he spend his whole life unable to escape his baggage?

He fired up his laptop and went to get a coffee while he waited for it to load. He still kept a few basics in the kitchen, although the pantry was mostly empty. He sat back down and opened his emails, scrolling through the new mail. An advertisement, a bill, a request from someone who wanted to book The Den for a birthday party, an email from one of his suppliers, another advertisement, and then he stopped. There, midway down the list, was an email from Jonathan Pride.

"Shit," he muttered. "Dad."

He immediately cursed himself for calling the bastard "Dad." He was a no-good absentee father. Not "Dad." That was a name reserved for someone who cared about their children. He hovered with a finger above the keypad, debating whether to open it or just delete and forget that he'd ever emailed his father in the first place.

Just do it.

He clicked the email and a dialogue box opened. He read quickly. Then re-read more slowly, anger heating his gut with each word.

Hi Logan,

It's been a while. I'm happy to hear from you. Hopefully the fact you're reaching out means you're ready to talk. I know your mum had years to poison you against me, and I'm glad you're ready to hear my side of the story.

Corinne and I were too young to be parents when she got pregnant with you. We weren't mature enough, and we had so much we wanted to do. Still, we gave it our best shot. The first few years had passed before I realized it. It's amazing how time flies when you have a new baby. We got along fine, for the most part, but changed in ways that meant we didn't suit each other anymore.

We should have separated then, but instead, we tried to stick it out and ended up pregnant with Kyle. As with you, the first couple of years after his birth flashed by, until one day I woke up and realized that neither your mum nor I were happy and if I didn't act, the life I'd wanted would slip by. It's scary when you see how easy it would be for your entire life to pass without you ever achieving your dreams.

When I moved out, we agreed to a custody arrangement, but your mum found excuses to keep you with her instead of sending you to me. Eventually, I got the opportunity to travel to Hawaii, which had always been a dream of mine. I went because I hardly saw you and your brother anyway, so I didn't think you'd miss me. But then I fell in love and how was I supposed to leave after that?

I tried to keep in touch, but I moved again and the time zones made it difficult. I'm sure your mother made the most of that to cast me in a bad light.

Anyway, when you stopped calling me and answering my calls, I assumed Corinne finally got what she wanted and that you were done with me. So that's the whole story. Corinne and I should never have been together. Separating was the right thing to do, and I know now that following my dreams and my heart was too. I hope you have managed to do the same in your life.

I'd love to hear more from you. I followed your professional surfing career closely.

Talk again soon,
Dad.

He stared at the email in a haze of fury.

What. The. Hell.

How dare he talk about Corinne like that? She had gone to pains to never shit-talk Jonathan, and God knew she'd had plenty of reason to. She'd been sensitive to Logan and Kyle's feelings and would never imply anything negative about their dad or suggest that because of them she'd lost some of the best years of her life. She was caring, warm, and more generous than Jonathan deserved.

Not to mention the fact he'd tried to blame her for all the times he'd bailed on them. Logan had been a kid, but he was old enough to remember the facts. Corinne was the one who'd had to explain to two disappointed boys why Daddy once again wouldn't be spending the weekend with them.

Logan shook his head. His jaw ached and he realized he'd been clenching his teeth. Then there was that part about following his dreams and his heart. Were his sons not part of his dream, or embedded in his heart? Did he have no fucking idea how much of an asshole this email made him sound like?

And what about that parting remark? Logan knew for a fact that he'd entered competitions near where his dad was living a few times, but the man had never shown his face. Either he was lying, or he knew that Logan would have told him to go to hell if he'd shown up.

"Asshole."

He shoved the chair back, wincing at the squeal of the legs against the floor. He paced the length of the room, went to the window, and took deep breaths, trying to calm himself.

It didn't work.

"Fuck." He kicked the couch.

He was related to that asshole? Shared a name with him? Maybe even a blood type?

To hell with that. He wasn't anything like Jonathan Pride. His father was a selfish flake who'd never loved his sons the way he should have. Perhaps they shared DNA, but Logan had been raised by Corinne, and he was more like her than he'd ever been like his father, no matter who said anything to the contrary.

Corinne had been everything they could possibly want

in a mother, and he was going to do her proud when it came time to raise his own babies. Screw Jonathan, and screw Logan for having been stupid enough to hold himself back because of a self-centered piece of shit.

GABBY STOPPED BY THE DEN AFTER SHE'D FINISHED AT WORK to pick up Logan. She'd dropped him off at the beach that morning for the last of his classes for the season. He'd told her he intended to surf on his own for a while afterward, before catching up on work.

She entered through the front, hoping to see Corinne, but instead, a stunning young blonde in the world's tightest tank top was behind the bar. This must be Peach. Their eyes locked. Peach's lips were bright pink, her hair streaked with lighter shades so that it looked sun-bleached, and her eyes appeared bright against her smokey eyelids and dark mascara.

Gabby faltered, struck by a bolt of insecurity. This woman was exactly the type Logan had hooked up with in the past. She knew because they'd discussed their histories, figuring it was best to get that out in the open. At the time, she'd thought they were being mature, but now she wondered if that knowledge had fed her insecurities.

Logan spent time around Peach, and he'd admitted that she flirted with him. Gabby hadn't liked that, but nor had she been too concerned by it. She'd figured that the fact he was being open with her about it meant Peach wasn't a threat. But now she was faced with the fact that the bartender was younger, blonder, and decidedly more svelte than herself. Heck, in this outfit, Gabby didn't even look pregnant, just fat. How could she ever hope to keep his attention?

"Hi." Peach's eyes flicked up the length of her body as if taking an inventory, but she greeted Gabby with a smile. "Can I get you anything?"

Gabby frowned. "No, I'm just—"

At that moment, the staff only door opened and Logan strode through. Peach immediately tucked her hair behind her ear and propped one hip against the bar, emphasizing her curves. Gabby's eyes narrowed.

"Hey, boss," Peach said. "Looking good today."

Gabby's gaze skimmed Logan. He did look good. His toned chest and shoulders were lovingly covered by a soft long-sleeved shirt, and denim cupped his lower half in all the right places. She glanced back at Peach, who was checking out Gabby's man, and her stomach hardened. She could see the other woman's interest.

"Thanks." Logan's smile didn't reach his eyes, which partially eased her mind. When he spotted Gabby, his smile widened, becoming more genuine. Her stomach relaxed. She should have known better than to doubt him. "Hey, beautiful."

He reached her in a few steps and kissed her on the mouth. She couldn't resist wrapping her arms around him and shooting Peach a look over his shoulder. He was hers. End of story.

"Let's go home," she said, taking his hand. She led him out to the car and they got in. He didn't say anything, which unsettled her. Usually, he loved to regale her with stories from his classes. By the time they were halfway to her place and he still hadn't broken the silence, she knew something must be wrong. "What's the matter?"

He jerked as if she'd startled him. "My dad emailed."

"Really?" She'd been under the impression he hadn't had contact with his father in years. "Does he email often?"

"This is the first time we've been in contact since I

stopped taking his calls when I was in high school. I, uh, emailed him after I found out we were pregnant. I wanted an explanation for why he left."

Her heart softened in understanding. Given his hang-ups, he'd probably thought that hearing the truth from his dad would help him be a better parent himself.

"What did he say?" She wasn't sure she wanted to know.

Logan scoffed dismissively. "He tried to blame Mum for keeping us apart. He said he'd just followed his heart and lived his dreams."

Ouch. Poor Logan. It must have been hard to hear that and know that his own father's dreams hadn't included him, and that his heart had led him away from his sons.

"What an asshole," she said. "I hope you didn't let him get to you."

He sighed. "I'm trying not to, but he's my dad. It's kind of hard to hear that and not take it personally."

"I get it." She wished she could track down Jonathan Pride and slap his stupid face. "His decision has nothing to do with you, though. He's just a selfish, thoughtless little man who's convinced himself he's the victim."

"Not so little," Logan said. "I get my height from him."

"Oh, shush. As far as I'm concerned, you get everything from Corinne."

To her surprise, his expression warmed. He gazed at her with tenderness, and her insides fluttered. "That's pretty much what I decided for myself twenty minutes ago."

She winked. "Great minds think alike." She hesitated, then added, "Are you going to email him back?"

Logan shook his head. "Nah. I thought about it, but it would only make me angry, and I want to get past that. I found out what I needed to, and it's time to move on. I can't let him hold me back forever."

Gabby pulled up the drive and parked outside their

house, then reached across and took his hand. "I think that's a smart decision."

She was amazed by how much more there was to Logan than she used to believe. Sure, he was fun, but he was also unexpectedly deep, and he felt things intensely. She admired that.

He leaned over and kissed her cheek. "Thank you," he murmured. "I won't let you down. I promise."

She wanted to believe him, but sometimes, even people with good intentions fell short. He seemed to expect a response. She couldn't give him the one he wanted so she settled for kissing him.

Please prove my doubts wrong.

23

LOGAN ARRIVED AT HIS APARTMENT AN HOUR BEFORE POKER night began so he could start the heater and ensure it wasn't too cold for his guests. He'd been debating whether to suggest they switch venues, but for now, the apartment was fine. When he rented it out, they'd need to organize something else.

"Good evening," Sterling said as he and Tione entered together.

"Hey. Take a seat. I'll be over in a moment," Logan called.

He heard the men pull chairs out, and then the sound of the door opening and closing again as he carried a platter of food to the table.

"What's this?" Jack—who must have just arrived—asked with a raised eyebrow as he scanned the assortment of fruit and vegetable sticks. "Isn't Shane supposed to be the clean-eating one? You're the chips and dip guy."

Logan shrugged, and tried to dismiss a prickle of unease. "If I'm going to raise a healthy baby, I have to up my game."

"And we're your test subjects?" Jack demanded.

"Who better?"

The door opened again and Kyle's smiling face appeared, with Gray's more serious one following behind.

"You're not the only one who needs to polish his daddy skills," Tione said. "Congratulations, Kyle." He stood and clapped Kyle on the shoulder.

Kyle turned pink. "Thanks. That reminds me." He turned to Logan. "Shane won't be here tonight because Faith isn't well."

Logan felt a twinge of sympathy. He'd seen how sick Gabby had been in the early days of pregnancy, and he wouldn't wish that on anyone. "No worries."

"No Michael, either," Jack added. "Apparently Wes is visiting this weekend, so he wanted to be home."

"He could have brought Wes with him," Tione said.

"No." Logan sat beside Jack. "He doesn't get to see Izzy very often, so he probably wanted to make the most of his time with her."

Wesley was Michael's brother and the father of his step-daughter. It was a weird situation, but they'd all gotten used to it. He was also, incidentally, the prime minister of the country.

"So, this is all of us?" Logan asked.

"I think so," Kyle said.

"Just deal and if anyone comes late, they can join then," Gray drawled. Despite having lived in New Zealand for years, he still spoke with a clear American accent. Of course, the fact he'd hardly interacted with anyone for the first five years he'd lived in the area probably contributed to that.

Logan passed the cards to Jack, who shuffled and dealt.

"So," Tione said as they checked their cards. "We're all partnered up." He glanced at Logan. "How does it feel to be off the market? Are you chomping at the bit to get back out on the playing field? It must be hard to be in a relationship after so many years without commitment."

They all looked at him expectantly. Kyle's expression was merely curious. The others were filled with humor, as if they fully expected him to be struggling. Did no one have faith in him?

If not, maybe there's a reason for that...

"It's good," he said firmly. "Really good. If you'd asked me a year ago, I'd have said you were crazy, but I'm happy to be taken. Gabby is everything I never thought I'd have."

"Or want." Jack grinned.

"Hey." Logan scowled at him. "I'm happy, okay? I know this is probably hilarious to you guys, but I'd really appreciate a bit more support."

Jack looked chastened. "Sorry, man. You're right. I shouldn't be a dick about it. For what it's worth, I'm glad it's worked out for you."

"We all are," Kyle said quickly.

Tione cleared his throat. "Yeah. We'll try not to give you such a hard time."

"I appreciate that." He doubted himself enough without them piling on.

"It's the start of a new era," Sterling said with a smile. "Why don't we toast?"

Jack raised his can of beer. "To happy relationships."

Sterling lifted his whiskey glass. "To happy relationships."

They all raised their drinks. Logan grinned, relief untangling the tension that had been growing within him. He'd always laughed at how mushy his friends got over their women, but he was one of them now, and it felt better than he ever could have guessed. He'd always thought that settling down would feel like the end of something, but it didn't. It felt like the beginning.

Hours later, when he got into bed with Gabby and wrapped himself around her, he breathed in her familiar scent and allowed it to welcome him home. He held her close, kissing the top of her head when she snuggled into him and murmured something sleepily. His heart was so full, he felt like it might burst. Perhaps he wasn't out hooking up with gorgeous tourists every other weekend, but he had something so much better.

Now don't screw it up.

GABBY SIPPED HER LEMON AND GINGER TEA AND PETTED Thomas, who'd curled on her lap. Karen sat on the arm of the sofa watching them as if deciding whether to grace them with her presence. Gabby was considering making breakfast when Logan sauntered in, his pajama pants slung low on his hips and his lean torso on delicious display. He stopped at the end of the sofa and gazed down, a smile flirting with the corners of his lips.

"Do you come here often?" he asked, hitching up one of his eyebrows suggestively.

Gabby smothered a laugh. "Was that supposed to be a pickup line?"

He winked. "Do I need one?"

Honestly, no.

She let her focus wander down his chest, past his tight pecs, over his grooved abdomen, and to the V that arrowed into his pants. She bit her lip. The annoying ass knew he was hot as hell.

"Are you just gonna look at me?" he asked mischievously.

She smirked. "I'm pregnant. I think that means you're supposed to do all the work."

To her surprise, he fished Thomas out of her lap and sat him beside Karen, then he slid his arms beneath her and scooped her off the sofa. She gasped in shock and clutched his shoulders.

"What are you doing?" she demanded.

"The work," he teased. "I would've thought that was obvious."

"But I'm too heavy."

He carried her to the bedroom. "Apparently not."

He set her gently on the bedspread and climbed over her, staring down at her with something unusually soft in his eyes. They'd been tender with each other before, but this felt deeper. Her pulse leaped. Could it possibly be love she saw looking back at her? Or was she projecting her own feelings onto him? Because she could no longer deny she cared for him deeply.

Her breath hitched and she rose up to kiss him. He kissed her back as though they had all the time in the world. There was no rush or urgency. Instead, he made love to her with his mouth, and her foolish heart squeezed and grew and yearned to give itself to him.

When they finally drew apart, her mind was pleasurably hazy. He removed her clothing piece by piece, kissing and caressing the skin revealed. He peppered the curve of her belly with kisses and rubbed his cheek against the smooth skin, setting off sparks in nerve endings she didn't even know she had. He shifted lower, using his tongue and lips to coax her senses to life until her entire body was humming with desire. She threaded her fingers through his hair and arched her hips, begging for more, now, please. She'd never been with a man who dedicated so much attention to her enjoyment and she knew, in her heart, that it wasn't only because of their chemistry. She meant something to him, and he was telling her so in the best way he knew how.

He entered her, holding her gaze, his expression almost fierce.

I love you.

She didn't say the words, but each time he sank into her, they echoed through her mind.

I love you.

I love you.

I love you.

Emotion swelled within her. Tears sprang to her eyes and she closed them so he wouldn't be able to see. She wasn't sure if he was ready for that. She wasn't sure whether she wanted to be that vulnerable either.

"Open," he grunted as the heat within her expanded like a balloon full of air, on the verge of popping.

She opened her eyes as she crested a wave of pleasure. His azure stare enthralled her and she held it as she fell apart, taking him with her. He mashed his lips to hers as he jerked within her. Slowly, the kiss gentled, and then his lips ghosted over her eyebrows, her nose, and her cheeks. Her heart tried to force its way out of her chest to go to him. She took a few slow breaths to calm herself.

"You are everything," he murmured, smoothing her hair off her forehead. "Everything."

Her lips parted, the words "I love you" in the back of her throat. In a millisecond, all of his possible responses flashed through her mind.

She closed her mouth. She wasn't that brave yet.

24

LOGAN PICKED UP A BOTTLE OF BAILEYS AND CHECKED HOW full it was, then set it back on the shelf. It was a Saturday afternoon, and he wanted to make sure he left the bar in a good state for Corinne and Peach to begin the evening shift. The Jack Daniels bottle was low so he went out the back to the storeroom to get another. He searched the shelves, plucked it down, and turned, only to nearly bowl into Peach, who'd entered silently and closed the door behind herself.

"Whoa." He juggled the bottle and managed to catch it before it hit the floor. He straightened and found her even closer than he'd thought she was. "What are you doing?"

She gave a sly smile and fluttered her eyelashes. "Helping."

He held the Jack Daniels up between them. "I've got it under control."

"Do you?" She nudged the bottle out of the way and trailed a finger down his chest. "You know, there's no one out there and we've got plenty of time before it gets busier."

"So?" He backed away.

She prowled forward. "So, why don't we have some fun?"

Her pink lips formed a pout. "I know you've felt the sparks between us. I catch you looking at me all the time."

"In alarm," he said. "Because you keep flirting with me even though I've told you I have a girlfriend."

Her sly smile deepened and she tried to cup his face but he swatted her hand away. A frown flitted across her expression but vanished as quickly as it had come.

"She doesn't have to know. It could be just our secret." She smirked. "It's not like I want a relationship with you, but I heard you know how to show a girl a good time. Think of it as sowing the last of your wild oats."

He stared at her, stunned into silence. It took a moment for him to gather his thoughts. "It's not about whether she knows or not. I'm with her, which means nothing is going to happen between us. And where the hell did you hear that anyway?"

She cocked her head. "Two of my friends vacationed here. They both said you were great in bed."

Oh, God. He hung his head. It was totally possible he'd taken a pair of friends to bed. Maybe even at the same time. Was his past constantly going to return to kick him in the ass?

"When I told them I'd gotten a job with you, they said I should take you for a test ride. That it'd be an easy, fun fling because you never turn anyone down." Her stare hardened. "But then you brushed me off."

"I'm *dating* Gabrielle," he pointed out. "I live with her. I don't know who your friends are, but I wasn't dating anyone when I slept with them." Although, fuck, he wished he hadn't been with them because then he could have avoided this shitstorm.

"What does it even matter?" Peach asked. "You got her pregnant accidentally, and you're trying to be a good guy and make the best of it, but I'm sure she expects you to slip up sometimes. I promise I'm even better than my friends."

"No." He lowered his voice, his tone becoming dangerous. "I care for Gabby. I'm not cheating on her, and if you do or say anything like this ever again, I'll have to let you go. Do you understand?"

Her lips pressed into a line. "I understand that you used to be willing to fuck any woman who showed you interest, but apparently, I'm not good enough. Well, fuck you, asshole." She raised her nose in the air then opened the door and stalked out.

Logan exhaled, relieved to have some distance between them. He waited for a few seconds before leaving the storeroom, then came up short when he saw Corinne standing at the foot of the stairs. How long had she been there? Had she been able to hear their conversation? And had she seen Peach leave?

Of course, there could be a completely innocent explanation for them both being in the small storeroom at once, with the door closed, but judging by the look in her eyes, that wasn't where her mind had gone.

"Mum—"

She shook her head. "There are customers."

She swept past him, and out into the pub. He swore. Damn it. Nothing was going according to plan today. He followed and tried to pull her aside to talk, but her jaw tightened.

"Later," she snapped.

His stomach sank. How could his own mother think the worst of him? Had nothing he'd done lately to put the past behind him mattered at all?

He glanced at the clock. His shift had officially ended. He needed to clear his mind.

He went to the beach and changed into one of his rental

wet suits, then took a board and hit the waves. There was nothing like the cold spray of the ocean to help him get perspective.

———

GABBY RESTED HER HEAD AGAINST THE EDGE OF THE BATHTUB and wondered how long she'd be able to hold out against the wrath of her hungry stomach. She should have thought to grab a snack before she ran the bath, but she'd been too distracted by her aching back. Now, the hot water had eased the ache, and her head was swimming in a woozy state between sleep and wakefulness, but her stomach had been growling for the past half hour.

She closed her eyes and focused on the way the water cocooned her limbs. So good. Her tummy rumbled and clenched, reminding her of how empty it was. She sighed. She'd just have to get food and return to the bath. There was no rule saying she couldn't lounge in the water while she ate. She'd been expecting Logan back any time now, so she'd been putting off eating because she figured he'd be hungry when he finished his shift and they could have something together.

Another growl. Time to stop waiting.

She slung one leg over the side of the bath. She felt so dozy, her muscles so languid, that she knew standing wouldn't be easy. She'd do it on the count of three.

One.

Two.

She pushed herself upright, one leg inside the tub and one leg out. Her vision flickered at the corners. Her pulse thumped in her ears. Black spots danced in front of her eyes and then she was falling. Her knee caught the edge of the tub and her head thwacked into the other edge.

Everything went dark.

An image popped into her mind. She was riding Princess through the fields. She touched her belly, confused. She hadn't been riding for the past month because of the pregnancy. But her abdomen was flat. Princess ran faster and faster, and no matter what Gabby did, she wouldn't stop. Gabby opened her mouth to speak but couldn't. She couldn't even breathe. She clutched her throat and tried to scream, but there was only silence.

She woke with a rush, jolting into a seated position. Water streamed down her face and she gasped for breath, her lungs straining to drag in air. Pain flared on the side of her head. She blinked, struggling to make sense of what had happened. Had she fainted?

She coughed, clearing her throat, and forced herself to inhale slowly and deeply. Her head spun as she reached shakily for the plug and pulled it out. The water swirling around the drain was tinged pink. She cocked her head, gasping as it throbbed again. She raised her hand to the area that hurt, and flinched when she touched it. Her hand came away coated in red.

Shit. She was bleeding.

She ran her hand over the cut. The side of her head was already swelling, but with how wet her hair was and the fact the water had diluted her blood, it was impossible to tell how bad it was. Was it just a nick, or a serious head trauma?

She needed help.

She eyed the edge of the bath but didn't try to stand again. If she fell, a second blow to the head might trigger a nasty concussion—assuming she wasn't already concussed. She scanned her surroundings and spotted her cell phone on the vanity. She reached for it, but it was too far away.

With difficulty, she scrambled onto her knees, clutching the side of the bath so she wouldn't slip. This time, she was able to get a hold of the phone with the tips of her fingers. She stared at the screen, trying to remember how to make a call. Her hands were wet, and water and blood dripped onto the phone. She reached over the edge for a second time and grabbed the bathmat, using it to dry her hands and the screen, then she found Logan's number and called. The phone rang and rang and no one picked up.

She blinked, and when she opened her eyes again, she was resting against the end of the tub, the phone slack in her hand. She must have passed out. Her stomach tightened. That wasn't a good sign.

This time, she found Shane's number in her recent contacts. Her finger missed the 'Call' button twice before she managed to hit it.

He answered on the third ring. "Hello."

"Hi." Her thoughts were muddled. What did she need him for? "Um, I've hit my head. I think I might have fainted. Could you come and get me? I probably need to visit a doctor."

Shane swore. Under different circumstances, the uncharacteristic cursing might have made her smile.

"Where are you?" he asked.

"In the bathtub." Her eyelids were heavy. They pulled down, but she resisted. If she closed them, she might sleep. "I'm afraid to get out in case I faint a second time."

"Okay. I'm coming for you." Sounds of movement came down the line, then muffled voices. "I'm going to pass you on to Faith," Shane said. "She'll keep talking to you until I get there. Don't hang up, okay?"

"Okay. Thank you." More background noise.

Gabby forced herself to sit upright. She folded the face cloth and pressed it to the side of her head, hissing as pain roared through her and her vision doubled.

"Hey, sweetie." Faith's voice filled her ears. "I hear you've hurt yourself. What happened?"

"Not sure." She tried to recall exactly what had happened before she fell. "Stood up too fast maybe."

"Such a dangerous activity," Faith teased. "Standing up while pregnant should be classified as an extreme sport."

Gabby was too tired to laugh. Her mind wandered. She longed to put the phone down and close her eyes. To rest. But she'd told Shane she'd keep talking, and she was going to do it.

"How are you feeling?" The words came out slow and thick.

"Better than you." Faith sounded worried. "I haven't thrown up yet today, which is a miracle."

"Good." Just saying that one thing took so much effort.

"Where's Logan?" Faith asked.

"Don't know." She pressed her lips together, battling to focus. "His shift finished an hour ago."

"He might still be at The Den," Faith said. "When I get off the phone with you, I'll call Corinne to check."

"Thanks." Seeing Logan would be really nice. She'd love for him to wrap her in his arms and assure her that everything was going to be all right. "I had a dream..."

"What did you dream, sweetie?"

"I was riding Princess. Wasn't pregnant. No belly." Her throat burned with emotion, on top of feeling raw from coughing up water. "Do you think the babies are okay?"

"I'm sure they are." Faith's voice was taut with emotion but uncharacteristically quiet. "You did well. You called for help, and now you're staying on the line with me even though I know it's hard."

Tears prickled in Gabby's eyes. "But what if that dream means I've lost them?"

"It doesn't mean anything," Faith said fiercely. "Your

babies are perfect. They're healthy and strong, and you're going to be a kickass mum."

"I hope so." She fell silent, unsure what else to say.

"Are you still there?" Faith sounded worried.

"Yes."

"Stay with me, sweetie. Okay?"

"Uh-huh. I'm here."

The water began to chill on Gabby's body, and she considered dropping the cloth from her head to dry herself but decided it was more important to slow the bleeding than to be warm.

Tires crunched over gravel outside, and then footfalls thundered up the front steps.

"I think he's here," she told Faith.

"Stay on with me until he's in the room with you," she insisted.

Gabby sighed. "You're bossy."

"Only with the people I love."

The bathroom door opened and Shane filled the frame. Gabby realized too late that she was now naked in front of her brother. He grabbed the towel from the rail and draped it over her, then knelt and looked her in the eyes.

"You're okay," he said. "Give me the phone."

She passed him the phone. He said a few words to Faith then hung up.

"Let me wrap this around you." He helped get the towel around her and then reached for the hand holding the cloth to her head. "I'm going to have a look. I'll be gentle, I promise."

She allowed him to remove the cloth. Nausea rolled through her when he touched her scalp, and she squeezed her eyes shut.

"The bleeding has mostly stopped," he said. "I don't think we need to worry too much. Head wounds always bleed a lot." He sat back on his heels and flashed the phone in her face. "I'm more worried about your pupils being slow to respond to changes in light."

"Since when did you become a doctor?" She tried to joke, but it fell on deaf ears.

"Teachers have to be certified in first aid," he said. "Come on. I'm going to help you out of the tub, and then we'll get you dry, put some clothes on, and take you to the hospital."

She didn't protest. It felt nice to have him take charge. He slid his arm around her shoulders and took the bulk of her weight as he bolstered her up. When she was upright, she held tightly to him as she got out of the bath. She stood meekly while he toweled her dry and stepped into the sweatpants he brought. She insisted on putting on her own bra, thank God, but allowed him to assist her in getting a t-shirt over her head.

When they were in his car and on their way to the hospital, she looked around for her phone.

"Need to call Logan."

"Faith just tried," Shane said. "He's not picking up. She's watching the boys, but Kyle has said he'll track him down."

"Okay." Gabby closed her eyes again. Her heart felt heavy. She wanted Logan with her. Where was he?

25

LOGAN WAS FLYING ALONG THE CREST OF A WAVE WHEN HE spotted a figure standing on the beach. He narrowed his eyes as he hurtled closer and realized it was Kyle. He leaped off the board before it hit the sand and hauled it out of the water. He'd have liked to have a bit more time to himself after the altercation with Peach, followed by his mum blowing him off, but it seemed like Corinne had sent Kyle to check on him.

"Hey, man," he said, striding up the beach toward his brother. As he drew nearer, he noticed brackets of strain around Kyle's mouth and a groove between his eyebrows. "Everything okay?"

"No." Kyle's one-word answer hit him like a blow.

He propped the surfboard up and leaned against it. "What's wrong?"

"Gabby fainted and hit her head on the side of the bathtub. It sounds like she knocked herself out. Shane took her to the hospital. Mum is on her way there too. She closed the bar." His lips pinched. "Shane says Gabby has been asking for you, but they haven't been able to get in touch."

"Fuck." Fear oozed through him, icy cold. "Is she all right?"

"She's in and out of consciousness." Kyle reached for the surfboard and Logan let him take it. He turned and started up the beach. Logan hurried alongside. "Shane thinks she might be concussed, but I haven't heard what the doctors have said yet."

The biting cold spread outward to his limbs. His heart felt frozen solid.

"The babies?"

Kyle glanced over, his expression creased with sympathy. "I don't know."

"We need to get there." Logan picked up the pace, rushing to his trailer, where he stashed the surfboard and stripped out of the wet suit without caring who might see. He tugged on his dry clothes and followed Kyle to his car. He felt sick. Gabby had hurt herself and he hadn't been there to help. She'd asked for him, and he'd been out chasing his bliss on the waves. She'd needed him, and he'd failed her because he'd been selfish.

God, he was no better than his dad.

He called her phone as Kyle drove, but it was Shane who answered.

"She's awake and her injuries seem minor so far, except for the possible concussion," he said without Logan's prompting. "The doctor is heading toward us now though, so I need to hang up. We'll see you soon."

"Thanks." At least Shane hadn't reamed him for not being there. He'd have deserved it.

The drive seemed to take forever. Kyle must have sensed his desire for silence because he didn't speak or play any music. Self-recriminations flew through Logan's mind. If he'd gone straight home from work, this might not have happened. If he hadn't felt the need to ride the waves, he could have been there for Gabby when it happened. Who knew how long she'd been alone and in need of help before she'd managed to call Shane? What if she'd fallen unconscious and drowned in the tub? He'd never have been able to live with himself.

You let her down. You're just like Jonathan.

Kyle pulled up outside the small hospital in Te Awa Tui and Logan threw the car door open and raced to the entrance. He asked for directions from the woman at the reception desk and took the stairs two at a time. When he reached the right corridor, he scanned the door numbers. He'd only gone a few steps when a familiar figure appeared in front of him. Cool blue eyes, wavy brown hair, clad in scrubs.

"You're here," Tristan said. "Good."

"I came as soon as I heard. Where is she?" He needed to see her. Until her beautiful face was in front of him again, he wouldn't be able to let go of the sense that something very bad had happened.

Tristan's pale eyes skimmed down Logan in a way that made him feel as though he'd been judged and found wanting. He couldn't blame the guy. Tristan was a doctor. If he and Gabby had been together and this had happened, he'd no doubt have been able to help her. He'd probably have been home with her, rather than trying to outrun his emotions, so they could have gotten here faster.

Don't waste time feeling sorry for yourself. Gabby needs you.

"Where?" Logan demanded.

"I just checked on her," Tristan said. "It seems like nothing is seriously wrong, but you'll want to speak to her personal doctor to confirm that." He pointed at a door a little further along the corridor. "She's in there."

"Thank you." He beelined toward the door without saying goodbye. He grabbed the handle and froze, suddenly afraid of what he might find on the other side. He opened the door slowly, revealing a small, private room with a single bed in the center. Gabby lay on the bed, her face deathly pale and a bandage wrapped around her head. His stomach plummeted as fear took hold. She looked terrible.

SOMETHING TIGHTENED AROUND GABBY'S HAND AND SHE lifted her heavy eyelids, peering out from under them.

"Logan is here," Corinne said. Her hand eased from Gabby's and she moved out of the seat beside the bed. A moment later, another hand clasped hers. One that was larger, manlier, and more welcome than Gabby could ever have imagined.

"Hi." She forced herself to focus on his handsome face. "You're here."

He raised her hand to his lips and kissed the back of it. "I should have been here all along. I'm sorry I wasn't home sooner." He sounded awful. As though he'd chewed gravel. His voice dripped with emotion. She opened her mouth to reassure him that everything was okay, but then, without her permission, tears began to spill down her cheeks.

"I tried to call you," she sniffed. "But you didn't answer."

"I'm sorry, sweetheart." He bent to kiss the uninjured top of her head. For some reason, the tender gesture just made her cry harder. "I'm sorry," he repeated. "I'm here now."

She wanted to ask if he'd been with the pretty young bartender. She'd overheard Corinne suggest to Shane that they try to get a hold of Logan by calling Peach since apparently he'd stormed out of the bar earlier and she'd followed him a few minutes later. Gabby wanted to trust Logan, but her thoughts were muddy and her fears were getting the better of her. She ached for him to comfort her but she also wanted to shove him away and demand to know where he'd been.

"What did the doctor say?" Logan asked one of the others.

"The babies seem to be fine, but she needs to be monitored overnight in case the concussion worsens," Shane said. "Someone has to wake her up every hour or two and get her to answer questions."

"I can do that." His hand tightened around hers. She closed her eyes and enjoyed the sensation, trying not to wonder if that same hand had been on another woman earlier today. "Did they say why she fainted?"

"A sudden drop in blood pressure," Gabby said, not liking the way they were talking about her as if she weren't there.

"That's right," Shane said. "Possibly caused by the rapid change of temperature when she got out of the bath, or by standing too quickly, and potentially exacerbated by the fact she hadn't eaten enough."

"You need to make sure she avoids hot baths, eats regularly, and moves slowly so it doesn't happen again." Corinne's voice was tight. Unusual for her when she was typically so warm and open. Perhaps she truly did suspect that Logan had been having an assignation with the bartender. Gabby's heart sank. If his own mother believed it, what hope was there?

She should have known not to fall for him. They'd only gotten together because of the pregnancy, and she'd always known she wasn't the type of woman that men changed for. Not Henry, and not Logan.

"I'm on it." Logan's lips brushed over her forehead. "I'm so sorry that I wasn't there. I'll do better."

"I thought I might lose the babies," she whispered, tears threatening once again. She already loved the little ones growing inside her. If she'd lost them, she'd have been devastated. Especially when she was so close to having the family she'd dreamed of. Fortunately, fate hadn't been that cruel. But it was still a wake-up call.

If she'd lost the babies, would she have lost Logan too? Without children to tie them together, he could theoretically go back to his carefree bachelor lifestyle. Would he want her if he had other options?

"You haven't," Logan said, glancing at the others as if to confirm. They nodded. "The babies are safe, and you're okay too. Everything is going to be fine."

She wanted to believe him, but she wasn't sure she did.

26

Gabby's head thumped, her heart ached, and her stomach was once again unsettled. She opened her eyes. Logan hovered above her, as he had every time he'd woken her during the night. Now, though, the gray light of dawn filtered through the curtains. At least they were home, rather than at the hospital. He'd brought her back late last night.

"What's your name?" he asked.

She rolled her eyes, then flinched when that hurt too. "Gabrielle Walker."

"What's my name?"

"The sleep police." She knew she shouldn't be annoyed. He was doing his best to look after her. But she was exhausted and it felt like every time she drifted off, he disturbed her again.

"Seriously, Gabs." His tone brooked no argument.

She sighed. "Logan Pride. The father of my twins. We're in Haven Bay. I'm thirty-one years old. The prime minister is Wesley Briggston. Can I sleep again now?"

He smiled and kissed her cheek. "I'm worried about you, that's all."

"I know." She felt like a bitch for being snarky. "Thank you for taking care of me."

Something throbbed behind her eyes. He may be taking care of her now, but he hadn't been there yesterday. A memory flickered through her mind. Corinne telling Shane to call Peach. An ache formed in her heart. She considered pretending she hadn't heard anything—she certainly wasn't in any shape for a confrontation—but she couldn't handle the idea of finding out later that, as with Henry, she wasn't his number one priority. Burying her head in the sand would get her nowhere. She loved Logan Pride, but if he was only with her because of the babies, she wasn't going to stand by and let herself get hurt again.

"Where were you yesterday?" she asked. "You weren't at The Den."

Guilt flashed across his face, and her stomach twisted in response. She'd wanted to believe she'd gotten it wrong, but maybe she hadn't.

"I was surfing," he said, stroking her hair back from her face. "I wish I'd come straight home. I'm sorry I wasn't here for you."

Surfing. That was plausible. But she needed to know for sure. She couldn't buy an excuse just because it was plausible. She shuddered to think how many times that must have happened with Henry in the past, and she'd had no idea what a load of bullshit he'd been selling her.

"Are you sure you were surfing and not with Peach? I overheard your mum say she saw the two of you in the storeroom together, and that you left and then she followed a few minutes later."

Logan's expression darkened and he stopped touching her. Gabby's stomach knotted even tighter. He looked furious—and worse, hurt. "Do you honestly believe I'm capable of betraying you?"

She rubbed her lips together. She hated seeing him in pain, but she needed to know for sure. He had to say the words. Her hesitation cost her.

"Huh." He stood and backed away from the bed. "Right." He tucked his hands into his pockets. The muscles of his neck tightened and his jaw worked. "You want to know what Mum saw?"

She nodded, even though she was starting to wish she'd never opened her mouth.

"Peach came onto me. I told her that if she did it again, I'd have to fire her." Anger was etched into his features. "I tried to explain that to Mum but she wasn't interested in listening, so I went surfing to clear my mind. If Peach left The Den after that then it's news to me because I didn't see her."

"Okay," Gabby whispered. Everything he said had the ring of truth, and shame descended over her. Even if he was with her because of the babies, she should have known he'd never do that to her. She'd just been emotional and in pain, and she'd let the insecurities Henry had created get the better of her. "I'm sorry. I shouldn't have asked. I just started thinking about how you wouldn't be with me if not for the babies, and it all spiraled."

He shook his head. "I can't believe you think I'd hurt you like that. If you don't believe me, Kyle can back me up. He found me at the beach. Do you want me to call him?"

"No, I believe you."

"For now. But how long until you wonder again?" He closed his eyes and took a breath. "Damn, Gabby." When he opened his eyes again, the fury had faded and been replaced by something worse: defeat. "I can't make you trust me. I know your ex burned you, but I'm not him. Yeah, maybe I slept around in the past, but those days are behind me. I care for you. *You*, you stubborn woman. Whether or not you're pregnant. And now I'm going out for some air before I say something I regret."

With that, he turned to leave.

"Wait!" Gabby called, guilt churning inside her.

He looked over his shoulder and raised an eyebrow.

"I'm sorry," she repeated. "I should have known better."

"Yeah," he agreed. "You should have."

Then he left the room.

Gabby's chest felt tight as she watched him go. She wished she could rewind the clock and start this morning over. She'd have thanked him for checking on her and asked him for cuddles. He was right. She did know him. Better, perhaps, than anyone else, even though they hadn't been close for long. He let her see a side of him that no one else did. But her fear and insecurities had gotten the better of her and she'd ruined it. She rested her head against the pillow and closed her eyes.

When she opened them next, Shane was sitting beside the bed. Her heart sank.

"Logan has gone into town," he said. "Can you tell me what my name is?"

LOGAN'S CONSCIENCE RAGED AT HIM AS HE DROVE INTO HAVEN Bay. He shouldn't have left Gabby when she was vulnerable, even if he'd waited for Shane to arrive first—and what an awkward conversation *that* had been. Still, he was Gabby's partner. The father of her unborn babies. Ergo, it was his responsibility to take care of her. But damn, her accusation had hurt, and he'd worried about what he might say if he stayed, especially when both of their emotions were heightened by what had happened yesterday.

His fingers tightened on the steering wheel. He could have lost her. For that, she did have the right to be angry with him. He should have been there. But as for her comment about Peach, that was way off base. He'd promised not to do that and thought that promise meant something to her. This proved otherwise. It felt like his reputation was an albatross around his neck and he'd never be able to get rid of it. Everyone expected the worst from him. Couldn't someone just believe he was capable of more?

He cruised a loop around the town square, unsure where to go. He didn't feel like surfing because no one would be able to get in touch with him if Gabby's condition worsened. On instinct, he turned towards Kyle's place. He and Charity shared a small home on the outskirts of the commercial area. As Logan parked outside, it occurred to him that he and Charity now had something in common. They both knew how it felt to have a reputation follow them around, and to not be trusted by a loved one because of their past. His stomach formed a hard ball at the thought of how he'd contributed to Charity's problems in that area. Without his interference, Kyle might never have worried about Charity's loyalty. Now the shoe was on the other foot. Maybe he deserved this.

As he walked up the path, he considered how charming the place looked from the outside and smiled. It was perfect for Kyle. He knocked on the front door and waited for his brother to open it.

"Hey." Kyle looked surprised to see him. "You want to come in?"

Logan entered, and Kyle led him to the living room, where he'd clearly been gaming with Charity. Charity greeted him with a smile and a nod. Kyle flopped onto the sofa and she stretched her legs across his lap. They both seemed to feel at home. He was glad they'd obviously settled in well.

Logan sat on the armchair.

"So, what happened?" Kyle asked. "After last night, I wouldn't have thought you'd want to be away from Gabby unless it was life or death."

Logan winced, wondering if that was a passive-aggressive reprimand. "Gabby asked if I was with Peach when she hurt herself."

"Peach?" Kyle frowned. "The new bartender?"

"Yeah. Apparently Gabby heard Mum mention that she thought I might be with her while she was at the hospital yesterday." A fact that stung. Surely Corinne knew he'd never let Gabby down like that. They'd talked about his insecurities. She knew how much it meant to him to be a good partner.

But then, other than the past few months, what did she have to compare his behavior to? A lifetime of flirting and sleeping around? Shame curled through him. There was nothing wrong with keeping things casual, but somewhere along the way, even his own mother had begun to doubt his integrity. If she couldn't look past his reputation, how could anyone else?

Kyle winced. "Mum shouldn't have said that around Gabby."

"She probably thought she was asleep."

"Still."

Logan raked a hand through his hair. His shoulders slumped. "Gabby doesn't trust me, and I don't know how to fix it."

Charity smirked. "It's rough when the people you love don't trust you, isn't it?"

"Yeah." He didn't blame her for taking a shot at him.

This probably seemed like karma to her. "It feels like shit. How did you get past it?"

She shrugged. "I had to stop and take a look at what I'd actually done to change people's perception of me, and accept that I couldn't wipe the slate clean overnight."

Logan mulled over her words. What had he done to change his reputation from playboy to devoted boyfriend and father-to-be? Definitely not nothing. He'd told people he was off the market. He'd treated Gabby well—or at least, he thought so, anyway. He'd prioritized her and setting up a future for their babies. But this had all occurred over a short period of time. Perhaps it had been a radical change, but it would take time for the people around him to start seeing the new version of him as normal Logan versus a phase he was going through. After all, if Jonathan had moved home and started saying he wanted to be a good dad out of nowhere, Logan would have been suspicious too. Trust took time to build.

"I get what you're saying," he allowed. "But don't I deserve the benefit of the doubt too?"

"Maybe," Charity agreed. "But you have to take her past into account. I don't know her full relationship history, but her ex wasn't faithful, right?"

"Yeah," Logan said.

Kyle scowled. "Asshole."

Charity smiled at him fondly. "He is." She turned back to Logan. "I don't know how it feels to be cheated on since it hasn't happened to me, but it can't be easy." She jostled Kyle with her foot. "Right?"

He nodded. "It sucks. I don't know how being cheated on feels either, but I know a bit about trust issues. It's like there's this voice in the back of your mind whispering things you don't want to believe, but it's hard to tune it out. In my opinion, all you can do is be patient and keep showing her through your actions that she can trust you. It might take longer than you'd like. Can you accept that?"

Logan buried his face in a cushion and closed his gritty eyes. He'd barely slept last night. "I can try." He dropped the pillow and met Kyle's eyes. "You don't have a ten-step list of suggestions for me to speed things up?"

Kyle's lips twitched. "No, sorry. If you find one, let me know."

Logan sighed. "Thanks, man."

"Remember," Charity added, "it may feel like your baggage will haunt you forever, but eventually, the load will lessen. Like Kyle said, you just have to be patient." She and Kyle exchanged a loving look. "It's worth it."

Logan glanced down at his phone, eager to avoid their obvious happiness when his life was falling apart. "I hope you're right."

"I am." Her lips curled smugly. "Pretty much always."

"Sure." He rolled his eyes. "Anyway, how are you feeling at the moment? Is everything going well with the pregnancy?"

"It is." Her smile grew wider. "It's been really smooth. I feel great."

"I'm glad to hear it." At least one of their partners was having an easy pregnancy. He turned to Kyle. "I suppose I'd better call Mum and explain everything to her too." Seeing as she'd decided to think the worst.

"Might be a good idea," Kyle agreed.

"Do you mind if I use the spare room?"

"Go for it."

Logan excused himself and dialed Corinne's number.

"Good morning," she said. "How's Gabby?"

"She's doing okay. Shane is with her now."

"And where are you?" Her tone sharpened.

"At Kyle's." He supposed he'd get straight to it. "Gabby

and I fought because she overheard you and Shane talking and she thought I was with Peach yesterday."

"Oh no! You didn't break up, did you?"

"No." He paced over to the window and looked out. The only view was of the side of the building next door. "Although we're going to have to talk about where we stand. I just wanted to call you to make it clear that I'm not having an affair with Peach."

"I know," she replied softly. "Kyle told me he found you at the beach. I still don't understand what I saw yesterday though."

He briefly explained the uncomfortable flirting and how it had come to a head.

"Why didn't you tell me?" she asked. "We could have discussed how to address it together." Great. She sounded hurt.

"Because I thought you'd believe I'd done something to encourage it. It's not like I haven't flirted with pretty much any woman in the past."

"Oh, Logan." She blew out her breath. "I like to think I'd at least have listened to you. Besides, it's your bar, not mine. You have a right to feel safe from harassment there."

His cheeks heated. "Hopefully she's got the message now."

"I think she has." Corinne laughed. "She emailed me a resignation letter this morning and asked me to forward it to you. She was probably so embarrassed she couldn't face you."

Logan felt a twinge of pity for Peach. Even though she'd threatened his relationship, she'd done so because her ego was on the line. She was young and self-centered, and felt like his rejection meant she was less desirable than her friends. She wasn't necessarily a bad person, but she had a lot of growing up to do.

He pinched the bridge of his nose. "Time to find another new bartender."

Replacing her would be a pain in the ass, but he was relieved he wouldn't have to see her again. Now he just needed to smooth things over with Gabby.

"I don't suppose you told Shane I didn't cheat on his sister, did you?"

27

"So." Shane fluffed Gabby's pillow into place behind her back and then passed her a mug of lemon and ginger tea. "How's your head?"

"Throbbing like hell." There were other, more colorful words she would have liked to use, but she reined them in. "I don't think the painkillers have kicked in yet."

"Hopefully soon." Shane sipped his own drink and studied her like she was a particularly challenging math problem.

"You don't have to babysit me," she said.

"I want to be here." He hesitated, then added, "I'm just not sure why Logan isn't here. He should be with you, but when I asked him about it, he wouldn't say why he was leaving."

She sighed. "I screwed up."

His brow furrowed. "How?"

She cringed, recalling the hurt in Logan's eyes and his stiffness as he walked away. "I basically accused him of cheating on me with his bartender."

Thomas butted his head against her chin and she scratched behind his ear, holding her drink out of the way.

He and Louise were keeping her company. The dog was curled on the end of the bed, glancing around every now and then, presumably to look for Thelma, who was outdoors.

Shane grimaced. "Is that because Corinne suggested I call her to see if they were together?"

"Yeah."

"Sorry, we thought you were asleep." He took off his glasses and wiped the lenses on the front of his shirt. "For what it's worth, they weren't. When I called her, she was alone, and Kyle found Logan at the beach."

"I know that now." If only she'd found out earlier. Although that still wouldn't have fixed the underlying problem. She closed her eyes, angry at herself for letting her shitty past interfere with their relationship. "I should have trusted him. He's treated me well throughout the pregnancy and it's been so easy to be with him. I guess I was waiting for the other shoe to drop."

She placed the mug on the nightstand and rested against the pillows before continuing.

"Everyone knows he never planned to settle down. He's told me so himself plenty of times. When he said he wanted to be together, I didn't trust him to stay with me because, well...no one else has. Henry and I wanted the same things, supposedly, and I still wasn't enough for him, so I didn't see how I could be enough to make Logan change his ways. I figured he'd realize before long that he was better off just being the babies' dad without also being my partner, and I pushed him away because of it."

"I wish I could have ten minutes alone with that asshole Henry," Shane growled through gritted teeth.

Gabby covered her smile. Her brother meant well, but he was forgetting that Henry was a professional athlete while he was a mild-mannered schoolteacher. It was for the best that they didn't come to blows.

"I suppose my attitude didn't help," he said. "I'm sorry if I made you doubt him—and yourself—too. I was trying to protect you. I didn't want to see you go through the same thing all over again, and if I'm honest, I was hurt that the two of you were sneaking around behind my back. I thought that in itself was evidence your relationship wasn't any different from the other flings he's had over the years." He sighed. "Logan is a good guy, but I've watched him go through a lot of women and I didn't want that to be you."

"I know it came from a good place." She gave him a little smile. "But I'm a big girl. I can look after myself."

"You don't have to though," he said. "That's what I'm getting at. I'm here for you, and whether I initially believed it or not, Logan is too." He scooted closer and took her hand. "I was wrong to mistrust him. I saw his face when he got to the hospital yesterday. He was terrified for you. He loves you, and he seems to make you happy—except for when you let your doubts get in the way—so give him a chance."

"What if he doesn't want me anymore?" she whispered. "He was really upset when he left."

"People can be upset without ending a relationship," Shane said. "And if this is about you not being good enough or anything else ridiculous, forget it. I think, deep down, you know that Logan loves you. You're just scared."

She shot him a glare. He was right. She knew he was. After all, Logan had showed her he cared in a thousand small ways. "Maybe."

"So, what are you going to do about it?"

She dragged her hand down her face. "I don't know. Apologizing and begging him to forgive me sounds like a good start."

"What about making some kind of gesture?" Shane suggested.

She bit her lip. "That's a good idea."

She needed to take a leap of faith to show Logan she trusted him, and then cross her fingers that he'd catch her if she fell. She loved him, but she'd been holding back out of fear. She'd been trying to protect herself, but if she wanted the future she'd always dreamed of, she couldn't get it without risking her heart.

"I have an idea," she said.

LOGAN HAD NEVER BEEN MUCH OF A GAMER, BUT THAT DIDN'T stop him from spending the entire day parked on Kyle's sofa, playing a hand-to-hand combat game he couldn't remember the name of. Hours passed, and he knew he should return home, but he wasn't sure what to say to Gabby, or how she'd react to his presence. It had been crappy of him to walk out earlier when she must have been feeling bad already. Finally, early in the evening, Kyle paused the game, stood, and stretched.

"It's time for you to go home," he said.

Logan blinked in surprise. "Are you kicking me out?"

"No." Kyle grinned. "Just nudging you along."

It felt like being kicked out. He pocketed his phone and let Kyle steer him to the door.

"If you let me stay, I'll cook dinner."

Kyle's grin widened. "Nice try, but you need to deal with what's bothering you instead of trying to avoid it."

"Isn't that my decision?"

"You know the best thing about being your brother?" Kyle asked. "I can stick my nose into your business all I want and you can't complain because you did the same to me."

Logan couldn't argue. It was true. But older brothers were supposed to protect their younger brothers.

"Fine." He gave Kyle a quick hug. "Thanks for everything." He turned to Charity, who was reading on the armchair. "You too."

She raised her hand in acknowledgement but didn't take her eyes off her book.

"No problem. Now go home." Kyle's tone was firm, and shockingly, Logan found himself wanting to obey. He waved goodbye and got into his car, intending to wait until Kyle had gone into the house before deciding on his next step, but Kyle didn't budge. Eventually, Logan realized his brother was waiting for him to leave.

"Stubborn idiot," he muttered as he pulled away.

He drove slowly, circling around the square, wondering whether to go to his apartment. Corinne was working at the bar and she'd given him clear instructions not to show his face. He was supposed to be looking after Gabby. Unfortunately, he wasn't sure whether Gabby would actually want to see him. He pulled over outside The Den and stared up at the dark top story. It didn't look welcoming. He wanted to be with Gabby. However she reacted to him, he had to make sure she was okay. Logically, he knew that Shane would have called if she wasn't, but she'd looked so small and tired in bed this morning.

He dragged his hand down his face. He shouldn't have lost his temper with her. She'd been overwhelmed, and she'd drawn the wrong conclusion. That hurt, but she'd apologized, and next time, they'd both do better.

He maneuvered back onto the road and didn't stop again until he was parked beside Shane's car, outside the home he now shared with Gabby. One of the goats raised its head and bleated at him. Another eyeballed him with suspicion. Princess was still outside too. He wandered over to the palomino mare and rubbed her muzzle when she pushed it into his hand.

"Time to go in." He walked her into the barn and slipped her a treat, then spent a few minutes brushing her. The movements were soothing, and she was good company. After a while, he felt calmer. "Bye, your highness."

He let himself out of the barn and headed for the back door. The door was unlocked and he took off his shoes and left them at the end of the hall before moving deeper inside. He flicked the light on and bent to greet Thelma and Louise as they crowded around his ankles.

"Have you looked after my girl?" he asked. They both gave him doggy smiles.

He heard the front door open and close and hoped it was Shane leaving rather than Gabby making a run for it. He passed by the empty bathroom, but when he came to the dining area, he paused. The room was lit with a golden glow cast by a dozen candles, and the scent of freshly cooked pizza permeated the space. He looked around, surprised at how tidy it was, and his gaze landed on Gabby, who sat at the end of the table with a bouquet of white flowers clasped in front of her.

28

GABBY STOOD AND APPROACHED LOGAN SLOWLY, UNSURE HOW he was going to react.

"Hi," she said softly.

"Hey." He scanned the candles once more, then his gaze settled on her face. "What's this?"

She offered him the flowers. They weren't much, but they were what the local florist had available on a Sunday afternoon. She was lucky the florist agreed to see her at all since they'd usually have been closed.

"These are for you," she said. "Can we sit down?"

He pulled out a chair and dropped onto it. She lowered herself slowly onto the one beside it. She still wasn't feeling particularly well, and she was wary of moving too quickly after what had happened yesterday. She interlaced her fingers on her lap and tried to remember the words she'd rehearsed.

"I'm sorry for what I said earlier. It was out of line. Everything between us has been so good, and when I talked to Shane, I realized that I was waiting for you to decide I wasn't enough for you. That's not fair to you, and I truly am sorry for it."

He held her gaze for so long that she began to squirm in her seat, then his expression eased and a twinkle appeared in his eyes. "I know you are. I'm sorry for how I reacted too. I've been trying so hard to get everything right, and when it seemed as if you hadn't noticed any change from how I used to be, it felt like my baggage was going to follow me around forever. Still, I shouldn't have lost my temper and left."

"You did the right thing. We both needed space." Her heart clenched. She felt awful for making him feel like his efforts didn't matter. She understood wanting to move on from the past. "You've been wonderful. The problem is me." She raised her chin, determined to get this out without falling apart. "I know I have trust issues, and they won't go away overnight, but I'm going to make an appointment with a therapist to try to work through my problems in a healthy way so I don't unload them on you again."

His posture loosened, and he cracked that lopsided grin she loved so much. "That's great, Gabs. For the record, you are not a 'problem.' Neither am I. We just have some things we need to get straight in our own heads so they don't come between us again." He hesitated for a moment, then glanced down. "You're not the only one with insecurities. The reason I don't like you talking to Tristan is because he's everything I'm not. Stable, successful, responsible. He's like your picture-perfect match."

Gabby's heart ached for him. "I'm sorry. I had no idea you felt that way."

He shrugged. "How could you?"

She should have noticed. She'd realized that he hadn't liked Tristan, but she'd had no idea this was why. She should have been more sensitive to his feelings. "You should know that however good Tristan looks on paper, there's a massive, massive problem with him."

"Oh yeah?"

"Yeah." She grinned. "He's not you. You're the one I'm crazy about, Logan."

His eyes were soft with emotion. "I'm crazy about you too." He cocked his head. "Hey, maybe I'll get the number for that therapist from you. I've never talked to a professional about how it affected me when Dad left. Mum offered, but I didn't think I needed it."

She shifted her chair closer until their knees were touching. "I think that's a great idea." Now, there was one more thing for her to come clean about, and it would be the hardest part of all. "I've got something to show you."

She slowly rose and offered him a hand. He ignored it and wrapped an arm around her once he was upright, supporting her. She rested her head against his shoulder for a couple of seconds, knowing she'd be happy if she never had to move. But it was time for her leap of faith.

"It's in the kitchen," she said.

They walked side-by-side to the kitchen and Gabby flicked on the light as they entered. She guided him to the counter, where eight cupcakes were spaced, each with a letter frosted on top of it. She watched Logan's face as he read the words. *I love you.* His eyes flicked to hers and a smile lifted the corners of his mouth and spread over his face, transforming him with joy.

"Really?" he whispered.

"Yeah." She rested her hands against his chest and looked up at him. "I love you, Logan. With every part of my heart. I want to be with you, whatever life brings. Even if, God forbid, we were to lose the babies, I'd still want to be with you. However our future might look, I'm here for it. Whether we marry or not. Have two kids or ten. None of that matters. I thought marriage and a white picket fence were what I wanted, but I was focused on the wrong thing. What I really want—what really makes me happy—is you."

Logan used a hand on the small of her back to shift her closer. "I love you too." He smiled helplessly, flashing his teeth. "You drive me nuts sometimes, but I'd rather lose my mind with you than do anything with anyone else."

"I—" She started to defend herself, but he put a finger to her lips. She narrowed her eyes.

"Just listen. All the reasons I avoided relationships were wrong. I had good intentions, but I was misguided." He removed his finger from her lips, but she kept them shut. "I want everything with you, Gabby. The marriage. The white picket fence. The children. Even your mismatched band of pets."

"Hey—"

"Uh-uh." He grinned. "I know it might take you a while to believe it, but I promise I'll make you happy, and I'm willing to wait until those insecurities disappear."

"I believe it," Gabby said. "I let doubt creep in earlier, but I'm done with that. I love you, and I want a future with you—in whatever shape it comes."

Logan kissed her. His past dropped away, leaving only the wonderful present. He felt weightless. He'd spent half of his life scared of falling in love with someone only to let them down, but now he knew that he never would—and if he slipped up, Gabby would call him on it. He deepened the kiss, wanting to get as close to her as possible. His soul yearned to be one with hers.

She pulled back, breathing heavily. Her pupils were dilated, and that was enough to remind him that she'd been through a trauma. No sexy times tonight. They could cuddle though.

"Want to put a movie on and eat these cupcakes in front of it?" he asked.

She laughed. "Way to segue. But yeah, that sounds great."

His stomach rumbled on cue, reminding him that he hadn't eaten since lunch.

"Maybe we should start with the pizza," she suggested. "I called your mum to ask what type your favorite is. I hope that's okay."

"God, yes," he said. "If it's any good, I might go pick out a ring."

She rolled her eyes. "Uh-huh. Because pizza is the determining factor of relationship success."

"Hey." He tilted her chin up with his finger. "It's not the pizza. It's the fact that you went to the trouble of finding out what I like and making it even when you had every reason not to leave bed today. I'd be a lucky bastard if I got to marry a woman who'd do that for me." Her cheeks flushed, and he kissed her forehead. "Let's eat pizza, and then we can have cupcakes for dessert."

He bent and swept her into his arms.

"Hey!" she protested. "What are you doing?"

"Taking care of my girl," he said. "You've spent enough time on your feet today. You need to rest." He carried her to the sofa and gently set her down, then stacked two plates with pizza and gave one to her. He sat beside her and pulled a blanket over their legs. Thomas jumped onto the arm of the sofa and tried to get to the food. Logan waved him off, chuckling as the cat tried to duck under his arm.

He bit into a slice and his eyes widened as he ate it. "This is really good."

"It has the Walkers' super-secret sauce recipe," Gabby said smugly.

"Really?"

She smirked. "No. I found the recipe online."

They finished their meal in contented quiet, then Logan took the plates to the kitchen, washed them, and returned with cupcakes. They snuggled together as they enjoyed the treats, which she and Shane had apparently bought from Megan at The Shack and redecorated. When they were done, Gabby cuddled against his chest.

He breathed in her scent, hardly able to believe that this was real. He finally had the woman he'd been hung up on, and he was excited for their babies to arrive in the world.

Mouse climbed into Gabby's lap and curled into a ball. Logan smiled. His life was pretty damn perfect.

EPILOGUE

CHILDBIRTH WASN'T FOR THE FAINT OF HEART. GABBY FELT wrung out and exhausted. She could barely lift her limbs, and she hurt in places she'd never hurt before. But seeing her two babies—Devin and Samantha—made everything worth it. She watched through a film of weariness as the nurse cleaned Devin, wrapped him in a blanket, and handed him to Logan.

Logan gazed at the little boy with such awe that she fell in love with him all over again. He'd been her rock throughout the past hours while she battled to bring their children into the world. He'd never left her side, even when she'd threatened to break his fingers and cut off certain appendages.

"Here, Mummy. Would you like to hold Samantha?" The nurse appeared at her side with the little girl bundled against her chest.

"Yes, please." She tried to take the baby, but her arms were too weak.

"You just stay right there and let me position you." The nurse shifted her into place and lowered Samantha gently onto her.

Gabby held her daughter for the first time, her throat tight, her heart full. "I love you, Samantha," she whispered. "You and your brother are going to be the most spoiled babies in all of Haven Bay."

"Can I see her?" Logan asked, his voice hoarse with emotion. He approached them with Devin and smiled down at Samantha and Gabby. "You did good, sweetheart. They're perfect."

Gabby overflowed with love, and tears slipped down her cheeks. "They really are."

There was a knock on the door and another nurse stuck her head in. "Are you up to seeing visitors?" she asked. "There are some people out here who can't wait to meet the twins."

Gabby caught Logan's eye and nodded. She sniffed and wiped her cheeks. She was tired, but she'd love to see their family. The door opened wider and the nurse ushered the entire Walker and Pride families inside. They clustered around the bed, exclaiming over the babies and congratulating the new parents. Gabby leaned back against the pillow and closed her eyes. She and Logan may never have expected to end up here, but she knew she was exactly where she was supposed to be. She was living her dream, and this was only the beginning.

"Are you okay?" Logan murmured near her ear.

She turned her face toward him for a gentle kiss. "I've never been better."

THE END

COME BACK TO YOU EXCERPT

LIAM

Is it possible to love and hate someone at the same time? - Unsent text message from Liam to Kennedy

The pub was relatively quiet. But then, it was a Monday night and most of the locals were at home, so that was no surprise. I sat at a table near the bar, cradling a pint of beer and listening to Toby brag about the hot tourist from the resort he'd been hooking up with. Apparently she was Swiss, blonde, and adventurous as hell, although I tuned out most of his colorful description. The state of my own sex life was nonexistent, and I didn't need a reminder of how great his was. It would only make me feel pathetic.

I drank more beer. Thirty should be too young to feel this old. Toby was only five years my junior and he was out there, playing the field. Why couldn't I bring myself to do the same anymore?

I reached for a chip and popped it into my mouth, scanning the other occupants of the pub while Toby rhapsodized about his hookup's killer body. Dad was behind the bar because it was Bailey's night off. Mum and a couple of her friends sat on stools, chatting to each other and bringing him into their conversation every now and then. A group of weather-beaten men clustered in the back, alternating between drinking and playing darts. They were doing surprisingly well considering how much beer they'd drunk. But then, these craggy old guys could put booze away like no one's business.

"...you, Liam?"

"Huh?" I snapped around. Toby and Asher, my best friend, were looking at me, both wearing wry smiles.

"I asked if you've been seeing anyone lately," Toby said, apparently unconcerned that I'd zoned out.

I huffed. "No."

"That makes..." Toby pretended to do math in his head. "A fucking long time without any action, am I right?"

Asher gave him a light shove. "Don't be an asshole. We can't all be as girl-crazy as you. Some of us actually have to work around here."

Toby launched into a protest about how being a ski instructor counted as a real job, even if he was technically only employed for half the year. I sent Asher a smile, grateful for the distraction. He knew I hated anyone prying into my affairs. Especially when there wasn't anything to talk about. I'd gone through a phase of sleeping around after Kennedy ended things, but lately something was missing. Hookups just weren't cutting it for me, and I'd decided not to bother.

I tuned back into the conversation, and that was when the pub fell eerily silent. I looked around, expecting to see that someone had broken a plate or a chair, but nobody cursed or shouted an apology. Instead, all attention was focused on the door, where a woman stood silhouetted against the rapidly descending darkness.

Fuck. It couldn't be.

I stared, taking in the long, blonde hair that was darker at the roots, the cute, upturned nose, and the unique eyes I'd never thought I'd gaze into again for as long as I lived.

Kennedy.

She was back in Destiny Falls. In the pub. Only a handful of yards away.

Why was she here?

Someone coughed, breaking the hush. Eyes burned into me as our audience waited to see how I'd react so they could follow my lead. The community had been a great source of support when she first made a name for herself in Hollywood. They'd rallied around me, boycotting everything Kennedy Carter. The store had refused to sell any tabloids with her picture on the front. The movie theater had never played films she starred in. And if someone ever happened to learn anything about her, they never mentioned it to my face. A few had gone further and helped shield me from reporters who'd come to town, trying to dig up dirt about Kennedy's time in Destiny Falls. Now, she was here. Inexplicably.

I had no doubt someone here would toss her out if I gave any indication that was what I wanted. Hell, either Asher or Toby would gladly volunteer for the job. I just needed to force myself to move.

"Liam." Someone jostled my elbow. Firm fingers gripped it. "Let's go, man."

It was Asher, trying to get me to leave. But I couldn't look away from the woman who'd crushed my heart and stolen my future.

"What the fuck is she doing here?" he muttered. "Come on."

I stood.

"Help me, Tobes," Asher urged.

Before my brother could move, Kennedy lifted her chin and crossed the room. I caught a waft of her scent as she stopped in front of me. Slightly sweet, but unfamiliar. My throat threatened to close over. I didn't even know what she smelled like anymore. Somehow, that made me want to kick shit down.

I could still read her face though. She was nervous. Rightfully so.

Asher tugged my arm again. "Liam has nothing to say to you," he snapped at her.

It wasn't true. I'd had plenty to say to her over the years. Questions, angry rants, random observations I knew she'd have appreciated. But she hadn't been around to share them with. Because she hadn't wanted me enough to stay—or rather, to come back.

"Can we talk?" Her voice was deeper than it used to be. Smoother. That tiny discrepancy jolted me into action.

"I wanted to talk eleven years ago," I snapped. "But you weren't interested. So no, we can't talk." I brushed past her, heading for the exit, Toby and Asher flanking me. As soon as the door swung shut behind me, I released a shaky exhale. "Did that just happen?"

"Yeah, mate." Asher clapped me on the back. "Come on, we're going back to your place."

"She's in Destiny Falls." I could scarcely believe it. Kennedy had become something of an urban legend in these parts. The Hollywood It Girl who'd broken the hometown boy's heart, discussed in whispers behind my back but never, ever to my face. "Why the fuck is she here?"

"Who cares?" Asher guided me to my Ute. "I'm driving. Toby, you get beer and meet us there. We're going to need lots of it."

Toby saluted. "Aye aye, Captain."

I climbed numbly into the passenger seat, registering

that it felt odd not to be driving my own vehicle, but my whirring thoughts kept me from dwelling on it as Asher started the engine. Kennedy Carter—or Cox, whatever stage name she was calling herself these days—had a lot of nerve showing up in my father's pub.

"She won't stay," I murmured to myself. I needed to remember that, and hold onto my anger at her for leaving without even giving me the chance to consider going with her. Many years had passed, but no matter what had brought her back here, I couldn't afford to let her into my life. Kennedy was a chapter of my past that needed to remain closed.

ALSO BY ALEXA RIVERS

Haven Bay

Then There Was You

Two of a Kind

Safe In His Arms

If Only You Knew

Pretend to Be Yours

Begin Again With You

Let Me Love You

Never Saw You Coming

Destiny Falls

Stay With You

Come Back to You

Always Been Yours

Little Sky Romance

Accidentally Yours

From Now Until Forever

It Was Always You

Dreaming of You

Little Sky Romance Novellas

Midnight Kisses

Second Chance Christmas

Blue Collar Romance

A Place to Belong

ACKNOWLEDGMENTS

Wow. I can't believe we've reached the end of the Haven Bay series. Four years ago, I sat down to create the beachside town I'd most like to live in, with a pencil, a piece of A3 paper, and very few artistic skills. Thus, Haven Bay was born.

I have had such a wonderful time getting to know Haven Bay and its inhabitants with you, and I hope you've enjoyed your visits. Thank you for coming along on this journey with me.

This series has taken a village to create, and I want to take a moment to thank some of the most important contributors.

First and foremost, thank you to Kate Studer for your hard work and valuable support on every single book in this series. Your feedback and ideas helped me polish these stories and make them the absolute best they could be. I so appreciate your thoughtful comments and constant cheer-leading.

Serena Clarke, thank you for letting me borrow your excellent brain to iron out details that I hadn't even noticed needed sorting out. Your input has been invaluable in adding realism.

Thank you, McKinley, for being the most wonderful, positive, enthusiastic cheerleader I could dream of, and for improving my knowledge of grammar.

Thank you to my beta readers and sensitivity readers. I appreciate you generously giving your time and thoughts.

Thank you, too, to my ARC readers. You guys make my heart happy.

Shannon Passmore, your covers have helped these books shine, and working with you is always a pleasure.

Thank you, Dinah, for taking the time to faithfully read each and every one of these books and spotting any typos that slopped through editing. You are wonderful.

Thank you to Shannon D for loving Haven Bay as much as I do. If I could move there with you, I would.

Last, but definitely not least, thank you to my husband, the love of my life, for your never-ending support, and for believing in me even when my own belief wavers. You are as perfect as any book boyfriend. Thank you, XO.

ABOUT THE AUTHOR

Alexa Rivers writes about genuine characters living messy, imperfect lives and earning hard-won happily ever afters. Most of her books are set in small towns, and she lives in one of these herself. She shares a house with a neurotic dog and a husband who thinks he's hilarious. When she's not writing, Alexa enjoys travelling, baking cakes, eating said cakes, cuddling fluffy animals, drinking copious amounts of tea, and absorbing herself in fictional worlds.